Eyes of Rain and Ragged Dreams

Eyes of Rain

and

Ragged Dreams

Coming of age in Edinburgh

by

Michael Elcock

Published by **Muckle Knock**
A Division of Pentland Steele Ltd.
Victoria, British Columbia, Canada
2017

Library and Archives Canada Cataloguing in Publication

Elcock, Michael

Eyes of Rain and Ragged Dreams / Michael Elcock.

ISBN   978-0-9958802-0-7

I.   Title.

Published by

Muckle Knock – A Division of Pentland Steele Ltd.
2-216 Russell Street,
Victoria, British Columbia
Canada V9A 3X2

Printed in Canada

For Charles and Hugh and Bobby and Roly and Alan
who didn't get through it all.
For Peter and Rig and Nick and Murray and Johnnie and
Willie and Duncan who did.
For Pat and Betty and Windy and Nobby, who knew about
it.
And for Mum . . .

Far 'yont amang the years to be
when a' we think, an' a' we see,
An' a' we luve's been dung ajee
By time's rouch shouther,
An' what was right and wrang for me
Lies mangled throu'ther . . .

Robert Louis Stevenson

Chapter 1 – The End of Summer

The stewardess was watching him. The hands told her the most, she decided. The rest of him was still and composed, but the long hands, grainy like miner's hands, with veins that stood out, clasped and unclasped all the time. He was just a boy, sitting, gazing through the window.

The aeroplane lurched in an air pocket as it banked for the run in to Nicosia. Grimmett steadied his rattling teacup, and listened to the beat of the Rolls Royce engines cutting through the morning air. The stewardess touched him on the shoulder.

"You should fasten your seat belt now," she said. "We'll be landing in a few minutes." He turned from the small square window and looked at her. His face was thin. It made his eyes look big. "I'll take the cup if you like." She held out her hand.

He passed her the cup, and reached for the grey webbing belt straps, and clipped them together across his lap. He leaned forward again, shoulders hunched, his face close to the window, misting the glass with his breath.

Below, the shoreline was tinged with white. Beyond it a dusty brown landscape rose from the blue ocean and blended into spiny, flour-grey mountains. Grimmett's ears

1

clicked as the pressure increased. Cyprus grew larger in the little window, until it filled out the horizon.

His father's letter had been clear. He wouldn't have to go back; he'd be able to stay here. He'd been awake most of the night thinking about it. Living in sunshine instead of lowered grey skies; thinking of travel and new people and places. Just him and his father, and no one to bother him with rules and things that had to be done. He hadn't slept on the long flight through the Mediterranean night thinking about it.

The Argonaut dropped over the Troodos mountains, rocking gently in the air currents. Outside the window the propellers arced bright red and silver in the early sunshine. Ugly black streaks from the engine exhaust smoked the top of the wing. They flew on over the Mesaoria, the plain that dissects the island. It was deserted and dry, with tiny villages standing in a network of dusty roads, and scattered windmill sails turning lazily, like toys.

They passed low over the airfield. Grimmett craned to look through the window, searching for his father, waiting for the aeroplane's wheels to thump onto the ground. His stomach churned as the motors suddenly opened up. The aeroplane roared a few feet over the runway, and then they were climbing back up over Nicosia, looking down into empty, narrow streets and a jumble of white, flat-roofed houses. He caught a glimpse of an old man standing in a small square, his head tilted back to watch as they passed overhead.

The aeroplane shuddered as it came round for a second time, its wing flaps fully extended. Dust flew up from the sparse brown grass beside the landing strip. They touched down with a bump, and the airframe shook as the pilot applied the brakes. The aircraft shuddered and slowed, and then they began to taxi in towards the little concrete terminal building. Grimmett bounced in his seat as the wheels jarred over the rough ground. The Argonaut came to a stop and the engines began to wind down. A steward opened the door, and a gust of sweet, cool air streamed through the cabin.

A cheerful cockney voice called from the back. "Ev'ry body 'aht."

2

Grimmett went down the steps, scanning the faces below him. Soldiers were sitting behind sandbags at the corners of the dilapidated airport building, fingering Bren light machine guns, their eyes shifting from the thin file of passengers to the far reaches of the dusty airfield and back again. At one corner of the concrete apron an armoured scout car stood dirt-grey in desert camouflage paint. Two R.A.F. Regiment soldiers in blue serge uniforms patrolled up and down in front of the sandbagged terminal, Lee Enfield rifles slung on their shoulders. The day was beginning to warm up. The soldiers looked uncomfortable. In the quiet, after hours of beating aero engines, Grimmett felt detached, as if he was watching the scene through glass.

An army officer led the passengers across the concrete to the building. Grimmett turned and stared back at the aeroplane, looking for his father. A small group of men in oil-spattered overalls stood staring up at one of the engines. He felt a hand on his shoulder.

"Are you Arthur Grimmett?" It was the army officer.

"Yes."

"Ah, good." The officer smiled. "Your father asked me to tell you that he'll be along in a few minutes. He's tied up just now. A . . . ah . . . small problem with one of the engines." He scratched the corner of his mouth with a fingertip. "Nothing serious of course. You can wait for him out here if you like. In the sunshine."

"Oh. Yes, all right. I'll wait here then."

The officer nodded. "Don't wander off though, there's a good chap. He'll be here in a minute." He waved a hand at the patrolling soldiers, and then ducked down the sandbagged alleyway that led into the building.

Grimmett put his overnight bag on the ground and sat on it, his back against the sandbag wall. He shuttered his eyes and squinted into the sun. It was warm now. He could feel the sun opening his skin out to the light. He began to relax, and his breathing slowed.

Four men were unbolting one of the aeroplane's propeller blades. They were standing high up under the engine on a scaffold they'd wheeled out from a hangar. Grimmett watched, listening to the clink of metal wrenches. A tinkle of bells floated across the airfield from a small flock

3

of long-legged sheep that were nibbling at the dry brown grass beside the runway. The sky had begun to mellow from a deep morning blue to a colourless wash. The aeroplane seemed to float in the rising heat.

A tall man stepped from one of the huts and strode towards the aeroplane. His step had a spring to it, his arms a familiar swing. Grimmett caught the movement from his half-closed eyes, and snapped awake. He stood up as the man detoured towards him in a wide circle. They shook hands.

"Hello father," he said.

"Hello Arthur. Did you have a good flight?"

"Yes. It was fine." They looked at each other.

Grimmett's father looked over at the aircraft. "It's good to see you. I shouldn't be more than a few minutes. I've got to make sure the aeroplane can carry on to Baghdad. I'll be with you as soon as I can."

Grimmett watched the white uniform recede towards the aeroplane, washing formlessly into the heat haze. He sat down again to wait.

Two mechanics came across the tarmac, bent under the weight of a propeller blade. They stopped and leaned it against the sandbags. One of them wiped his sleeve across his forehead.

"Warming up," said a soldier at a machine gun nearby.

The mechanic pointed at the propeller blade. "Not a very neat little 'ole is it?"

The soldier stood up for a better look. "Christ! So that's what happened."

Grimmett twisted round. The propeller blade glinted in the sunlight. It was silver-grey, with a red horizontal stripe near its tip. Half way down it there was a jagged hole nearly three inches across.

The mechanic ran his finger carefully round the hole. "Lucky shot I'd say. I didn't know they had anything that big up in the mountains though."

A scout car sped across the grass, trailing a whirlpool of dust, its radio aerial swaying and jerking, tugging a tiny triangular pennant at its tip. Sheep scattered out of its way.

4

Grimmett watched his father walk back through the heat haze.

"Right! Come on son," said his father. He laid his hand on Grimmett's shoulder. "We can push off now. We might as well go home."

Cyprus was a short-term posting for Grimmett's father, and the airline had provided him with an apartment on the outskirts of Nicosia. It was small and clean, with white walls and cool marble floors. The furnishings were impersonal; a couple of cushioned wicker chairs in the living room, a polished wood dining table, two chairs in a corner next to the kitchen, and a glass-topped coffee table.

Grimmett's father showed him his bedroom. White walls with a print above the bed of a man leading a donkey laden with oatmeal-coloured sacks down a dusty track. It could have been biblical, or it could have been contemporary. The bed was narrow and hard, with a red and white-squared bedspread. Beside it stood a small table. A jar of water and oil sat on top of it; a cork with a wick in it floating at its centre. A varnished wooden chair sat by the window next to a small chest of drawers. A blue and white vase full of pretty yellow flowers sat on top of the chest.

Each morning a maid came to clean the house, and prepare an evening meal. She was a short, olive woman who hardly spoke any English. She put fresh flowers in Grimmett's room every day, and hummed tunelessly while she worked. She called Grimmett 'Pehtheemoo', but when he spoke to her she only smiled, and nodded her head up and down like a little bird.

The days passed. Grimmett's father took him to the beach to swim and lie in the sun, and they drove up to the old walled town of Kyrenia. They spent an afternoon talking lazily at a table outside a café beside the harbour at Larnaca, drinking coffee and orange Fanta, and watched the fishermen mending nets with pointed wooden awls and untidy heaps of twine. A woman joined them there that day; a woman who knew his father and smelled of soap, and gave him a small buss on the cheek, and looked away when he caught her eye. His father introduced her as Hillevi and told him she was Danish.

"Eoka—the terrorists—seem to be pretty well entrenched in the mountains," said Grimmett's father one evening. They had moved the chairs outside, so they could sit on the veranda and watch the short Mediterranean twilight mark the changing of day into night. Luminescent purple bougainvillea trailed over a corner of the balcony.

"It's rough country up there; ideal for guerrilla operations. Our troops don't seem to be able to winkle them out. Anyway, the airline has decided to re-route its Far East flights round by Istanbul and Beirut because of this . . . ah, unpleasantness . . . so very soon now there's not going to be much for me to do here any more." He emptied a bottle of beer into a silver mug. The bottle chinked on the glass tabletop when he put it down. The wicker chair creaked.

"The Parachute Regiment flew in from London yesterday. They're moving up into the Troodos Mountains today." Jack Grimmett rested his feet on the wrought-iron railing and cradled his beer mug somehow between his hand and his wrist. The moon poked over the hills in a wafer crescent, like a delicate ivory tusk. Early that afternoon there had been a bomb explosion in the middle of the town.

They were silent for several minutes. Then, "You must be starting to miss Edinburgh by now," said Grimmett's father.

"No. I don't miss it at all. I like it here."

"Aren't you ready to go back?"

"No." The question made Grimmett uncomfortable.

Jack Grimmett studied the glass in his hand, turned it round with his fingers. "You know you have to go back," he said.

Grimmett stared at his father, noticed for the first time the thin lines on his face, the grey hair at his temples. "The letter you sent. You said I'd be able to stay here."

His father looked at him, and looked away. "I know. That's what I wanted too. But it's not as easy as that. Things have changed now. It's not going to be possible for you to stay with me."

Grimmett stared into the darkness. A dog barked in the street below. Further off a door slammed. A car started up.

"It's not safe for you here just now," said Grimmett's father. "Not until this Eoka business has been sorted out and they catch this Dighenis character; the leader. It's not safe for any of us." He took a sip from his glass. "And I don't expect to be here much longer myself anyway, if they're shutting down the station. I'll be getting a new posting in the next few weeks, and I've got no idea where they'll send me." A moth flapped on the lampshade between them.

"Look at this." He indicated the apartment with a wave of his arm. "This is no place for you to live. It wouldn't be any sort of life with me at the moment. You need to be with your friends; have your own things around you . . . And of course the schooling's important." He looked at his son. "I always wanted you to have the best."

Grimmett stared out at the night. "I don't have any friends. I don't care about any of it. I don't want to go back there."

"I'm sorry if my letter misled you," his father said. "I thought it might be possible . . . you know. . . To have you with me."

Grimmett stood up. It was difficult to speak. "I think I'll go to bed now." He turned away.

"There's . . . ah . . . one more thing," said his father. He waited until his son turned to face him. "I'm thinking of getting married again."

Grimmett lay awake for a long time. Clouds of stars filled the open window, infinitely high in the black sky. The intermittent crackle of a cricket came from a lemon tree in the garden. Beside Grimmett's bed the candle floated and flickered, and sputtered shadows onto the wall. He remembered the fights between his mother and his father. He remembered his father coming home on leave with a beard on his face, and his mother refusing to kiss him or give him dinner until he had shaved it off. He remembered picnics on a spread tartan blanket among whin bushes on the side of a hill with a stream chuckling past, and skylarks overhead.

And the truth of it came to him in the early morning, before the sun rose, long after the crickets had gone to sleep. His father would marry the Danish woman. There would be no room for him with them. He would be in the way.

Chapter 2 - Meeting

"Grimmett!" Dodson grabbed the weight from his desk. With a short sweep of his arm he sent it sailing through the air. It was a small lead ball the size of an apple. A century before, it had been shot out of a Turkish cannon at Sebastopol, where it had smashed through a window and taken off the arm of an Armenian moneylender.

The cannonball landed with a crash on Grimmett's desk and fell on the floor. Grimmett jerked upright in his seat.

"Were you asleep Grimmett?"

Sunlight slanted through the high squared windows, throwing geometric shadows across the room. A fly buzzed in the waiting silence, flinging itself repeatedly against the windowpane.

"Bring it to me boy!"

Grimmett picked the ball up from the floor. It was smooth and cold; like ice, heavy for its size. He walked slowly down the row of wooden desks to the front of the class and held it out.

"The ablative singular of 'mensa', Grimmett, is 'mensae'. It's an easy one. You should have learned it years ago. Were you asleep?"

"No sir. I was thinking."

8

Henry Dodson stared at him over the top of half-moon spectacles. He gripped the sides of his desk top, elbows out. Insolence or indolence? It was hard to tell from the boy's eyes. He leaned forward as if he had a stomach ache. The class waited. The master's face creased into a thin smile, lips drawn across yellowed teeth.

"Well, you'll have plenty of time to think this evening. You can write out for me one hundred times, 'The ablative singular of 'mensa' is 'mensae'. Do you understand?"

"Yes sir," said Grimmett. He remained in front of the master's desk. The fly attacked the window again.

"You may return to your desk."

"There is one thing sir." There was a slight tenor in Grimmett's voice.

"What is it, boy?" The master's voice rose.

"It's just that . . . I think it's dangerous sir." He looked at the weight sitting on Dodson's desk. "It could kill someone."

Dodson leaned back and stared at him. He'd been using that weight his whole teaching career, all thirty-six years of it. No one had ever had the temerity to question it. The corner of his eye twitched. This was not indolence. He gripped the sides of the desk and leaned forward again, his voice just under control.

"I don't like you Grimmett," he said. "I don't like you at all. You don't work and you're lazy. You're just a good time Charlie!"

"Yes sir."

The master opened the drawer of his desk and reached inside. He withdrew a dull leather strap, thick and tightly coiled. He placed it on top of the desk. Released from the confines of the drawer the belt unwound itself a little. Grimmett stared at it in fascination.

With neat, precise movements Henry Dodson took off his jacket and draped it over the back of his chair. He rolled up the right sleeve of his shirt, uncovering a thin, bony arm. Grimmett blinked. He hadn't meant to initiate this.

"Stand on the spot!" said Dodson. He pointed at a large black dot on the scuffed wood floor.

Grimmett moved a pace to his right.

9

"Hold your arm out and pull back your sleeve."

The strap made a whistling sound as it cut through the air. The leather tore into Grimmett's hand, stung fiercely, wrenched at his wrist. Dodson grunted with the effort. "We . . . must . . . make . . . sure . . . that . . . you . . . . stay . . . awake . . . for . . . the . . . rest . . . of . . . the . . . class." Dodson swung the strap again. Grimmett's hand went numb. The crack of the leather filled the space the buzzing fly had occupied. "And we must teach you to do as you're told." Dodson brought the strap down a third time. "I will not tolerate insubordination in my class!"

Back at his desk, Grimmett held his hand between his thighs. After a few minutes he inspected it surreptitiously. Three weals rose livid-red from his fingers and scored across his palm. The thongs had torn the soft skin on the underside of his wrist and left a thin line of blood. The red part was already swelling. His whole hand throbbed. Dodson was an expert.

Dunphy caught up with Grimmett in the school yard after the class. "Did it hurt?" he said. Grimmett walked on without answering.

"Do they do that often here?" Dunphy was new at the school. He was Canadian.

"Yes." Grimmett continued walking.

Dunphy jogged along beside him. "He'll break someone's wrist someday doing that," he said.

"He already did. Last year. He's not supposed to use it any more."

Dunphy stared at Grimmett's hand. Grimmett was squeezing his wrist, as if he was trying to push the blood back into his fingers. The skin was scarlet.

"You were asleep you know," said Dunphy. "You snored."

It was difficult to keep up with Grimmett's long strides. Dunphy was short and pear-shaped; stumpy-legged. Exercise made his face flush with round, red imprints on both cheeks, like tennis-ball marks. He was having trouble with the customs at the school, difficulty assimilating. Grimmett hadn't spoken to him before.

Grimmett glanced at him, and slowed his pace. "I did?" he said.

Dunphy nodded. "Are they all like him? The other masters?"

"Not all of them. Some of them are worse. Even Dodson isn't too bad most of the time. There are worse ones than him."

Dunphy took a deep breath. It was hard to keep up.

Grimmett shortened his step. He was almost a foot taller than Dunphy. He had a high, bony forehead over deep brown eyes. Some of the boys at the school called him 'Moonman' because of his long, almost skeletal hands, and the watery blue-green veins which stood out on the backs of them. Dunphy had assessed him as either intelligent or eccentric. He wasn't sure which.

They came to an untidy line of boys at the tuck shop window.

"Let me buy you a bun," said Dunphy.

"It's all right," said Grimmett. "I've got some money."

They stood in silence, shuffling forward as the line shortened. The girl behind the counter regarded them. "What do you want?"

"A bun please," said Grimmett.

The girl shooed a fly from the tray and pushed a bun towards him.

"And you?" She looked at Dunphy.

"Two buns, and a Bounty bar."

They took their purchases and moved off to a stack of metal crates full of half-pint milk bottles. Dunphy pulled out a bottle and poked a hole in the tinfoil cap with the end of a straw. He sucked slowly at the straw.

"How long've you been here?"

"Since I was six."

"Do you like it? I mean, what do you think of the place?"

"Not much. I try not to think about it." Grimmett pressed the palm of his injured hand against the cold glass of the bottle. "Mostly it's boring. The days go by very slowly." He swallowed the last of his milk and rattled the empty bottle back into the crate. He looked at Dunphy. "Why did you come here?"

Dunphy laughed. "The Diplomat made me. That's my father," he said. "He works at the Embassy in Glasgow. The Canadian Embassy. Said it would do me good and teach me manners. Said it might give me an education as well."

"Why do you live in Edinburgh if he works in Glasgow?" said Grimmett, taking a reluctant interest.

Dunphy laughed again. "Diplomat's a bit of a snob I guess. Said he'd been to Glasgow before. In the War. Didn't like it. Said it's dirty; full of factories and slums and the people there drink and fight too much. He likes it better when it's at the other end of the railway line."

They walked under a stone arch outside the dining hall. "Why are you here?"

Grimmett shrugged. "I won't be here for long. I'm leaving soon."

Chapter 3 - The Gym

The changing room under the gymnasium was cold like a cavern. It smelled of stale sweat.

"'H'all 'rite lads," said Crampsey. "Change into your togs and be upstairs in two minutes." He wheeled round and disappeared out the door.

Dunphy selected a peg next to Grimmett's and hung his blazer on it. He sat down on a wooden bench and began to untie his shoelaces. A steady drip of water came from the showers, and they could hear a slow 'thump-thump-thump' from upstairs as Crampsey warmed up on the wooden floor.

Dunphy rummaged in the bag at his feet. He straightened up. "Forgot my sneakers," he said.

"Careless," said Grimmett. "He won't like that."

He stood up and pulled on his shorts. "He won't let you off. He was a Commando you know. He won't care if you get splinters from the floor. He doesn't think we're tough enough as it is." He gestured at the showers. "That's why he makes us take cold showers." He tied the laces of his gym shoes, and sat down to wait for Dunphy. He shivered; the damp seemed to ooze right through the stone walls.

"Come on," Grimmett said after a minute. "We'd better get up there. I don't want to be kept in afterwards."

13

Dunphy pulled on his shorts and stood in his bare feet on the cold stone floor. Grimmett started up the stairs. At the door of the gym he turned and looked back. "It's boxing," he said.

Crampsey was tightening the ropes around a boxing ring. It was set, with wooden benches arranged around it, in the middle of the floor.

"Right," said Crampsey. "When you're not boxing, you'll watch." He glared at them from under bushy eyebrows. "That should stop any pussyfooting about. Makes you fight when there's people watching. Only way to toughen you up. Make men of you."

He leaned into the ropes and grunted as they bounced him upright. He swung an arm around the class and pointed.

"You and you!" he barked. "McCue and Rowland. On with the gloves and into the ring. Three one-minute rounds." He looked over the class. "You, Newberry. You're the timekeeper. Get on the bell."

"Sir," said McCue. "Excuse me sir."

"What?" Crampsey unhooked a stopwatch from a string around his neck. He handed it to Newberry.

McCue coughed. "It's not a very fair fight sir. I'm a lot smaller than Rowland."

"Smaller!" said Crampsey. He glared at McCue. "You're not frightened of him are you McCue?"

"No sir." McCue cleared his throat. "But I'm not . . . well, I'm not a fighter and he'd probably . . . enjoy it more against someone who's as big as he is."

Crampsey bent forward. He glared at McCue, his face inches away. "You're an artist right? Delicate sensibilities and that sort of thing. Well, I'll leave that to the art department. It's my job to make you into a man." He straightened up. "I'll referee," he said. He grunted as he ducked through the ropes. "Size doesn't matter in a refereed fight. If you're smaller you'll perform beyond your capabilities."

Half way through the first round McCue's nose was bleeding freely. He was fending off Rowland's blows with feeble pawing motions, and trying to turn his head away.

"C'mon box!" shouted Crampsey. "Fight like a man!"

14

Rowland crashed two more blows to McCue's stomach then stepped back, waiting for Crampsey to stop the fight.

"Whatsamatter?" shouted Crampsey, waving his arms. "Get stuck in there!"

The carnage continued until the bell rang at the end of the round. Newberry the timekeeper helped McCue out of the ring, and led him down to the washrooms.

"God," whispered Dunphy. "That was awful."

"Yes, well, he wasn't an officer you see," said Grimmett.

Dunphy looked at him, and Grimmett said, "Crampsey. It makes a difference." He ducked as Crampsey threw a towel across the ring at him.

"No talking," he said. "Take that and clean up the floor."

He spotted Dunphy's bare feet. "You," he said to Dunphy, "and . . ." his finger wavered, until it was pointing at Macgregor. "You."

Dunphy sucked in his breath. Macgregor was a front row forward on the school's rugby team. He was known for his temper.

Dunphy squeezed through the ropes. Grimmett helped him to put on the heavy boxing gloves. "Try not to hit him," said Grimmett. "You'll just make him mad. Stay out of his way. I'll throw in the towel if he hits you."

Dunphy ran his tongue over his lips, and nodded. He looked up as McCue walked slowly back across the gymnasium floor; his nose swollen and red, shining like a clown's.

McCue lowered himself onto a bench beside Grimmett. "It's barbaric," he said, speaking through his mouth, as if he had a bad cold.

The bell rang. Macgregor jumped up and immediately dropped into a crouch. Dunphy walked slowly towards the centre of the ring and offered his glove in a handshake. Macgregor hit Dunphy's glove out of the way and moved forward, jabbing the air in front of Dunphy's face. Dunphy backed away with an ungainly dance step. He spent the rest of the round running backwards, moving with surprising agility. When the bell rang at the end of the round Dunphy was unmarked.

"Well done," said Grimmett, as Dunphy collapsed onto the seat in the corner. "Keep it up and you'll tire him out."

Dunphy looked up. He was breathing hard. "He's really trying to hit me," he said.

Grimmett fanned him with the towel. The bell rang. Dunphy rose slowly to his feet. He dashed out of the way as Macgregor lunged across the ring. As he turned, his bare feet slipped on a wet patch where Grimmett had mopped McCue's blood off the floor. He cannoned into Crampsey as a wild overhand punch from Macgregor flailed over his head.

"Fairies!" The ex-Commando picked himself up from the floor. He stuck the whistle in his mouth and gave it a blast. "Fairies! Call that boxing? Neither one of you's landed a punch yet!"

He grabbed Macgregor's gloves. "Take 'em off. Take 'em off," he wrenched at Macgregor's wrists. "I'll show you what boxing is." He looked wildly around the class.

Dunphy might have been all right if he hadn't opened his mouth. "Not me sir," he said. He retreated towards the ropes, breathing heavily.

"Yes, you sir!" roared Crampsey, pulling on the gloves. He blew the whistle and spat it out of his mouth. It dropped to the end of the cord around his neck. Dunphy backed away.

Crampsey dropped into a crouch with his left hand in front of his face, his right glove wavering protectively in front of his groin. He advanced, jerking his head unpredictably from side to side. Dunphy skipped into a corner and bounced off the ropes.

Suddenly Crampsey lunged, bringing his shoe down on Dunphy's unprotected foot.

"If they won't fight," he said through clenched teeth, "You've got to bring them to bay."

Dunphy let out a yelp and poked a glove in Crampsey's chest. It was a mistake. Crampsey answered with a quick rat-a-tat-tat on Dunphy's stomach, and a stiff blow to his chin. Barely pausing, he boxed Dunphy's ears with his gloves open, as if he was clapping his hands. Dunphy reeled away and fell down on the floor.

16

"Come on! Come on!" shouted Crampsey, motioning with his glove. "Get up and fight. What's wrong with you?" Dunphy crawled towards the ropes. The ex-Commando stared down at him in disgust.

"Next!" he shouted, whirling round to face the class. His face was flushed. Nobody moved; every one avoiding eye contact.

Grimmett stood up and helped Dunphy to his feet. He started to unlace Dunphy's gloves.

"You then!" roared Crampsey, pointing at Grimmett. Dunphy tottered to a bench, and sat down and cradled his head in his hands.

"No sir," said Grimmett.

"What?" Crampsey's face was purple.

"I don't want to sir."

Crampsey thrust the gloves into Grimmett's hands. "You're scared are you?" He straightened up. "Well, it's my job to make men of you. You'll box."

Grimmett held the gloves for a moment, and then pulled them on. McCue helped him to lace them up.

"If this wasn't so sickening it might almost be funny," said McCue, his voice thick. "A grown man too." His nose was stuffed with cotton wool to stop the bleeding.

Grimmett opened his mouth to say something, but thought better of it. He bent through the ropes into the ring. Crampsey advanced towards him, darting his head from side to side like a puppet.

"The bell sir," said Grimmett.

"The bell," roared Crampsey.

Newberry rang the bell. Crampsey dropped into his crouch, and came forward with his head to one side. He shot out a glove and hit Grimmett on the ear. The blow stung. Grimmett backed away. Crampsey made a wheeling motion with his gloves, beckoning Grimmett forward. Grimmett continued to retreat.

Crampsey feinted with his left and slapped Grimmett on the top of his head with his right hand. Then he lowered his gloves and glared at Grimmett. "This is a boxing lesson," he said, as if he'd suddenly regained his equilibrium. He stuck out his chin and did a cocky dance step. "Come on," he said. "Hit me."

17

Grimmett hit him on the point of his chin just as he was changing feet in his little dance step. Crampsey twirled around and fell on the floor with a crash. Grimmett stared down at him in shock. The ex-Commando lay on his back with his arms and legs splayed out like a child playing dead, his head twisted to one side. No one moved. No one spoke.

Crampsey's right arm twitched and he tried to lift his head. His eyes opened and he grinned stupidly up at Grimmett.

"Goo' shot," he said. "G' punch." He rolled awkwardly to his knees, knuckling his gloves on the floor for support. Grimmett helped him to his feet and piloted him to the side of the ring. The ex-Commando wrapped his arms round the ropes as his knees sagged. Grimmett waited, unsure what to do next, suddenly thoughtful of the consequences.

"Don't unnerstand," mumbled Crampsey, stumbling as the ropes gave under his weight. "Shouldn't've happened." He waved an arm at the door. "Dismiss'," he said. "Class dismiss'."

"Poor guy," said Dunphy when they were outside. They had changed quickly.

"He's a bully," said Grimmett. "He likes seeing people hurt. Besides you didn't think that earlier when you were in the ring with him."

"No," said Dunphy. "But it's different now. I feel sorry for him."

"He's got a chip on his shoulder as big as the gym there. You wait; he'll make it up on me. Next week or the week after."

Dunphy shook his head. "I feel sorry for people like that."

"That's because you don't really live here," said Grimmett. "You'll leave here and go back and live in Canada with your family and have nothing more to do with this place. So it doesn't make any difference to you does it?"

Dunphy was taken aback by the bitterness in Grimmett's voice. He started to speak, but then he realised he didn't really know what to say. He turned to walk away.

"He'd have beaten you up you know," Grimmett called after him.

Chapter 4 – Poachers

They were lying side by side on the grass bank, staring into the pool. The water sparkled in the sunlight that filtered through the branches above them. On both banks the ground rose dapple-shadowed into the woods.

"There. See!" Grimmett pointed at the far bank, where mud and roots met the water. A slim brown shape glided into deeper water, glinting as it passed through a patch of refracted sunlight.

"See the spots on its back?" The fish flicked its tail and moved slowly across the pool towards them. Grimmett pulled back his sleeve, his eyes fixed on the fish.

"Watch," he said. "Don't move." He slid his hand into the water, careful not to make a ripple. The fish was facing into the current, almost motionless now, except for tiny movements of its tail to keep it facing upstream.

Grimmett eased his hand through the water and brought it carefully up to the fish, until his fingers hung under its belly. The fish's tail bent in a small eddy.

"Come on. Come on." Dunphy's teeth were clenched with tension. Grimmett began to stroke the fish's stomach. Dunphy could see its gills opening and closing as it breathed. He watched Grimmett's hand caressing seductively, working up towards the fish's head.

19

Suddenly the water churned as Grimmett seized the trout behind the gills and flipped it struggling onto the bank. Grimmett jumped up, his foot slipping into the water. "Damn," he said.

The fish leapt about on the grass, beating the ground with its tail. Dunphy twisted round and sat up.

"Fantastic!" he said. "Where did you learn to do that?"

"We'd better kill it," said Grimmett. "Here." He reached past Dunphy and picked up a fallen branch. The wood broke as Grimmett brought it down on the trout's head. The fish jumped once and lay still.

Dunphy gazed at it. The fish's mouth was open, its eyes dull and glassy.

"My father showed me how to do it, a long time ago," Grimmett said. "He's better at it than I am." He looked around, searching the line of the woods. "We'd better get going. It wouldn't do for us to get caught in here. They can take you to court."

He shook the water out of his shoe, and looked down at the fish, damp on the grass. "We should get rid of it in case we're caught," he said.

"Get rid of it?" said Dunphy. "You've just killed it! You can't waste it like that."

"There'll be big trouble if we get caught with it."

"What did you catch it for then? You can't just go round killing things like that. Even fish."

Grimmett stared at him. He shrugged his shoulders. "I don't know. For the fun of it I suppose."

"It's not right," said Dunphy.

"Well then, we'll have to get it out of here," said Grimmett.

The trout was about a foot long. It was a warm day, and Grimmett was wearing shorts and a grey shirt, splashed now with water from the stream. He looked at Dunphy.

"You'll have to carry it." He bent down and picked up the fish. "You'll have to put it down your trousers so the gamekeeper won't see it if we bump into him." He indicated his own clothing. "Shorts. I can't hide it, and we've got nothing else to conceal it with."

A look of dismay passed over Dunphy's face. He scrambled to his feet. His lip curled.

"I'm not putting it down my trousers," he said. "It's all slimy and wet."

Grimmett shrugged. "You were giving me the lecture about killing it. You'll have to, or else we'll have to leave it here . . . and we'll have killed it for nothing."

Dunphy backed away as Grimmett advanced towards him with the fish. "You'll have to," said Grimmett. "You just said we can't waste it."

"I didn't know you were going to get me into this kind of trouble," said Dunphy. "You should've told me first."

"We're not in trouble yet." Grimmett bent down and began to push the fish up the leg of Dunphy's trousers. "Here. Stick your hand in your pocket and hook your fingers through its gills."

He stood back to study the effect. One of Dunphy's legs looked fatter than the other, but the fish was hidden.

"It'll have to do," said Grimmett. "If we meet up with anyone I'll try and walk in front of you so they won't see it." He started to climb up the bank to the path, passing through lines of sunlight streaming past tree trunks, so that it looked to Dunphy for a moment as if his movements were being projected in a slow motion film.

Dunphy clambered up to the path. "Slow down a bit," he said, puffing.

On the path Dunphy stumped along with one leg stiff, rolling his body from side to side.

"You should have a stick," said Grimmett. "It looks as if you've got a bad leg or something."

They walked on through the woods, until a few minutes later they saw a stocky, tweed-jacketed man coming towards them. The Gamekeeper stopped, waiting for them to reach him. He was dressed in plus fours, standing with his feet planted a little bit apart. He watched them as they approached, his head tilted to one side under a deerstalker hat, a shotgun crooked over his arm.

"'Efternoon lads," he said. "And what hae' ye been up tae in here then, eh?"

"We've been out for a walk," said Grimmett. "Exploring the countryside."

"Yer no' frae 'roon here though," said the Gamekeeper.

"No," said Grimmett. "We're just out for the day from Edinburgh."

"Ye'll not know then that you're no' supposed tae be in here," said the Gamekeeper, holding a pleasant note in his voice, but dropping his tone. "This land belongs tae Lord Lothian. Ye'll not have noticed the sign then, back up at the road?" He swung the shotgun muzzle round to indicate the direction of the road.

Grimmett shook his head. "No. We must have walked round in a big circle and come on to the property without knowing it."

The Gamekeeper studied him for a moment, then switched his gaze to Dunphy. He narrowed his eyes. His nose twitched, as if he'd just caught a whiff of some odour. "Ye'll know now," he said. "I'd not like tae catch you in here again." He nodded. "Guid day." He signalled them to continue with a lift of the gun muzzle, and stood and watched as they walked away.

Dunphy whistled through his teeth when they were out of earshot. "Jeez," he said, without looking at Grimmett. "Didn't like the look of him."

Grimmett turned and looked back down the path. The Gamekeeper had his back to them. He was climbing down the slope towards the stream, casting his eyes to his right and left.

"Oops!" said Dunphy. The trout slid out from the bottom of his trouser leg, and flopped onto the ground.

"Quick. Grab it." Grimmett shot a glance back at the Gamekeeper, but he had disappeared into the trees. The woods stood empty and silent. Grimmett knelt down and pushed the fish back up inside Dunphy's trousers, until Dunphy could hook his fingers into the gills again.

They reached the road and followed it between drystone walls to a small village with smoking chimney pots.

"Why have they got fires on?" said Dunphy. He pulled a handkerchief from his pocket and wiped his face. "It's a hot day." His nose wrinkled. The fish was beginning to smell, and his leg hurt from the effort of keeping it straight.

"They need the fires for cooking," said Grimmett. "Most of them still have coal stoves."

The green and white bus wound its way down country roads towards Edinburgh. There were only two other passengers on board, and they quietly removed themselves to seats near the front. Grimmett and Dunphy had the back of the bus to themselves.

Grimmett stood up and opened the window so that the breeze would dilute the smell of fish. They passed through a copse and emerged by a field of tall green barley. The wind flushed dark patterns through the waving stalks. Three dead crows hung upside down on a fence.

"How did you know about that place?" said Dunphy.

Grimmett looked up towards the front of the bus. "We used to live out that way. A long time ago, before my father went overseas. I like to go back there sometimes."

The bus drove past the first houses of the city; squat brown and grey stone bungalows with red tile roofs.

"The fish," said Dunphy. "What do you want to do with it?"

"You take it," said Grimmett. "My mother would know where it came from. She's a bit funny about these things. She doesn't like the idea of me going back there."

Dunphy looked down at the fish. It stared glassily back at him from the floor of the bus.

"I'm not sure they'd like it," he said. He waved his hand vaguely.

"Tell them it's a gift from Lord Lothian," said Grimmett. He stood up and grasped the back of the seat in front of him. "I've got to get off here." He pushed a red button under the luggage rack, and a bell rang up by the driver. "It wouldn't be right to leave it after we caught it. And killed it."

The bus slowed. Grimmett raised his hand, and moved down towards the front.

"See you Monday," called Dunphy, and watched through the window as Grimmett stepped onto the pavement, and the bus accelerated away.

"Where have you been all day?" Grimmett's mother was frowning, her face clouded. "You know I asked you to clean your things out of the spare room, and to fix the shed door."

Grimmett stood in the doorway of the living room. The television flickered black and white pictures of a tennis match across the screen. A glass sat on a table by his mother's elbow.

"Who's playing?" he said.

"Laver and Cooper. Get me a gin and tonic, there's a dear. There's some lemon in the fridge."

Grimmett picked up her glass with the King George IV crest on it, and went through to the kitchen. The level in the gin bottle was low. It was only two days since he'd helped her in with the groceries. The bottle had been full then. He levered two cubes of ice out of the metal tray from the tiny freezer, and dropped them into the glass. The ice crackled as he poured gin over it.

"Uncle Ronald's coming for supper," his mother said, as she took the glass. "I need you to fix that shed door. We'll be putting some things in it soon and I want to be able to lock it. And the spare room's a mess." She took a sip of the gin and tonic. "Tomorrow," she said. "I want it done this weekend. By tomorrow."

Uncle Ronald wasn't a blood uncle; he was a friend of Grimmett's mother. She'd told her son to call him 'uncle', but the relationship remained distant. The two of them were oblivious to Grimmett at supper, and talked to each other as if he wasn't there. His mother called out as Grimmett carried the dishes through to the kitchen.

"Uncle Ronald and I are going out for a little while dear. We'll leave you to do the dishes and clean up. We won't be late." And then they were gone, disappearing up the road in Uncle Ronald's old Rover.

Grimmett opened the front door and sat down on the step and looked west over the roofs of the houses on the lower side of the street. The sun was hanging just above the tops of the hills, throwing great sections of them into shadow. It was on the other side of these hills that he'd spent the afternoon with Dunphy. Already it seemed infinitely far away.

Chapter 5 – The Ace of Spades

Henry Dodson was class master for Grimmett and Dunphy. It was his job to shepherd them through the year, receive information about them from other teachers, field complaints about them, and occasionally act on them. It was Dodson's task to teach them and prepare them for the future, and so it was through the years of the school, one teacher passing his pupils on to another.

Dodson had taught at the school since the end of the Second World War. Before that, he had gone straight from Cambridge into the Army. The Army had shipped him to France early in 1940, where he had lasted until a small engagement outside a village called Wimereux, a few miles from Boulogne on the Channel coast. He had collected a bullet in his thigh there, and lost a lot of blood, and so he was left in the village with a doctor and a small company of wounded colleagues, including some Frenchmen—while the rest of his Regiment pulled back to Calais and then Dunkirk. The next day the Wehrmacht had driven into the village. Dodson had spent the rest of the war in prison camps in Germany and Poland.

It was only his love for the classics that had kept him going. He had memorised the Aeneid in the camps, and even now, many years later, he could still recite it in its entirety. At the end of the war he had been repatriated, to join former colleagues and contemporaries who had come out of the war as Colonels, one as a Brigadier-General. But Dodson remained a Second Lieutenant, his career and his rank frozen in time by his capture.

It had been more than his wife could take, although they had tried together to start again. But eventually she found that she missed the regimental parties, and the whole social milieu she'd grown used to with his friends while he was a prisoner-of-war. Elevated social activities that were not fully open to Dodson now in peacetime, because he was still a junior officer. It had become clear to him that his return was causing awkwardness for his wife, and for some of his old friends. In the end it was better to forget it all, and accept that he would have to go in a different direction. But it had left a piece of him stunted in some way—unsure and not quite grown up, and subject to sombre moods and uncertain tempers.

"Grimmett," he said now. "I want to see you after the class."

Grimmett looked up from his exercise book. "Yes sir."

Dodson walked slowly up the aisle between the desks. He stopped and looked over a boy's shoulder to check on the assignment he had given. "Move over," he said to Newberry, and squeezed onto a small square of seat beside him.

"What's that?" he said, pointing at the paper on Newberry's desk. Dunphy stopped writing and waited.

"It's a picture of the Faeces, sir," said Newberry. "The rods and the axe. The Roman rule of law." He pointed at his drawing, neatly titled in a calligraphic hand.

"The Fasces!" shouted Dodson, erupting suddenly. "It's nothing like it. Looks like something the cat threw up. What's that?" He tapped his pencil at a point on the page.

"That's the twine that binds it all together, sir."

"God help us. It's more like something from the other end of the cat." He glanced around, as if to measure the effect of his joke. Newberry laughed uneasily. His face was pale.

"Ha, ha. Yes sir." Dodson stood up and pulled Newberry's ear.

"You can do better than that Newberry." His voice had an unnatural cadence. His wife had found it irritating when he was annoyed. Grimmett felt the muscles tighten in his stomach.

"What do you think your father would make of that Newberry?" said Dodson. "A son who can't tell the difference between authority and excrement. He's a magistrate of some stature I believe. Do you think he'd appreciate that?"

Newberry sat stiff in his chair, staring in front of him.

"Well, would he?"

"No sir." Newberry's voice was almost inaudible.

Outside, the bell pealed across the playground. No one moved. Dodson walked back to his desk, his shoes clicking on the wooden floor. He sat down and stared at the open book in front of him. It was a full minute before he looked up. "All right," he said. "You can go now. Except for you Grimmett."

The boys stood up, and gathered books and papers before passing to the front of the room and out the door. Grimmett stayed at his desk.

"Collect your things," said Dodson. "I don't intend to talk to you here. We'll go to my study."

Grimmett followed him out of the classroom into the schoolyard, walking half a step behind, aware of the shouts and laughter of break time around him. He looked straight ahead as he walked. They reached a drab brownstone building in the corner of the schoolyard, and Dodson pushed open an opaque glass door. This was the entrance to the Master's Common Rooms. Grimmett had never been in the building before.

"In here," said Dodson. He led the way into a short hallway by a narrow staircase, and opened a door to his right. Grimmett heard the front door close behind them on its spring.

"And here. Come on boy." He showed Grimmett into a spare, cold room brightened only by northern light from a frosted window. There was a desk with a straight-backed wooden chair, and an oaken bookcase with no books in it against one wall. There was nothing else in the room.

Dodson turned to face him. "You know why you're here?"

"No sir."

"All right then, I'll tell you." Dodson's voice was thick. "You came into my class in September. That is, you were put down a level from last year because your marks were poor. You were therefore expected to excel in my class, it being a lower standard to that which you had previously aspired. This despite the fact, in my considered opinion— and in that of my colleagues who have had the doubtful benefit of your company—that your intelligence warrants your presence in the top stream of pupils." He cocked his head to one side. "What do you have to say to this?"

Grimmett stood with his feet together, hands by his sides. "I don't know sir."

"You are now half way through your first term with me," said Dodson, "and I find that you are near the bottom of my class." Dodson too was standing almost at attention.

"Now, I consider myself a very good teacher. My record speaks for itself. Some of our most successful barristers, bankers and stockbrokers have passed through my hands. So your poor performance can be no fault of mine. What do you have to say to that?"

"I don't know sir."

"There can only be one conclusion Grimmett. It is that you are not working. Not working because you are lazy. There is only one way to deal with people like you. That is to knock some sense into you. If the carrot doesn't work, we have to use the goad."

Grimmett bit his lip. He felt his left knee shake. Dodson continued, his voice rumbling around the dark panelling on the walls. "This time I won't take it any further than something which lies between you and me Grimmett. But I intend to beat you. Can you give me any reason why I shouldn't?"

Grimmett looked at the floor, and said nothing. Dodson reached into a drawer in the desk and pulled out a thick, coiled strap. He placed it on top of the desk. Grimmett lifted his head and stared at it, worn and shining in the flat light. God, he must have one in each of the rooms he uses.

Dodson took off his jacket and hung it over the back of the chair. He turned to face Grimmett and wound the heavy leather thong round his wrist. Suddenly he swung it to one side in an arc. The tawse cut through the air with an

28

audible swish. Dodson grunted. Grimmett could feel his heart beating.

"We'll do it differently this time, shall we Grimmett?" Dodson's voice was controlled, still in that uneven cadence. "I want you to bend over and stick your head under here." He pointed at the desk. "That way you'll keep your head down and the seat of your trousers stretched tight across your bottom."

Grimmett bent forward and pushed his head under the desk, and felt the cold wood on the back of his neck. He waited, apprehension and anger mixed together. Dodson stepped back and with no more warning swung his arm. Grimmett's head jerked involuntarily upwards and cracked the underside of the desk. The strap cut through the air again, then four more times. Grimmett made no sound, and let the desolation and shame of it wash over him. He could hear Dodson breathing heavily.

"You can go now." Again that controlled voice. "But you had better buckle down, or we'll meet here again. You can count on it."

Grimmett straightened up and walked out of the room into the pale sunshine. He limped across the yard to the classroom, the shouts of play pushing at him.

"How was it this afternoon?" said Dunphy. They had been in separate classes since Grimmett's interview with Dodson. Now it was nine o'clock at night. They had arranged to meet by the cathedral in the High Street.

Grimmett took Dunphy's arm and steered him past a great grey plinth carrying a statue of King Charles on a big charger. He walked Dunphy into a narrow lane behind the great church.

"It was perfectly bloody," said Grimmett. "I've got to get out of that place. I don't want to put up with any of that crap any more." He took his school cap off his head and stuffed it in his jacket pocket. Outside school they were allowed to wear sports jackets instead of blazers, but the rules stated that they always had to wear the school cap and tie.

"Must've hurt," said Dunphy. He was wearing a short white raincoat against the uncertain weather.

29

They reached the end of Parliament Close. "Take your cap off," said Grimmett, "unless you don't want to come."

"Where are you going?" Dunphy reached automatically for his cap. He folded it into a pocket of his raincoat. "We'll both get beaten if anyone sees us. Do you like it or something?"

"Come on," said Grimmett. "Don't dawdle. The place opens at nine and I want to get in there before many customers turn up." He looked up and down the street. "It's safer that way."

"What are you talking about? You'll just get yourself in a heap more trouble."

"Look. It's the only way I know to get out of this whole business. If I can make some money then I can leave this place. Otherwise . . ." He stared at Dunphy for a moment. "It's different for you," he said, and walked on.

Dunphy wavered, and then walked quickly after him. He pulled his collar up, and they fell in step as they passed the door of the Sheriff Court. He hunched his shoulders and tried to appear inconspicuous. A moment later he realised that Grimmett had disappeared.

"Psst!" Dunphy spun round and peered about him in the gloom. "In here!" Grimmett beckoned from the shadowed entrance of an alleyway. Dunphy followed him under an archway.

The lane curved, cobblestoned and slick with drizzle, down towards the Cowgate. They descended a steep hill, past dank, musty courtyards, towards a glistening, slate roofscape. The alley was badly lit and running with rainwater. Greasy cobbles reflected the dim light from windows. Garbage lay heaped in dark doorways, and sodden pieces of paper lifted in the wind that curled and twisted between dripping walls. Grimmett's steel toe-caps clipped on the slope.

"Where are we going?" said Dunphy.

"Here." Grimmett stopped at a green door beneath a weak neon sign which flickered out the name 'Ace of Spades'. "I told you. I've got to get some money together." He pushed a bell in the wall by the door.

It was quiet except for the desultory sound of traffic filtering up from the Cowgate. The door opened a few inches. A pale face stared out at them. After a moment of silent scrutiny the door opened wider, and they were ushered inside.

"Card?" The woman held out her hand. She was wearing a high-necked red gown, her face layered with make-up. In the faint light Dunphy could see that she was about forty years old, and trying to look younger. Grimmett pulled a creased green card from his pocket. The woman studied it for a moment and handed it back.

"Your guest?" She nodded at Dunphy.

"Yes."

"Okay," she said. "What's it to be tonight?"

"Chemmy," said Grimmett. He avoided looking at Dunphy.

"Follow me." The woman set off up a narrow staircase.

Dunphy pulled at Grimmett's arm. "What are you playing at? This is unbelievably dangerous." His voice was higher than normal. "I don't believe what we're doing here."

At the top of the stairs they followed the woman down a dimly lit corridor. She stopped at a door and ushered them inside.

Two men were sitting at a green, baize-topped table overhung by a long, wide light suspended three feet above the cloth. One of the men wore a velvet-collared evening jacket, and a white, frilled shirt topped by a black bow tie. He was short and burly, and he looked bored. His jacket was buttoned at the waist. It was a size too small for him. The breadth of his shoulders pulled it wide at the lapels, and gave him a barrel-chested look.

The other man was wearing a lounge suit that sparkled in the cone of light from an overhead lamp. He turned to stare at Grimmett and Dunphy, a cigarette at the corner of his mouth. Dunphy hung back, staying near the doorway as Grimmett stepped into the room.

"Sit down Jimmie," said the man in the dinner jacket. He indicated the semi-circle of vacant chairs around the table.

"We'll just watch for a minute if you don't mind," said Grimmett. Dunphy moved up beside him, his hands in the pockets of his short raincoat; wishing he were somewhere else.

"Take yer coats off then," said the croupier. He indicated a line of hooks on the wall, and turned to the man in the sparkling suit. He dealt a card from the wooden shoe before him, and flicked it across the table.

The door opened behind Grimmett, and a thin man with thin, straight hair, strode into the room. He walked directly to the table and sat down in the chair beside the croupier.

"Deal me in next hand," he said. He extracted a packet of cigarettes from his pocket, lit a cigarette, and placed the packet on the table. He exhaled the smoke noisily, and it hung under the hooded light.

Grimmett and Dunphy watched the game for several minutes. "This is madness," said Dunphy, in a whisper.

"You can go if you want," said Grimmett.

Dunphy twisted inside his raincoat. He cleared his throat. "What game is this anyway?"

The man in the dinner jacket, the croupier, reached out a long wooden spatula and flipped the cards back towards him. He stuffed them into the shoe behind a plastic separator, and gave Dunphy a withering look.

"Chemmy," he said. He switched his stare to Grimmett. "Are you in now?"

"Yes." Grimmett pulled back one of the chairs and sat down. Dunphy hovered behind him, as if he was ready for flight.

"You! Jimmie!" said the Croupier. "Sit!" He pointed to a chair with the spatula. "We'll no' have any of that in here."

"He thinks you're going to try and look at the cards," said Grimmett. "You'd better sit down."

Dunphy flopped into a seat, and then sat upright, on its edge.

The croupier flipped a card to each of the three players. "Place your bets," he said.

Grimmett turned his card over. It was the three of diamonds.

"What do you have to do?" said Dunphy.

"Ssshh. I'll tell you in a minute." Grimmett took a ten-shilling note from his pocket. He tossed it on the table.

The other players placed their bets. The croupier tossed another card across the table. Grimmett picked it up, and gathered it to his chest. It was the ace of hearts.

"Any more bets?" said the croupier. Grimmett shook his head. The man in the sparkling suit dropped a five-pound note on top of the money he had already wagered. The thin man pushed a pound note in front of him, and dragged on his cigarette. The croupier stared at Grimmett for a second, then reached forward to deal another card to the older man in the lounge suit.

Grimmett stopped him. "I think I'll put something on," he said. He placed another ten-shilling note beside the first one.

"How much money have you got?" said Dunphy. "I've only got five shillings."

"Three pounds," said Grimmett.

"God. It's nothing."

"Banquo," said the thin man, drumming fingers on the table. The croupier ignored him, and glared at Grimmett.

"Make up your mind," he said.

"Carte a la banque," said Grimmett.

The croupier tossed him a card. It flipped over on the table top, exposing itself as the nine of spades. Grimmett stared at it and looked up.

"Carte," he said again.

"That's your carte," growled the croupier. "The nine there."

"It turned over. I don't want it."

"Whadya mean you don't wantit. That's how you play the bloody game, Jimmie," said the croupier. "That's yer carte!" He reached forward and deftly removed Grimmett's two ten-shilling notes with his spatula. He placed them on top of a pile in front of him.

"Oh no," said Dunphy. "Now you've only got two pounds left."

"Ssshh," said Grimmett. "I'll do better next time."

Dunphy saw tiny drops of perspiration on Grimmett's forehead.

The croupier dealt again. Grimmett's first card was the Queen of Hearts. He put another ten-shilling note on

33

the table. His second card was the King of Clubs. He put a pound note on top of the ten shilling note.

"All or nothing this time," he said.

Dunphy rubbed his eyes.

"Carte a la banque," said Grimmett.

"Come on, Jimmie." The croupier was short of patience. "Stop pissing about. Put some money on."

"My name's not Jimmie," said Grimmett, reaching into his pocket.

"What? What's that?" The croupier rose half out of his chair. He banged the spatula down on the baize table-top. "Just watch it sonny or ye'll be out of this place!" He subsided back into his chair, glaring across the table at Grimmett.

Grimmett put his last ten-shilling note on the table. His next card was the eight of diamonds. The other players both took extra cards. The man in the lounge suit grunted in disgust and threw his hand into the middle of the table.

"It's a bit like pontoon or blackjack," said Grimmett quietly to Dunphy. "Only you've got to get eight or nine."

The croupier dealt his own hand openly. He drew a card from the shoe with the flat of his hand and flicked it over in front of him. It was a nine of diamonds. With the two of spades and the Jack of Diamonds already in front of him he had no useful score. He scowled at Grimmett, and pushed two pound notes across the table at him. Fifteen pounds went to the thin man beside him.

Dunphy poked Grimmett in the ribs.

The next game was easier. Grimmett was dealt an ace and an eight for a total of nine. The croupier dealt himself a three and a five. He looked across at Grimmett. His face dropped when Grimmett showed his hand. Grimmett collected four more pounds.

Grimmett played carefully for the next hour, and lost only two or three games. In the games he did lose, he had placed his bets conservatively. He gathered up a small pile of notes from the table and pushed his chair back. He stood and turned to leave.

"Hey! Wait a minute Jimmie," said the croupier, lifting his hand from the table. "You're not leaving the now?"

"Yes," said Grimmett. "I am."

The croupier looked round the table. He stared back at Grimmett. "You've got to give the bank a chance to redeem its losses," said the croupier, his teeth clenched. "It's not sporting to leave like that."

"I'm sorry, I've got a bus to catch," said Grimmett. He moved quickly to the door, and let himself into the corridor. Dunphy hurried after him. Downstairs, they let themselves out to the alleyway with only a glance from the woman at the table in the lower hallway.

Dunphy chuckled as they climbed up the hill to the High Street. "You sure showed them," he said. "How much did you make?"

Grimmett pulled the banknotes out of his pocket and counted them. "Twenty-eight pounds," he said.

"Twenty-eight pounds," said Dunphy. "That's a lot of money. I didn't know you knew all that stuff."

"I've been there a couple of times before," said Grimmett. "But it was the woman who was dealing both times. I lost."

They came out of the alleyway. Groups of people were walking down the pavement on either side of the High Street. A bus drove past, throwing light over them.

"Better put our caps on," said Dunphy, reaching in his pocket.

"Oh, to hell," said Grimmett. "I'm sick of all that stuff."

"Don't wreck it," said Dunphy. "You've done all right up to now. There's no point in just breaking their rules for the sake of it."

"There's always a point to it. Can't you see?"

Chapter 6 – The Champion and the Hare

"There's a letter for you from your father." Grimmett's mother pointed at the hall table. "He sent me one too." There was a grim smile on her face. She went into the living room.

Grimmett picked up the letter. He went into his room and closed the door. The front of the envelope was postmarked with Hindi symbols. The stamp had a picture of a tall, fluted column in a rich maroon colour, with the word 'India' at the top. He sat on the edge of his bed, and ran his finger up the side of the envelope, and opened it.

116, Palam Cantonments,
New Delhi

Dear Arthur,
Your letter took some time to reach me because of my move. It was sent back to HQ in London and eventually out here. As you see, they have now posted me to Delhi. I expect to be here for about a year, but you never know with the airline. They could move me somewhere else at short notice, or keep me here longer.

36

I have found a nice house on the airport side of the city. It is part of a new housing development. There is a police station across the road and the policemen play volleyball outside in the mornings. They are playing now as I write. It's hot, very hot—but I have a refrigerator to keep my beer cold. I have three servants; one to cook (Cookie), a dhobi to do the laundry (Dherma), and one to run the household and act as a kind of waiter (M'Habbia).

The most important thing that has happened is that Hillevi—whom you met at Larnaca—and I got married last month. I know you will be pleased that I have a chance at happiness with someone now. Hillevi has been given a posting to the Danish Embassy here and will join me in two weeks. I hope you will get to know her in time and come to care for her as I do. I know you will.

As to the request in your letter, we did discuss that when you were in Cyprus old chap. It really is impossible right now. There is no proper schooling out here—at least none which would be adequate. And of course my circumstances remain unreliable, as the company might choose to re-assign me at any time. It just wouldn't do.

Please give my salaams to your mother, and write to me from time to time, and let me know how you are getting on.

As ever, your Father.

Grimmett's mother pushed the door open, and came into his room. "Uncle Ronald's coming over this evening," she said. "We'll probably go out for a while. Your father all right?"

"Yes."

"I got a letter from him too," she said. "He told me he was getting married."

"Yes. That's what he's done."

She sat down beside him on the bed. "I have tried, you know Arthur," she said. "I've always tried to do what's best for you. You won't let me down will you?"

"No." He cleared his throat.

37

"Uncle Ronald's a nice man," she said. "He likes you, you know." She stood up and went to the door. "He likes us both." She went out.

The history master was drawing a diagram on the blackboard to show the manoeuvrings of the armies before the Battle of Waterloo. Grimmett was doodling in his notebook with a pencil. The master's voice floated in and out of his consciousness.

". . . and General Blucher's force entered the scene from here," intoned the history master. He indicated a spot on the blackboard with his pointer. He cast an eye around the class.

"Now, during the Napoleonic Wars the horses of the French Grand Armée consumed about twenty-five tons of hay every day. In the end the French were not able to cope with that. What do you call supply problems of that kind?" He shot out an arm and pointed. "McCue?"

"Hayburners," muttered Dunphy, not quite under his breath. He snorted at his own joke, and started coughing.

"Logistics boy!" said the history master. "Logistics! The secret of winning wars." He stared at them. "Tonight you will each write me a short essay on the logistical problems you would expect to occur in armies of that size and type. I want it by tomorrow. That's all." He rose from his desk and went out of the classroom, his black gown billowing behind him like a rain cloud.

"Well," said Dunphy. "That's screwed up the evening all right. It'll take all night to write that."

Grimmett put his hands behind his head. He leaned back and stared at the ceiling where cobweb strands hung out of reach of the cleaner's broom.

"To hell with it," he said. "I'm going out tonight."

"Where are you going?"

"Want to come?" said Grimmett. "It'll be an adventure for you. Something different."

"I don't know," said Dunphy. "Your last adventure was almost too much for me; the cards and that place."

"Tonight'll be different." Grimmett stood up. "It's up to you though. I'm going anyway."

Dunphy hurried out of the classroom behind him. "You're up to something aren't you," he said. "You've got some kind of a plan going on in your head."

"I've already told you," said Grimmett. "I want to get myself out of this place."

"Yes, but you'll just get yourself into a whole lot of trouble."

"You've told me that before."

"You've got twenty-eight pounds already from the other night," said Dunphy. "You should quit while you're ahead."

Grimmett laughed. "I need a hell of a lot more than that," he said.

"Oh Christ," said Dunphy. "And that essay won't get done for tomorrow either."

They slipped through the turnstile at Powderhall Racetrack. It was a cold night, and low clouds reflected the soft glow of the streetlights. It was threatening to rain, and the tenements which overlooked the track gave out an air of gloom and quiet struggle.

Grimmett was wearing an old, green, army greatcoat, and a Tyrolean hat with a short red feather in its brim. Dunphy had borrowed an overcoat, and a cloth cap that was too big for his head. It sat down over his eyes so that he had to tilt his head back to see properly.

"Diplomat's old clothes," he said. "Found them in a cupboard." They would be in trouble if they were seen anywhere near the racetrack by anyone from the school.

Inside the arena they were jostled by hurrying punters. "Keep your hands in your pockets," said Grimmett.

"What for?" said Dunphy.

"Pickpockets."

In front of them a man was gesticulating in the middle of the crowd. Dunphy's step faltered. He stared at the man, astonished. The man was standing on a wooden box, waving his arms in sweeping arcs, periodically tapping his elbows with his fingertips, the top of his head and his chest.

"Tic-Tac Man," said Grimmett. "He gives the odds to his pal over there." He pointed at another man who was making similar motions at the back of the crowd. "It's all sign language. Mumbo jumbo."

Dunphy followed Grimmett through the crowd to the wire barrier at the edge of the track.

"This is a good spot," said Grimmett. "We can see everything from here."

Eight sleek greyhounds trotted onto the track beside their handlers. Each dog wore a tiny coloured vest with a number on it. The handlers looked like lab technicians in long white coats. They paraded up and down in front of the grandstand for several minutes, and then led the dogs round behind a bank of wire-mounted traps. The handlers unhooked the leashes and pushed the dogs inside the traps.

The crowd went quiet as a loud whirring noise filled the stadium, and a mechanical hare sped jerkily around the inside of the grass track. The hare flashed past the traps and the gates sprang open. The dogs surged out in a wave, straining after the hare. Dunphy watched, fascinated.

The crowd began to shout for their favourites. A man beside Dunphy let out a roar of pain, and threw a pair of tickets down into the dirt at his feet.

"Feggin' porridge!" he said. He thrust his hands into the pockets of his coat and trudged off towards a sign which read 'Snacks'.

Grimmett stared down at the crumpled tickets.

"Sometimes," he said, "they give a dog porridge to eat before a race. It slows it down."

The dogs ran past the finishing post and a marshall tossed two big chunks of meat onto the track. The greyhounds immediately veered away from the hare and pounced on the meat in a rabble. The handlers pounced on the dogs, hooked the leashes on, and led them away. A scratchy, indistinct voice began to intone the result of the race over a loudspeaker.

"Now, in the next race," said Grimmett, lifting his programme to the light, "there's a dog called Black Diamond. They daren't do anything to slow him down because he's the Scottish champion. He's bound to win." He looked at Dunphy. "If you want to back a certainty, he's it."

"Me? Bet?"

"Why not?"

"Well, I might," said Dunphy. "I've got my mid-term train money on me. The Diplomat gave it to me."

"Why not?" said Grimmett again.

"What are the odds?" said Dunphy, grasping the terminology.

A light drizzle had begun to fall. Grimmett squinted at a bookie's signboard a short distance away.

"He's four-to-five on," he said. "It's not very good really. If you put five pounds on him and he wins that means you get your stake back and make another four pounds. And if he loses . . ." he shrugged his shoulders. "But he won't."

Dunphy shifted his feet. "I . . . don't know," he said. "It's the money for my train fare to London. I'm sunk if I lose it. I won't have enough to get down to my aunt's."

Grimmett regarded him for a moment. "Okay," he said. "But I'm going to put something on. A tenner I think."

"Wait!" said Dunphy, as Grimmett turned away. He reached into his pocket and pulled out a thin bundle of notes. He peeled off five. "You put it on for me." He thrust the notes into Grimmett's hand.

"All right." Grimmett took the money and made his way through the crowd to the bookie's stand.

Grimmett returned in a few minutes and handed Dunphy a receipt slip. A new batch of dogs was led onto the track, and paraded in front of the spectators.

"There." Grimmett pointed across the stadium. "That one." He glanced down at his programme. "Number seven. Black Diamond."

Dunphy tilted his head back and stared out under the brim of his cap. The dog looked groomed and cared for. There was a symmetry and an economy of movement in the way it walked that seemed to place it apart from the other greyhounds. The dogs disappeared into the traps.

The hare began to circle the course, throwing out a small shower of sparks as it rattled round the curve at the river end of the track. A puff of smoke hung in the floodlights to mark its passage. It whirred round the track towards them with a faintly audible grinding noise.

The hare flashed past the traps, and the dogs sprang out in pursuit, and dashed down the straight. At the river bend they skidded sideways on the wet turf, their legs and bodies pumping and undulating as they fought to retain their balance. One dog fell in a scrabbling heap and crashed into the side netting. The hare released another shower of sparks, and a loud bang reverberated through the stadium. The hare slowed visibly, and the dogs began to gain on it. Black Diamond stretched his lead to a yard.

Suddenly the hare let out another cascade of sparks, and lurched drunkenly on its side. Black Diamond was gaining on it with every stride. Sideways now, the hare continued to career round the track, trailing a thickening plume of blue smoke. The crowd fell silent. But Dunphy was jumping up and down.

"Come on! Come on Black Diamond!" he shouted, oblivious to the tension.

"Ssshh!" said Grimmett, tugging at his sleeve. "It mustn't catch it."

Black Diamond lunged at the hare and took it in his jaws, and wrenched it from its mechanical platform. A loud explosion shook the stadium and a great flash lit up the grandstand. The champion and the hare fell together at the side of the track and lay motionless for a second, and then they were set upon by the trailing dogs. There was complete confusion. The handlers ran onto the track with their white coats flapping, and fought to separate the snarling, snapping dogs. Men were shouting. Then the stadium lights went out.

"Broke down," said the ferret-faced man next to Dunphy, back from the snack bar. "Haw, haw, haw. The feggin' thing broke down." He poked Dunphy in the ribs. "Didya ever see anythin' like it, eh?" He grinned mindlessly out at the track where the marshals, handlers and dogs were milling about.

Dunphy turned to face Grimmett. "What happens to my money?" he said. His face was pale; his head back as he peered out from under the brim of his cloth cap.

"I don't know," said Grimmett. "Maybe they'll make an announcement."

It took the officials fifteen minutes to clear the track. The inert body of Black Diamond was wrapped in a blanket and carried off. A thin, tinny voice came over the tannoy system. Dunphy couldn't decipher it.

"It says," explained Grimmett, "that there will be no payout on the last race. All bettors will get their money back."

Dunphy sighed with relief, and felt in his pocket for his betting slip. He tried the other pocket. Panic mounting, he unbuttoned his overcoat and reached into the pockets of his jacket, then his trousers. He slapped his chest and lifted his feet to look on the ground.

"I've lost it," he said. "I've lost the receipt."

"You can't have," said Grimmett. "Look again."

"I've looked in every pocket twice. It must have gone through a hole in the lining." He flapped the coat in anguish, his hand thrust right through the material where the pocket should have been. "What'll I do? I don't have enough money now to get to my aunt's."

"You could put something on the next race," suggested Grimmett.

Dunphy felt himself drifting inexorably into the morass of the gambler. Grimmett pulled out the programme to study the form for the next race. Dunphy stared over his arm at the page.

"I don't understand this stuff at all," said Dunphy. "What do all these numbers mean?" He pointed at the page.

Grimmett pushed the Tyrolean hat back on his head. "That's the form," he said. "These figures in front of each dog's name are the results of its last six races." He scratched his nose. "The trouble is that it's hard to tell where a dog's been racing before. It only tells you sometimes and not others."

"That makes a difference?"

"Of course it does, you idiot. All the tracks are different, and you get different classes of dogs at each one. So if a dog like . . ." his finger moved down the page, ". . . like Speedy Knight wins two or three races at Wallyford it doesn't mean it can win here. It's a different class of racing. The dogs that go there aren't so good."

"I like that one," said Dunphy, reaching over Grimmett's arm and putting a finger on the page. "Ironsides."

"Hmmm . . . not bad," said Grimmett. "Not bad. Let's see . . . two seconds, a third and two firsts in its last six races." He scanned the information after the dog's name.

43

"Raced at Ayr and Perth. Not quite the same as Powderhall, but it might be worth a flutter."

He looked over at the tote board. The Tic-Tac Man was waving his arms about. Dunphy tilted his head back, and followed Grimmett's gaze.

"Ten to one!" Dunphy's voice was excited. "The odds are ten to one!"

"Yes, yes. I can see that," said Grimmett. He thought for a moment. "If you take my advice you'll put no more than a pound on it. That'll cover the lost ticket if you win, and put you a little bit ahead."

It was at this point that Dunphy slid a little off the rails. He heard himself say, with the gambler's irrefutable logic, "I've already lost five pounds, so I haven't got enough money for the train ticket down to my aunt's place anyway. I might as well go for broke. If I win I can travel First Class. Or buy her a nice present," he added. He thought for a moment.

"Right," he said. "Five pounds. You put it on for me again." He pulled his cap down over his eyes, and looked about in case he'd drawn attention to himself. "Er . . . ah . . . you were lucky for me the last time."

Out on the track two men in grimy overalls were screwing the mechanical hare back together. The new hare sat lopsidedly on its little sled. The explosion had twisted the metal frame, but it was still workable. The men stood up. One of them motioned to a third man in a wooden hut further round the track. The hare began to move tentatively along the electrified rail, making a high-pitched whine. As it came to the straight, the operator increased the speed, and the hare swayed and dipped as it raced towards the river bend. At the curve the hare leaned out from its platform like a motorcycle sidecar racer. As it clattered past the grandstand a derisive cheer went up from the assembled punters, then the hare slowed and came to a stop beside the waiting men in overalls.

One of them made another adjustment, and stepped back and waved at the operator again. The hare launched itself round the course once more. This time the mechanics appeared satisfied, and before the hare returned they disappeared beneath the grandstand.

Dunphy felt something jostling his left arm. It was the ferret-faced man. He'd been to the snack bar again. Now he was eating a greasy pie and chips, wrapped in a dirty copy of the Evening News. He offered a chip to Dunphy. Dunphy shook his head.

"Haw, haw, haw," guffawed the ferret-faced man, waving a half eaten chip in front of his face. "Funniest thing I ever saw." He popped the chip in his mouth, and punched Dunphy on the arm with a bony knuckle. "Feggin' dug went up in smoke."

Dunphy smiled nervously at him and looked around for Grimmett, second thoughts gnawing at him. But Grimmett was lost in the crowd in front of the bookie's stand.

"Godda bet on this race?" enquired the ferret-faced man through a mouthful of pie. He studied Dunphy, his jaws working.

"Er . . . ah . . . yes," said Dunphy.

"Watsit on?" He thrust his face close to Dunphy's.

Dunphy blenched before the odour of pork pie. "It's, ah . . . a dog called Ironsides."

"Ironsides! Haw, haw, haw," chortled his new companion. He slapped his thigh. "Ironsides! Haw, haw."

"Why? What's wrong with that?" said Dunphy. He felt a stab of apprehension.

"Notta chance. Notta bleedin' chance," said the ferret-faced man. "Feggin' dug's never run more'n a quarter mile." He thrust his programme under Dunphy's nose.

"See that?" He tapped the page with a chip, pointing at the numbers by the dog's name. "Never run more'n a quarter mile."

He lowered the sheet and looked at Dunphy. "Wellington Boot," he said.

"Pardon?"

"Wellington Boot," said the man. "That's yer best bet." He wagged a piece of pie at Dunphy. "That's what I've got my money on. He's won here before."

Grimmett arrived just as the dogs were parading from the grandstand to the traps.

"Grimmett," whispered Dunphy. He glanced over his shoulder at the ferret-faced man, who was standing with

45

his head sunk deep into his upturned collar. Dunphy jerked his thumb in the man's direction.

"He says that Ironsides has never run more than a quarter mile." Dunphy's voice sank to a moan. "What'll I do? That's all my money down the drain."

Grimmett leaned over so that his face was close to Dunphy's ear. "It's a quarter mile race," he said.

"Ha, ha, ha," laughed Dunphy, only slightly reassured.

The hare rattled past the traps. The gate sprang open and seven dogs leaped out, straining and jostling for the inside of the track. It was a long moment before the ferret-faced man realised that Wellington Boot was not among them. His mouth fell open as a long nose dragged slowly out of the eighth trap. On its tiny vest it wore the number five.

The other dogs were already racing round the top bend, skittering on the wet surface. The mechanical hare churned convulsively past in front of Dunphy and Grimmett.

The ferret-faced man let out a howl of indignation.

"Fix!" he screamed. "Feggin' fix." He looked wildly about him. "It's been got at. The Boot's been done." With a sweep of his arm he hurled the remains of his pie supper onto the track in front of the speeding dogs. The effect was electric. Instantly the dogs forgot the mechanical hare and dived, snarling and biting, onto the greasy, newspaper-wrapped pie. It disappeared in a second and the dogs started fighting amongst themselves. The crowd roared with anger.

Dunphy was horrified. Pale, he turned to confront the ferret-faced man. But the man had disappeared. The marshals were running round the track towards the spot where Dunphy and Grimmett were standing. The punters around them melted away, leaving them in the middle of a small, accusing circle.

Dunphy turned distraught to Grimmett. "Ironsides was in the lead," he said. "He was winning."

Grimmett grabbed him by the arm. "Come on," he said, staring at the white-coated marshals. "We've got to get out of here. They think it was us." He pulled Dunphy into the crowd.

Dunphy gazed through the rain-flecked window as the bus laboured up Dundas Street towards the lights of the city centre. The earlier drizzle had turned into a downpour. Rivers of rainwater ran freely down the gutters, bouncing reflections from the streetlights and the drawing room windows of the New Town flats. The rain drummed on the metal roof of the bus, audible over the straining engine, and the windscreen wiper thumped back and forth beneath his feet.

"I'll never make it down to my aunt's," said Dunphy. "The Diplomat'll kill me if I ask him for more money."

Grimmett sniffed. He'd caught a cold, and had problems of his own. The loss of eight pounds was a serious setback to his plans.

"He's pretty good about money. Stuff like that," Dunphy went on, as if he were talking to himself. "But he'd never forgive me for losing it at the dog track." He twisted round in his seat.

The bus changed down a gear and jerked them forward. Water dripped from the brim of the Tyrolean hat and fell inside Grimmett's collar. He shivered. "I'll lend it to you," he said. "I've still got twenty pounds. I can give you the ten you lost. You can pay me back out of your pocket money."

Dunphy received a Canadian standard of weekly allowance. His father had liberal ideas about teaching the value of money. He cheered up right away. "Thank you," he said. "It'll save my bacon. I'll pay it back as soon as I can."

Grimmett pulled the money from his pocket. He counted off ten notes, and handed them to Dunphy. He stared at the small pile of money left in his hand for a moment, and then put it away.

"Not much left," said Dunphy.

"No. I won't get very far on that."

"It'll work out," said Dunphy. "You wait and see."

Chapter 7 – Newberry

The train snaked through the small, grimy towns that dotted the countryside to the south of Edinburgh. It chugged down shallow valleys hung with triangular slag heaps and the detritus of old coal mines. The smoke from the engine was snatched away by the early winter wind, to drop its residue of soot onto green, wet fields and dripping trees.

Newberry dug into his holdall and pulled out a toilet roll. He stood up and slid back the compartment window, and let the slipstream unwind the roll in a long white streamer as the train began the run down from the village of Heriot into the long valley of the Gala Water. Grimmett watched with interest. The toilet paper writhed for a moment at the end of the roll, and then the wind snatched it away towards the back of the train.

"I've always wanted to do that." Newberry sat down. He leaned back into the upholstery with a smile on his face, and crossed his legs. He looked at Grimmett. "You've got no idea what it's like to get out of that boarding house," he said. "It's like . . ." he searched for a metaphor. "It's like— coming out a tunnel."

Grimmett nodded. He knew he wouldn't like to live in the school's boarding houses.

"Why are you coming down this way?" said Newberry.

"I've got cousins near Hawick," said Grimmett. "They live on a farm. I'm going down there for the mid-term break."

They gazed out the window. Streaks of rain slashed stripes across the glass. Sheep and cows speckled the misty hillsides.

"Have you met my father?" said Newberry. "He comes up to the school sometimes. He's a Trustee."

"No." Grimmett was surprised by the question. None of them talked about their parents.

"I thought you might have met him at Prize Day or something."

Grimmett shook his head. He looked up as the door slid open. The ticket collector came in, punched their tickets and left. The door closed. The carriage swayed as the train rumbled over a bridge.

"We don't get on very well," said Newberry. "A weekend's about as long as we can last without getting on each other's nerves." He frowned. "That's why I board at school I suppose."

"You're going home for the weekend then?"

"If you can call it that. My mother's dead. It's always been difficult since then; between my father and me, I mean."

Grimmett couldn't think of anything to say. He knew that some parents paid high fees for a private education in order to get their children out of the way.

Newberry reflected his thoughts. "My father's too busy for me to live there all the time. He's a magistrate."

Grimmett remembered the Roman history class, and Dodson's jibe at Newberry's simple mistake. The train shuddered and slowed as it approached Stow. The slow-moving river was spotted with circles of raindrops. A flight of ducks beat their wings soundlessly on the water. The train's brakes started to squeal.

The train drew into the country station in a dirty cloud of steam. The square tower of the old church stood across the road, its red-brown stonework stained dark with rain. The clock on the tower showed five minutes to eight.

49

"It always says five to eight," said Newberry. "It's quite suitable really. Time seems to have stopped here. It's a very conservative place." He wiped the window with his hand, and left a smear on the glass. "My father fits in well down here."

"What sort of magistrate is he?" said Grimmett.

"He's a Judge. He sends people to jail."

Family confidences were a private affair. Grimmett knew little about Newberry's life outside the school. He felt himself being drawn into uncharted territory. It made him uncomfortable.

A door banged shut. The train gave a lurch and stopped. A whistle blew. There was a hiss of escaping steam. The train moved forward, pulling slowly out of Stow. Newberry sat, stocky and red haired. He pointed out farms and country houses as the train puffed down the valley. He said no more about his father. Ten minutes later they drew into the station at Galashiels.

Newberry lifted his bag down from the luggage rack. He inclined his head towards the platform without looking out the window. "There's my father," he said.

Grimmett looked out of the window. A tall man was standing by himself, austere and pinched in the cold air, his breath misting in front of him in small, quick patches. He was wearing a black homburg hat, and a long black overcoat buttoned up to his neck. He carried a rolled umbrella in one hand, and shifted his weight impatiently from one foot to the other. Grimmett noticed dark tufts of hair at his cheekbones, and dark, deep-set eyes.

Newberry said goodbye and went out of the compartment into the corridor. Grimmett watched as he stepped onto the platform and walked up to his father. He saw the frown on the Judge's face, and then the attempt at a smile. The effect was hard and dispassionate. It startled Grimmett, and he saw Newberry's circumstances with a clarity that had evaded him about his own. Then for the rest of the weekend he forgot about Newberry and his father.

Grimmett walked slowly across the school yards. It was the first day back after the half-term break. He had just been given his Latin marks for the first part of the term. They were not good. One desk in the class had been empty;

Newberry's desk. Newberry's half-term marks had not been read out. The class list had jumped down the alphabet from McCue to Phillips.

Dunphy was coming towards him. "Did you see this?" He thrust a newspaper into Grimmett's hand. "Page three." He pointed as Grimmett turned the page. "There!"

The headline was small, tucked into a corner under a sub-heading entitled 'Border News'.

'Schoolboy Dead', it read. Grimmett felt a chill, and dropped his eyes to the story.

'Police are investigating the death of David Newberry, 17, son of Galashiels magistrate Judge Morton Newberry. Newberry was found dead from gunshot wounds at his house on Monday morning. Foul play is not suspected.'

A thin line cut across the column at the end of the piece. Grimmett drew his eye past it and read the next story, which had no heading.

'Galashiels police are investigating an outbreak of vandalism which occurred in the centre of town on Sunday night. Several street lights and neon signs were smashed, apparently by gunshots. Damage is estimated at over £1,000. No arrests have been made. A man is helping police with their enquiries.'

Grimmett stared across the yards, letting the newspaper fall. The vignette came back to him, like a clip of old black and white film with the reel stuck and replaying itself. A man meeting his son after a long absence; impatient with waiting; stern and distant, and dominant. It began to rain. He walked away.

"Are you all right?" called Dunphy, clutching the newspaper.

Grimmett was sitting at his desk after lunch when McCue walked into the classroom. He was a friend of Newberry's. McCue had relatives in Melrose, a small town near Galashiels.

51

"You went down in the train with Newberry, didn't you?" said McCue.

Grimmett nodded. "Yes."

"How was he? Did he say anything on the journey?"

"No," said Grimmett. "Not much. Just a bit about his father. He said they didn't get on."

"I'd have been on the train too,' said McCue, "but I had a dentist's appointment, so I had to get a later train." He looked round the classroom. Two boys were poring over a crossword puzzle. "Can we go outside?"

The rain had stopped. The wind tugged streamers of smoke from the tenement chimneys across the street, and clouds hurried over the wet slate roofs. The school bell tolled to mark the end of the lunch break. Schoolboys, on their way to the classrooms, crossed the yards in dark patterns.

"Don't pay any attention to the bell," said McCue. "I need to talk about this."

"It's okay," said Grimmett.

"I saw him on Sunday afternoon," said McCue. "He didn't seem right. Not himself, if you know what I mean. He'd had problems at home over the weekend."

He gazed up at the clouds. "Problems with his father." He looked at Grimmett. "His father was a bastard you know . . . a right bastard. I think he blamed Newberry for his mother's death somehow, but you never really know these things . . . it's just something he said once. I've known him for a long time." He was using the present tense, as if Newberry was still alive.

They reached the great iron gates that separated the school from the street. McCue grasped the bars with his hands and rested his forehead against the metalwork. A white delivery van was unloading boxes at the confectioners shop across the road.

"Did he tell you he was beaten here on Friday?"

"No." Grimmett's hands were deep in his pockets, his shoulders hunched forward.

"He was beaten after classes because he'd dropped all the way down from top place to nearly bottom. That happened to you too, didn't it?"

Grimmett didn't answer. McCue went on. "He got six from Dodson for that. Dodson was in the army with

52

Newberry's father at the beginning of the war. He telephoned Newberry's father about it.

"Oh God," said McCue. He leaned his forehead against the gate. "There was trouble about that when Newberry got home. From the little bit he told me on Sunday there was a big scene with his father. All about letting down the family name, disgracing the memory of his mother." He drew in his breath. "Dodson had known his mother too. He'd brought her name up when he was beating him." He shook his head. "That's bad enough, but then it's rubbed in by your own father . . . you'd wonder if there was anyone on your side at all."

They walked back across the empty, windswept schoolyard, bent forward with their hands in their pockets, their heads down and moving together in unison.

"It seems there was an argument and Newberry left the house," said McCue. "You know, in a strange sort of way he liked his father. I could never understand it, but he always seemed to need his father's approval. He never got it though; never got any respect for what he was. He seemed to need that. I could never understand it," he said again. "The man's a complete bastard . . . but I suppose if you don't have anyone else . . ."

They turned round the side of the grey, stone school building, and the wind died away. A shaft of light shone out of a classroom window onto McCue's face.

"My uncle's an Inspector in the Galashiels Police," he said. "He told me what happened on Sunday night. Newberry apparently walked out of the house and went to the garage and took his father's car. What no one knew until later, was that he'd also taken his father's shotgun."

McCue let his breath out slowly. A gust of wind blew his hair over his eyes. He brushed it away. "We'll never know what was going on in his head, but he drove off into Galashiels, and each petrol station he came to, he wound down the window and shot out the lights. You know, the big neon signs; a Shell one in the High Street, an Esso one on Eildon Street and a BP one down by the Nethergate. There might have been one or two others."

Grimmett's voice was flat. "I saw his father at the station on Friday. He looked," he hesitated, ". . . cold."

McCue didn't seem to hear him. "After he'd done that he went back to his house, put the car in the garage and went up to his room and shot himself." He stared at Grimmett. "His father had gone out. He always played Bridge on Sunday nights with friends down the street, so there wasn't anyone in the house. It wasn't until nearly midday on Monday that he found Newberry. He went up to his room to see why he wasn't all packed; ready to catch the train back to Edinburgh."

They moved around behind the main building. "Lunchtime on Monday," said McCue. "Can you imagine that?" The rain had started again, angling in on the wind.

Grimmett looked for the shelter of a doorway.

McCue continued walking. Raindrops skipped across the black tarmac at his feet. "How can anyone understand something like that?"

Chapter 8 – Plunkett the Cat

Newberry's death put Grimmett into a depression for days. He hardly spoke to anyone at the school, and remained uncommunicative at home. Dunphy tried to cheer him up, but Grimmett met his efforts with monosyllabic replies. Dunphy had liked Newberry, and his death made him sad. It was a waste, but in it Dunphy found no connections to his own life. Years of circumstance and tradition had been at work on Newberry's fragile psyche, and that was beyond Dunphy's grasp.

A week passed, and Dunphy realised that Grimmett was avoiding him. Grimmett was disappearing out of the school's back gate during the daily breaks, spending time alone by the stream that ran behind the nearby row houses. This was against the rules, for none of them were allowed to leave the school during the day. But Grimmett's thoughts were focused on Newberry, and on his own circumstances. Newberry's death was a harsh thing, and he saw it with an awful clarity. A wealthy family background, and a status in the community through his father's position had given Newberry the best education that money could buy—but none of the things that really mattered.

Grimmett walked for hours by himself, kicking at stones; standing under the trees by the stream, staring at the brown water, trying to think it through. But he couldn't find answers. The only thing he could think was that he had to get away. It was the solution he returned to, time after time, as his mind spun round and round like the anemometer on the little grey box outside the school library as it picked up the wind in its tiny cups. Grimmett was missing classes. It was evident that he would get himself into trouble again if he couldn't sort through his bitterness.

The resolution when it came was inadvertently brought about by Dunphy. In his own unique way he succeeded in re-focusing Grimmett's thoughts.

"Qu'est-ce que vous faites la?" The French Master's voice rose an octave.

Dunphy tried to stuff the photograph in his pocket, but it fell from his fingers onto the floor beside Grimmett's desk. The French Master swept down the aisle with his gown unfurling behind him like a banner.

"Qu'est-ce que c'est?" he enquired, and bent down to pick up the photograph.

"It's a . . . ah . . . photograph," offered Dunphy.

"En francais, monsieur. Parlez en francais s'il vous plait!"

"Say oon foto de . . . de ma tante," said Dunphy.

Dr. Fischer held the photograph close to his nose. He lifted his spectacles with one hand and peered at the picture.

"Votre tante!" His eyebrows moved upwards. "Votre tante! Mais elle est tres jeune, non?" He frowned at Dunphy, and glared at Grimmett. "Et elle n'est pas en portant des vêtements."

He transferred the photograph to his waistcoat pocket. He leaned over the top of the desk and stared into Dunphy's eyes. Dunphy tried to avert his gaze as his face slowly turned pink. Dr. Fischer straightened up.

"Dunphy, et vous aussi Monsieur Grimmett, je veux que vous me visitez apres cette classe ici." He turned round and floated in his gown back to the front of the room.

"Well, that's a bit much," said Grimmett.

"Sorry about that," said Dunphy. "Didn't mean to get you into trouble as well. I mean it could have been my aunt for all he knew."

It was difficult to stay upset with Dunphy for long. Despite himself, Grimmett could see a glimmer of humour in the situation.

"Hardly! It's not likely you'd have a photograph of a naked aunt in your pocket," he said, "lying on a leopard skin rug across the bonnet of a Ferrari with 'Visitez-moi dans le Cote d'Azur' written across it. Where did you get it anyway?"

"I found it in a book I was reading at home. The Diplomat must've been using it as a bookmark."

"What was the book?" said Grimmett.

"I don't know. Tropic of something. I thought it might help me with a geography essay I was trying to do."

"So now we've got to dig Fischer's garden on Saturday morning."

"Well, it's not as bad as ordinary detention," said Dunphy. "At least we'll be outside instead of sitting in a stuffy classroom."

"It'll be raining."

"I just remembered," said Dunphy. "I'm supposed to go through to Glasgow with the Diplomat on Saturday. For the day. How will I explain that to him?"

Grimmett retreated back into silence.

"You'd think they'd be pleased to see a picture of a woman in this place," said Dunphy. He'd been looking forward to going off with his father. "The French are supposed to be keen on that sort of thing aren't they? I mean whoever heard of a school without any girls in it. I tell you, if any of my friends in Canada saw me in this place they'd think I'd gone strange." They walked on.

"Fischer's not French," said Grimmett after a minute. "He's from Ipswich." He scratched the side of his nose. "I'm supposed to clear out the spare room on Saturday. My mother's been on at me about it for weeks. Uncle Ronald's moving in."

"Moving in? That's a turn up."

"Yes. He's a right turnip," said Grimmett, without wit. "A right neep. I don't want him living with us."

"Is he moving in for good, or just for a while?"

"Not for good. He's got a job in Africa, but it doesn't start for a few weeks. I suppose he'll stay with us 'till he goes. He wants my mother and me to go out there for Christmas."

It took Mrs. Fischer some time to come to the door after Dunphy rang the bell. She stood inside for a long minute and regarded them through the stained-glass panel before she opened the door. The two boys were standing in drizzling rain at the top of a flight of stone steps.

Mrs. Fischer was keen on fitness. She ran every morning in a tracksuit round the school playing fields. One of the boys outside, she noted, was overweight. The collar of his raincoat was turned up against the rain, and the belt was twisted and stretched round his stomach. His cap sat on top of his head with the brim canted off-centre, so that it sat over one eye. He looked untidy and wet.

The other one was tall with a thin nose. He didn't look as if he should be trusted with anything lying about the property. She decided she didn't want them in the house. She opened the door and contemplated them for a moment before she spoke.

"Dr. Fischer is out at the moment," she said, holding the door close with her foot, "but I've been expecting you. I shall see that you get started, and I will keep an eye on you from the kitchen window."

She pointed to the side of the house. "Go round to the shed in the back garden and you will find a spade and an edger which Dr. Fischer has put out for you." She stared at them. "I shall give you instructions from the kitchen window."

She closed the door. Dunphy led the way down a gravel path and round the side of the big Georgian house. He shrank into his coat as the rain started to come down harder. He heard Mrs Fischer's voice as they turned into the back garden.

"Plunky! Plunky, Plunky!" she called. "Plunky, Plinky!" There was a moment's silence except for the sound of rain. "Plunkett! Come on pussy. Puss, Puss!"

They wandered into Mrs. Fischer's range of vision, and she started, as if she hadn't seen them before. "There," she called from the kitchen window. She pointed at the garden shed, its peeling green paint running with rainwater. "The tools are inside the door."

Dunphy detoured across the lawn, his shoes squelching on the wet grass. He opened the door and a shapeless orange bundle flung itself at him and shot across the lawn towards the house. Dunphy reeled backwards.

"Plunkett!" shouted Mrs. Fischer. "Where have you been? Oooh, Plunky!" She reached down and lifted the cat into her arms.

She stared at them through the rain, stroking the cat. "He wants you to dig around the roses." She pointed. "You've to turn the soil over properly and get rid of the weeds. After that you can tidy along the edges of the lawn. When you've finished that, you can go." She pulled down the window.

Grimmett stared at the tools. The shovel was a heavy gravedigger's shovel, with a long thin handle. It was the kind that caused blisters. It was caked with mud. Dunphy picked up the edger and ran his finger along the sharp, semi-circular blade.

"This is ridiculous," said Grimmett. He looked over at the kitchen window, the warm, yellow light inside. Mrs. Fischer was preparing food at a big wooden table.

Grimmett started digging. Dunphy worked beside him for a while, pulling up weeds. The rain fell steadily, soaking dark patches onto their coats. Water ran down Dunphy's cap onto the back of his neck and dripped from the brim onto his nose. Soon he was coated with heavy, cloying mud. It covered his shoes and spattered his trousers. His fingers were cold and slippery, and black under the nails with dirt.

Dunphy was sitting on his haunches pulling weeds when the cat leaned heavily against him, toppling him slowly to one side. He tried to jump to his feet but sat down instead, in the dirt.

"Aw, come on! Get away!" He shooed the cat away from him, and stood up to wipe the mud from his coat. He only smeared more of it across its front.

"She must have let it out again," said Grimmett.

"Ugly thing. Don't know why anyone would want a cat like that," said Dunphy. Plunkett purred and rubbed itself against his leg. Dunphy flicked at it with his foot. "Go away!" he said. He looked up at the kitchen window. Mrs. Fischer had her back to them, working at the table.

Grimmett leaned on his shovel. "You know," he said. "I think it likes you. I don't mind cats, but they don't seem to like me. They always like people who don't like them."

Dunphy sneezed. "I'm allergic to them. I wish it would go away."

"We'll be sneezing a lot more than that by the time we're finished here," said Grimmett, looking up at the sky. The cat started to dig with its paw in the soil. "I thought cats didn't like the rain."

"Well, it's almost stopped now. Maybe it wants to go to the bathroom." Dunphy sneezed again. The cat lifted its tail and stalked off across the grass. Dunphy picked up the edger and started to slice the perimeter of the lawn.

"An ordinary detention," said Grimmett, bending to his shovel, "would have been infinitely preferable to this." The rain had plastered his hair to his head, giving it a curious, pointed appearance.

They worked on in silence. Dunphy moved slowly round the lawn, slicing off thin clods of earth with the blade of the edger.

"It's not a very straight line," said Grimmett. He pointed at the grass, where Dunphy's progress was marked by ragged, zigzag indentations along the edge of the lawn.

"What do you mean?"

"Well, look at it. You should mark out a line before you start on the next side."

Dunphy sneezed again. He bent forward and continued cutting. Out of the corner of his eye he saw the cat approaching. Without thought, he turned and shooed it away with a sweep of his arm. Too late he realised he had the edger in his hand. Like a slow motion film he saw the sharp, half-moon blade lop the cat's head neatly into the rose bed. Plunkett rolled over and lay still.

Dunphy stared at the headless cat, and then looked quickly over to the kitchen window. The kitchen was empty, although the light was on. "Quick! Quick! Dig a hole!" he said.

Grimmett turned from his shovel.

"Dig a hole! Quickly!" said Dunphy in panic. "We've got to hide it before she comes back in the kitchen."

Grimmett saw Plunkett's inert body lying on the grass. "God, you've killed it!" he said. "Now we're in trouble." He looked up at the window, then began digging furiously between the roses.

Dunphy dropped the edger and stared down at the dead cat.

"I didn't do it on purpose," he said. "I didn't know I had it in my hand." He sneezed again.

"Bring it here," said Grimmett. "No, not the edger. Bring the cat. Oh hell!" He strode over and scooped the cat up with the shovel. "Throw its head in." He started shovelling dirt on top of the body.

"Plunky, Plunky!" Dunphy swung round in fright. Mrs. Fischer was standing at the back door. "Plunkett! Puss, puss!" She stared at Dunphy and Grimmett. "Have you seen my cat?" Her eyes pierced through her spectacles.

Dunphy looked around wildly. "Um . . . ah . . . no. That is . . . not for a while."

"He was here about fifteen minutes ago," said Grimmett.

"Plunky!" she called, and closed the kitchen door.

"Come on," said Grimmett. "Let's get this finished. We'd better get out of here."

Half an hour later they put the tools in the shed and walked up to the house and knocked on the back door.

"We're finished now," said Grimmett. "Do you mind if we go?" Dunphy hovered behind him, unable to look at Mrs. Fischer.

"Have you done everything? All the edges? And the rose bed too?"

"Yes."

"All right," said Mrs. Fischer. "I suppose you can go then. I expect my husband will speak to you on Monday." She closed the door.

The rain was falling hard as they walked round the side of the house. They heard her voice again from the bottom of the steps.

"Plunky, Plunky! Puss, puss, puss. Where are you Plunkett? Time for din-dins. Plunky!" The voice followed them up the road.

"I'm going to speak to the Diplomat about Africa when he gets home tonight," said Dunphy as they turned the corner. "Mebbe I should go there with you; leave the country for a while."

Chapter 9 - The Golf

"Grimmett!" said Dunphy down the telephone. "Have you got any golf clubs?"

"Er . . . yes. I think I've got some somewhere. What do you need them for?"

"I've got to play golf this afternoon. Gotta fill in for the Diplomat." Dunphy sounded relieved. "He's gone off to a conference somewhere, and he was supposed to partner one of the neighbours."

"You've got to play golf?" The most athletic thing Grimmett had ever seen Dunphy do was tie his shoelaces.

Dunphy sighed down the telephone line. "My mother's having a fit. The neighbour's a big Company Director, and he's invited two guests to his club. Something about an important contract. Anyway the Diplomat's supposed to make up the foursome, and now he's gone off to this conference and forgotten all about it. Mother says I've got to play instead."

"So why don't you use your father's golf clubs?" asked Grimmett.

"That's the thing. He's taken them with him to this conference. I need to come round right away and get yours. We've got to tee off in an hour. I'll get my neighbour to pick me up at your house."

Grimmett went through to the living room. His mother was sitting with Uncle Ronald. Uncle Ronald had taken up residence with them, and had moved into the spare room. He was kneeling on the floor surrounded by coils of fine wire and dismembered pieces of the mantelpiece clock.

Grimmett's mother looked up from a book. "Run into the kitchen and get us both a little lunchtime drink will you dear?" she said. She held out two empty glasses.

Grimmett took the glasses. Uncle Ronald had crinkled brown hair and wore spectacles. He believed he could mend anything electrical or mechanical. He refused to spend money on appliance repairmen. He swore softly under his breath as the screwdriver slipped.

Grimmett stared at the sliding door that opened out to the back garden. "Why are those green strips on the glass door?" said Grimmett. "They spoil the view."

Uncle Ronald swore again. Grimmett's mother looked up from her book. "Oh," she said. "Uncle Ronald put them there. He thinks the door's dangerous."

"Damn right I do," muttered Uncle Ronald, struggling to hold a spring clip and insert a short piece of wire with his other hand. "Damn well just about killed me; that's what it did."

"What happened?" said Grimmett.

"Uncle Ronald thought it was open yesterday. He walked into it by mistake."

Grimmett noticed the bruise on Uncle Ronald's forehead.

"Damn!" There was a click, and the spring clip released itself and scattered tiny screws and minute but important clock parts across the carpet.

"It was working darling," said Grimmett's mother. "It was only running a little bit slow."

"Those golf clubs of Uncle Willie's," said Grimmett. "Do you know where they are?"

"They're in the attic, dear. I put them up there after you hit Mrs. Mainwaring's car."

Grimmett remembered the incident. He'd been taking practice swings on the tiny front lawn. Mrs. Mainwaring's car had passed just as he'd lifted a divot with the toe of the driver. The mud had dropped neatly onto her

64

windscreen and she'd swerved into the kerb and burst a tyre.

Grimmett poked his head through the trapdoor into the attic. Thick cobwebs trailed from the rafters, and the air smelled musty. He pulled himself up, balancing carefully on the beams. The attic didn't have any floorboards. A wrong step would put his foot through the floor and into the room below. He found the golf bag on top of a tin trunk next to the water tank. It was covered with a thick coat of dust.

The bell rang as Grimmett was climbing down the ladder into the hallway. He opened the front door.

Dunphy stared at the grimy canvas golf bag Grimmett was carrying. His face fell. "That's not it," he said.

"Yes." Grimmett gave the bag a wipe with his fingers, smearing dust across it. "Uncle Willie's clubs," he said. "They're good clubs. They might be a bit old, but they don't make golf clubs like this any more. I'll clean the dust off."

"I can't play with them," said Dunphy. "I've got to fill in for my father. This place we're playing isn't just any old Golf Club you know."

"Well," said Grimmett, "they're the only clubs I've got. If you don't like them you'll have to get some other ones."

Dunphy pulled the clubs out one by one and looked at them. The head of the Driver was charred, as if it had been burned at some time in a fire. The Three Wood was scarred, as if it had been flung against a wall in a long-forgotten fit of anger. The twine that joined the shaft to the club-head was loose. As well as the two wooden clubs, the golf bag held a Four-Iron, and a Nine-Iron with the word 'Wedge' imprinted on its metal head. The last club was a vicious, curved weapon stamped with the words 'Mashie Niblick'. The carrying strap on the bag was frayed, and the handle was broken at one end.

"Where's the putter?" said Dunphy.

"There's no putter. You use the Four-Iron. Uncle Willie broke the putter before he died."

"But there's only five clubs," said Dunphy. "Where are all the others? There's supposed to be fourteen."

"Uncle Willie only used five clubs," said Grimmett, "and the putter of course. He said there was no need for any more clubs if you played the game properly." He paused.

"Uncle Willie was the Edinburgh Chemist's Champion. He was the only man at his golf club who could go round the course in less strokes than his age."

"Must've kept his own score if he used these," said Dunphy. "Look at them, they're prehistoric." He clicked them together with the flat of his hand. "They must be at least a hundred years old."

"They're Auchterlonies," said Grimmett. "Auchterlonie was the greatest golf club maker in Scotland. They're probably worth a fortune."

The doorbell rang. Grimmett went to open it. A man in a Harris Tweed jacket and cavalry twill trousers was standing on the front step.

"'Scuse me," he said, "but is George Dunphy here?"

Dunphy appeared at Grimmett's elbow. "Be right with you," he said. "Only be a minute."

"I've left the motor running," said the Company Director, motioning at a silver Bentley idling at the kerb. "We're a little bit late." He lifted his arm to look at the gold watch on his wrist. "You chaps should get a bend on. We have a tee off time of a quarter-to-two. I'll wait for you in the car."

"Right!" Dunphy ducked back into Grimmett's hallway. "We'll have to use these," he said, gathering the golf bag up in his arms.

"We?"

"Didn't I tell you? He said you could caddy for us."

The first setback came at the door of the Bentley. The Company Director shook his head through the window as Dunphy tried to open the back door to admit the golf bag. He motioned to the back of the car. While Dunphy was putting Uncle Willie's Auchterlonies in the boot, Grimmett squeezed onto the back seat beside the Director's golf bag, which nestled on the lambswool seat cover.

The Bentley drew up the gravel driveway to the Royal Lothian Golf Club. Dunphy stared at the ivy-covered walls of the old sandstone clubhouse, and cast his eyes over the Jaguars, Rolls Royces and Bentleys in the car park.

"We can go in and change," said the Company Director, switching off the engine. "Your chum can wait here with your clubs for the time being." He turned to Grimmett. "Won't be long."

Dunphy cleared his throat. "Yes . . . ah . . . that's fine, but I'm . . . . ah . . . already changed."

The Company Director looked at Dunphy's plaid shirt, baggy windcheater and crushed brown corduroy trousers. "Golf shoes?" he said.

"Er . . . these." They stared down at Dunphy's scarred sneakers.

The Company Director sighed. "In that case I'll just run along myself then. I'll meet you chaps by the first tee, in . . ." he consulted the watch ". . . ten minutes."

Dunphy and Grimmett walked round the side of the clubhouse. Dunphy stopped at the front door and wiped his shoes on the ornate metal foot stanchion beside the front steps. The chink of china and cutlery came from the open window of the Member's Dining Room. When they reached the first tee, Dunphy sat down on a white-painted bench to wait.

"Don't know about this," he said. "There seem to be some complicated protocols I ought to know about. You've got to help me out here Grimmett. Can't let the Diplomat down or he'll never forgive us."

Grimmett leaned Uncle Willie's golf bag against the bench and sat down beside him. "Well," he said after a minute. "At least you've got your own personal caddy."

The company men strode briskly down the concrete path from the clubhouse. Each of them had a golf cart. The first one walked with a limp, and trailed his cart behind him. Then came Dunphy's neighbour, who had changed into a pair of tailored brown golf slacks and a belted tweed jacket. Behind him stumbled the last member of the foursome. Grimmett stared at him. He wore green velveteen plus-fours over bright red stockings. A blue gabardine jacket barely fitted round his midriff. His pale white forehead was offset by red, puffy cheeks and bright blue eyes.

"He looks like a beach ball," said Grimmett.

The Company Director made the introductions, and the two men shook hands with Dunphy. Grimmett was not introduced. The large one sniggered as he caught sight of Dunphy's golf bag.

"I say," he said. "You oughtn't to play with those. They must be jolly valuable. Ought to be in a museum, eh?" He slapped the man with the limp on the shoulder.

"They're Auchterlonies," said Dunphy.

"Quite, quite," said the large man.

Dunphy's neighbour flipped a coin. "Righto," he said. "You go first Charles. Then I'll go next." He looked at Dunphy. "Hugo next, and young George last."

Charles limped onto the tee. On the ground he placed a small cup attached to a piece of coloured fluff. Carefully he peeled the cellophane wrapper from a new ball, and bent down and placed it on the little cup. He stepped back and took a practice swing, his back-lift long and laboured. He addressed the ball, and hit it smoothly, ending his stroke by lurching gently forward onto his right foot. The ball floated down the centre of the fairway.

The Company Director hit his ball, and it disappeared towards the green, hooking slightly. Hugo walked solemnly onto the tee. He addressed the ball for a long time, waggling the club head and flexing his forearms. His swing was wide and flat, and hampered by his girth. As he brought his driver down his whole body rotated, and the ball sliced viciously off the club head, flashing in front of a group of golfers walking up the eighteenth fairway.

"Fore!" shouted Hugo. He swore under his breath. The golfers scattered.

Dunphy took the Three Wood from the bag. It seemed a safer bet than the scorched Driver. He stepped up and faced his ball. He hadn't played golf since his father had paid for him to have lessons two summers before. He drew the club back and swung.

As the club connected with the ball, the wooden head flew off and sailed down the fairway, unravelling black twine from the shaft as it went. The ball jumped a few inches off the tee and rolled into a clump of coarse grass. Hugo guffawed.

"I say," he said, "that's unfortunate. Never seen anything quite like that?" He grinned at Dunphy's neighbour.

"Dreadful," said the Company Director. He frowned as Dunphy tried to reel in the club head. "We could have got you some decent clubs you know."

"Sorry," said Dunphy. "Had to borrow these at the last minute. Didn't know . . ." His voice tailed off.

"Well, it's still you."

"Pardon?" said Dunphy.

"Still you, old boy. Still your shot." The Company Director indicated Dunphy's ball lying in the long grass at the front of the elevated tee.

Dunphy turned to Grimmett. "Wedge!" he said, holding out his hand. Grimmett pulled the Wedge out of the bag. Dunphy took a difficult stance with one foot down the bank at the front of the tee, and the other bent awkwardly underneath him. He flailed at the ball and it soared into the air.

The others strode off without waiting for him. Grimmett hoisted the bag onto his shoulder. The bag's bottom gave way and the clubs clattered onto the ground. The three partners stopped and turned to stare. Dunphy waved at them, and they turned and walked on.

"God, Grimmett, now the bag's broken too," said Dunphy. "When did you last use these clubs anyway?"

"I've never actually used them myself. Uncle Willie left them to me in his Will. I don't play golf."

"You should have told me. At least I could have rented some decent clubs. This is just awful, and we've still got eighteen holes to go."

Hugo caught up with them after playing his ball from the middle of the eighteenth fairway. He looked at the broken bag and snorted. "Hardly need the bag at all old chap," he said, "what with only four clubs to carry now. Hardly need a caddy either." He chuckled to himself and went off to play his third shot.

They watched him select an iron from the array of shining clubs in his leather bag. He swung the club and the ball flew from it, straight into a tall beech tree. They watched in silence as a crow fluttered to the ground and lay still. Hugo dragged his cart up to the crow and turned it over with his foot.

"Dead!" he called over to them. "Quite dead. Extraordinary!"

"Never seen anything like it," said Dunphy's neighbour.

Hugo addressed the ball for his fourth shot, a dozen yards from the tree. He stood with his legs splayed apart, facing at an angle in order to miss the tree. They watched the heavy, flat swing. The ball shot off the tip of Hugo's club and hit the trunk of the beech tree with great force. Hugo flung himself flat on the ground as the ball rebounded past his head and flew up the fairway, back towards the tee. Dunphy began to shake. Tears came into his eyes. Hugo slowly picked himself up and began to walk back the way they'd come.

"This might be all right after all," said Grimmett.

"If your golf clubs last the round," said Dunphy. He wiped his eyes. "But I think I've figured it out. These people are just a bigger kind of bull-shitter." He walked on with a smile on his face.

They completed the first hole in silence. The next few holes passed uneventfully. Dunphy lost two balls in a pond at the sixth and ordered Grimmett to wade in and retrieve them. Grimmett refused.

"You're my caddy, and there's only one ball left in the bag," said Dunphy. "Why didn't you tell me there were hardly any golf balls in it?"

"I didn't look," said Grimmett. "Besides, there were plenty of balls in it when you started. Who'd have expected anyone to lose eight balls in six holes?" He gazed at the dirty pond. "I'm not going in there. It'll be full of worms and bloodsuckers. Besides, it's the end of October. I'll get pneumonia. If you need more balls you'll have to go in there yourself."

The matter became academic at the seventh hole. Hugo hooked a ball through a stained glass window of the exclusive Ladies College that bordered the fairway. They watched from a distance while he underwent a visibly difficult interview over the fence with the school's Headmistress. The discussion ended with Hugo reaching into his pocket, and writing a cheque for the damage.

Hugo took out a huge divot as he played his replacement ball, and then claimed to have sprained his wrist so badly that he was unable to continue. He also remembered a forgotten dinner appointment. It began to rain. The Company Director decided to call it a day.

"The Diplomat was a bit upset about the golf," said Dunphy on Monday. "Something about a contract that's fallen through. The neighbour'd been working on it for months apparently. Had the nerve to say it was something to do with me, and your golf clubs."

"There's nothing wrong with the golf clubs," said Grimmett. "Uncle Willie played at St. Andrews with them many times."

"The Diplomat said they weren't right for the Royal Lothian Golf Club."

"Well, he should have remembered that it was him who was supposed to play there in the first place," said Grimmett. "He should thank you for trying help him out."

"Settle down," said Dunphy. "I spoke to him about Africa. He says I can go out there with you at Christmas. Thinks it'll be good for me. Give me some solid colonial education, he said."

Chapter 10 - On the Way to Africa

"Uncle Ronald and I are going to get married," said Grimmett's mother. They were standing in front of the fireplace, holding hands. Uncle Ronald smiled, and his spectacles flashed in the overhead light. The clock lay in pieces behind them on the mantelshelf.

"We're just going to have a quiet do at the Registry Office," said Uncle Ronald. "No guests or anything like that, but you can come if you want to."

"Uncle Ronald says he wants to get to know you better," said Grimmett's mother. "He says he knows he can't take the place of your father, but he'd like to be the next best thing."

Grimmett stared at them. He had no idea what to say. He felt unaffected by it all, as if he wasn't in the room, as if they were talking to someone else. He remembered something his father had told him a long time ago, when they were a family together. His father had known Uncle Ronald when they had both started out in the working world. They'd worked in the same office for a while, and both of them had cycled each day to work. Grimmett's father told him he'd taken a long route to work each day, cycling miles out of his way in order to avoid having to make the journey with Uncle Ronald.

"I'll be flying out to Africa the week after next," said Uncle Ronald. "Your mother's going to come with me."

What was it that Uncle Ronald did? Grimmett tried to remember. Something to do with farming; sheep and cattle and experimental programmes. He couldn't get a job in Britain, so he'd been forced to look overseas. They were still standing in front of the empty fireplace, as if they expected him to say something.

"I've spoken with the Dunphy's," said Grimmett's mother. "You can stay with them until you come out at Christmas. It's all right. They'd like you to stay with them." As if it was a surprise that anyone would want it. God, the thing had a momentum of its own.

"George will be coming out with you for the holidays of course. That's all agreed too."

George. Who was George? Grimmett realised she was talking about Dunphy.

Dunphy's father was an older version of his son. He had the same ruddy complexion, and had long ago given up fighting his waistband.

"It's for my country," Grimmett had heard him say once. "We Consuls have to do a lot of entertaining; a lot of eating and drinking in the name of service to the flag."

Grimmett liked him. He wondered at the refined vowels that marked his accent, and where they'd come from; so different from his son's Canadian accent.

Dunphy's mother was small and energetic; half the size of her husband. She knew it had been a mistake to christen their son George after his father. Now whenever she called his name, two voices answered her. Or neither did, conspiring silently to avoid whatever task she wanted them to undertake.

Mr. Dunphy took Grimmett's suitcase and looped an arm round his shoulders. "We've been looking forward to having you to stay," he said, in his curious, booming, diplomatic-service voice. He walked Grimmett into a living room cluttered with a pleasant disorder. A coat was draped over the back of a chair. A pile of newspapers sat beside the fireplace, next to blocks of wood which looked as if they'd come from a carpenter's bin. An untidy cat was spread along the back of the sofa, balanced like a woolly

73

antimacassar. A fire blazed in the grate, warming the room with soft light.

"Coal and wood mixed together make the best fires," said Dunphy's father. "When we're in Ottawa it's hard to get coal, and it's difficult over here to buy wood for burning." He chuckled to himself. "But I managed it."

"Here you are dear," Dunphy's mother handed Grimmett a cup of hot chocolate. "This will warm you up."

The taxi had brought Grimmett here on its way to the airport with Grimmett's mother and Uncle Ronald. He looked around the living room.

Things had happened quickly in the last few days. The Salvation Army people had taken away a heap of old possessions—sheets and blankets, sweaters, shoes and magazines. They'd even taken Uncle Willie's golf clubs. Pieces of his growing up had gone off to clothe the poor and needy, his old toys for their children to play with. The dustman had made a special collection too; bent wire from days spent fishing with his father, a punctured soccer ball, broken lead soldiers he hadn't touched in years. None of it was valuable, but most of it had been important.

Grimmett's mother had organised it all without telling him. Hardly anything had been left. "We're going to start again," she'd said. "It's just dreadful though that they don't appreciate Uncle Ronald's abilities in this country."

Dunphy's father was speaking. "George will be here in a few minutes. He's gone out to get fish and chips." He rubbed his hands. "What a treat. It's one of the great benefits of living over here."

"They get more heart attacks in Scotland than anywhere else in the world dear," said Dunphy's mother. "It's because they eat so much deep-fried fish and chips."

"Nonsense," said her husband. "They're perfectly good for you as long as you buy them from the Italians."

Dunphy's mother looked up. She was seated on the edge of a print-covered armchair by the fire, sewing a button on one of her son's shirts. "Whatever are you talking about?"

"The Italians change their fat every night. The Scottish fish and chip shops use the same fat for weeks. Italian cooking cuts down on the stuff that clogs the arteries. It's much healthier."

The door burst open. Dunphy ran in with a steaming pile of newspapers in his arms. "Quick, get the plates." His father jumped up and ran through to the kitchen. He returned in seconds with a tray of plates and cutlery, vinegar and salt. Grimmett had never seen anyone's father respond to his son like that.

Dunphy's mother put down the shirt. She pushed a pile of books to one side of the table to make space. They chatted while they ate; about the events of Dunphy's father's week; about a Scottish literature course Dunphy's mother was taking at Edinburgh University; about the school. Grimmett was astonished to find that Dunphy's father's opinion of the school was not a positive one.

"Why did you send . . . er, George to it then?" said Grimmett.

Dunphy's father wiped his mouth with a napkin. "Well, to tell you the truth I thought it would sort him out." He smiled, and let it fade.

"I thought . . ." he glanced at his wife. "We thought it would give George a good grounding in the classics and the humanities. And it probably will. The school's well known for its sports, and we thought it might give George an aptitude for that. Leadership and responsibility—that sort of thing." He sighed. "But it probably won't do that."

He picked up a piece of fish with his fingers, and studied it for a second before popping it in his mouth. "They know their stuff all right, these teachers at your school. Some of them have very impressive backgrounds. The trouble is they don't know how to get it across. Communication; there's no point in sending a message if the receiver doesn't work. Human receivers can't be made to work like mechanical ones; they have to be taught to work—encouraged and stimulated and rewarded. The trick with learning is to get people to enjoy it. But I'm afraid that takes qualities and talents that few of the teachers at your school seem to have."

It was like that for the next four weeks. Grimmett was wrapped in the warmth of the Dunphy household. He was sorry when it was time for him to leave.

"I'll see you out there next week," said Dunphy, as they shook hands at the airport. He was to visit his aunt in

England for a week. After that he would fly out to West Africa for the rest of the holidays.

"They've liked having you stay," he said. "The Diplomat thinks you're all right."

Chapter 11 – The Traitor

Grimmett stood on the whitewashed stoep, listening to the buzz of crickets. The strains of Benny Goodman's clarinet came from the living room. The air was heavy and oppressive, thick with the scent of frangipani. Brooding storm clouds were gathering over the hills across the valley.

"It looks as if it's going to rain," he said.

"Not a chance," said Uncle Ronald. "It never rains before March."

Thunder rumbled faintly in the distance. Grimmett's new stepfather walked inside to the brown walnut hi-fi set. He put on a different record and came back outside, warbling along with the singer.

I never gargled
I never gambled
I never smoked at all
Until I met my two good amigos
Nick Teen and Al K. Hall.

A bright red MG sports car came up the road towards the house, dragging with it a tail of tan-coloured laterite dust. It turned into the driveway as a streak of lightning flashed across the hills.

"Hah!" said Uncle Ronald. "Here's Rex. You'd better go and have your bath now."

Grimmett glanced at the parrot as he passed. It was sitting quietly in its little aviary. It tilted its head to one side and regarded him through the wire mesh. Grimmett crossed the cool parquet floor and walked through the living room to an inner veranda. He pushed open a spring-loaded screen door.

A big red spider was trying to scale the steep enamelled sides of the bathtub, slipping and sliding each time back to the bottom. Grimmett watched it for a moment, and then turned on the tap and tried to catch it in a stream of water. Nimbly the spider avoided the cascade, and moved to the far end of the bath. Grimmett reached over and took a glass from a holder beside the basin. He filled the glass with water and flushed the spider down the tub towards the drain. When it was in range he flicked on the tap again, and watched the spider disappear down the plughole.

Grimmett lay back in the bath and watched a company of egrets through the window as they strutted back and forth, uncoiling their long white necks as they picked at insects in the grass. A butterfly alighted on the window's wire screen. The breeze ruffled its purple and red wings, and brought a rich scent of dry soil and damp air into the bathroom. He heard the intermittent crack of ripening bean pods as they burst on the tree outside and scattered seeds like shotgun pellets across the roof.

He'd been here for three days, and the shock of his arrival was beginning to wear off. He'd stepped from the cool aeroplane into furnace heat at the top of the passenger steps, and come face to face with his father. It had taken him long seconds to absorb this. He'd stood there frozen, passengers pushing into him from behind as they tried to leave the aeroplane. In that brief moment he'd gone through a complicated series of thoughts. There had been a mistake. It had all been put right between his parents. There had been no second marriage for either of them.

"Hello Arthur." His father had reached out his hand, and Grimmett had found himself shaking it.

"Hello father." He'd caught a glimpse of red behind his father, across the tarmac. His mother was standing behind a fence, in a small enclosure in front of the terminal shed, waving a red handkerchief.

His father had looked embarrassed. He'd pulled him to one side to let the other passengers past.

"We should get off the steps," he said. "We're blocking the way." They'd descended onto the tarmac apron. "I've been posted here for a few months to relieve the station manager. He's catching up on some overdue leave, and then he's got to take a course in London."

Grimmett didn't know what to say. He caught sight of Uncle Ronald standing beside his mother in the enclosure.

"I didn't tell you because I . . . we, that is . . . thought it would be a nice surprise." They'd walked towards the terminal, heat rising in waves from the hardstand. "We can see a bit of each other while you're here if you like." His father cleared his throat. "Hillevi and I have taken over the station manager's house while he's away. It's not far from here, so as soon as you've settled in you can come over for dinner. Hillevi would like to get to know you a little better. I know she would."

Grimmett's father had gone off then to attend to the aircraft before it flew on to Lagos. His mother and Uncle Ronald had met him outside the Customs Hall. They'd driven him off to their house on the University grounds. Since then he'd heard nothing from his father at all.

Grimmett stepped out of the bath and dried himself on a rough, white towel. He padded across warm red tiles to his bedroom. The bedroom smelled of sandalwood, and the dry, earthy scent of chopped grass came to him through the window mesh. A single sheet was pulled back in a triangle on the bed. He put on a pair of white shorts and a white shirt.

Rex Mayhew was sitting with Grimmett's mother and Uncle Ronald on the stoep. He climbed to his feet as Grimmett walked through the French doors. One hand went absently to his head, and he held out the other. Grimmett shook it.

Uncle Ronald made the introductions.

Rex said, "Good to meet you squire, I've heard a lot about you. Have a good flight?" He sat down, his toupee slightly twisted on top of his head. It made him look as if he was on the point of turning round to look behind him. Rex had lost his hair in a burning Lancaster bomber in 1944. The wig was a bad fit, but he didn't seem to care about it. He'd never taken the trouble to buy one that was better shaped to the contours of his scalp.

"Rex here stepped on a snake today," said Uncle Ronald. "Jumped down from a rock in the middle of the new golf course and a Puff Adder bit into his boot." He grinned. "My man Montgomery says he's never seen anyone jump so high in his life."

"So would you have," said Rex. He drained the remains of his whisky, and rattled the ice cubes in his glass. Grimmett's mother reached down and tinkled a small brass bell on the table beside her. The houseboy appeared.

"More drinks please Campbell," she said. Campbell moved to the sideboard and picked up the drinks tray.

"It's the second one in a week isn't it Rex?" said Uncle Ronald. "I heard you ran over a Boomslang in your car the other night, and took it home to show the kids."

Rex said something unintelligible. He held his glass out for Campbell to fill.

Uncle Ronald was enjoying himself. "I heard it woke up before you got home and you had to abandon the car on the Achimota Road." He turned to Grimmett. "The Boomslang's one of the most dangerous snakes there is, lad. Just you remember while you're here; the brighter the colour, the more dangerous they are."

Even Grimmett knew that wasn't true. Uncle Ronald was giving him the benefit of his few weeks' experience in the tropics.

Campbell circulated slowly, dispensing drinks from the tray. Grimmett sat down on the warm step and watched an aeroplane approach the airport's main runway, which sat on the top of a range of low hills a few miles in front of the house. Lightning flickered silently above the plane, darting from cloud to cloud.

Rex was speaking. "It is a bit provocative," he said. "But I don't think they're deliberately trying to antagonise us. I just don't think they see anything wrong with it."

"They're a bunch of Commies, that's what they are," said Uncle Ronald. "I've always said that the government here is going that way, and now it's getting more obvious every day. Now that they've hired this . . . this spy, it just confirms it. It's only a matter of time until the Russians move in and take the place over completely."

"Who's a spy?" said Grimmett. They looked at him.

"Oh, no one dear," said his mother. She rang the bell again for Campbell. "It's just someone they've appointed to be head of the Physics Department."

"He's a spy, and we shouldn't go to this reception thing tonight on principle. The man's a bloody traitor." Uncle Ronald was working himself into a state.

"We've got to go to it dear," said Grimmett's mother. She held her glass out to Campbell. "All the department heads have to go. It wouldn't look good if you stayed away, and besides, we don't have to stay for long." The dying sun caught in the folds of her brown hair.

"He wasn't much of a spy," said Rex. "He only got fifty pounds from the Russians for those secrets."

"Fifty pounds or fifty thousand pounds, it doesn't make any bloody difference." Uncle Ronald was annoyed. No one else seemed to share his passion about the matter. "The man's still a traitor. They should have hung him."

"Perhaps," said Rex. He studied the whisky in his glass. "Perhaps they should have just kept him in jail." He stared at Campbell's retreating back. Grimmett's mother accidentally knocked the bell as she stood up. Campbell turned round.

"Although I've always considered that his was a crime of belief and passion, rather than one of criminal intent," said Rex.

Uncle Ronald jumped to his feet. For a moment Grimmett thought he was going to lose his temper. Rex held up his hand. "Nunn May always claimed that he didn't do it for the money. He always said that he didn't know the Russians had put fifty pounds into his bank account. He maintained all through his trial that he wasn't interested in personal gain, that he'd only done it because the atom bomb was such a terrible weapon it was vital for the whole world to know about it."

"That's nonsense!" said Uncle Ronald. "You're defending him." He grabbed the soda bottle from the drinks tray and squirted some of it into his glass. "The man has no concept of loyalty. Where do you think he got his education and training? Britain! And who paid for it? The good old British taxpayer!" Uncle Ronald sat down. "And he gave it all away to the Russians."

Rex leaned forward in his chair. The wicker creaked beneath him. "I'm not defending him Ronnie. I'm simply trying to present a balanced point of view." He took a sip from his drink. "It's a different way of thinking. Nunn May thought the world would be a safer place if the bomb wasn't a secret any more. You think the opposite. You think that if the British and the Americans were the only ones who knew about it they could be trusted to be the world's policemen—all wise and benevolent."

"Rubbish!" said Uncle Ronald. He disliked being called Ronnie. "Nunn May didn't think anything of the sort. Power and money, that's why he did it. The man's a criminal; completely evil. They should have hung him."

Grimmett's mother had left the room a minute or two before. She came back out onto the stoep now, trailing a film of chiffon. "Come on dears. We must be going. The invitation said six o'clock." She hiccupped, and put her hand up to her mouth.

"You look very nice dear," she said to Grimmett. She smoothed his shirt collar with her hand. She lowered her voice. "You mustn't talk to that man when we get there. He's been in prison."

Uncle Ronald stood up. In the distance, on the other side of the valley, four big tailplanes stuck crookedly into the shivering atmosphere. Beside them the runway lights danced softly in the evening haze.

"Look at those things," said Uncle Ronald. "Just look at them. The government paid millions for those Russian planes, and all they've done is sit there. One flight each, and now they can't get spare parts for them. Illyushin 16's," he said. "Illusions more like. And we can't get any money to spend on research so we can feed these people properly."

"It said on the radio today that they were going to trade the aeroplanes for some tractors," said Rex, grateful for the shift in subject.

"Right," said Uncle Ronald. "You know what'll happen then don't you?"

82

"What's that?"

"They won't be able to get parts for the tractors."

Grimmett squeezed into the red sports car with Rex Mayhew. His mother and Uncle Ronald climbed into their second-hand, black Volkswagen. They drove down the driveway under purple jacaranda trees, and accelerated out onto the road.

"What did he do?" said Grimmett over the noise of the sports car's engine.

"Who?"

"Nunn May."

"Oh him." Rex pushed the gear lever into third. "He gave the atom bomb plans to the Russians after the war. He and a chap called Klaus Fuchs. They were caught and sentenced to jail, but then Fuchs was swapped for a prisoner the Russians had. Nunn May only got out a few months ago." He looked at Grimmett. "He'll be an old man now I think. I expect he's quite harmless."

Grimmett was thoughtful for a moment. "Was that true about those aeroplanes?"

Rex changed down through the gears as the car climbed the hill. "More or less. They've been sitting out there for months. It's all dreadfully inefficient. They never seem to think these things out properly. But they want independence and freedom; not control by Europeans who think they know best. I've decided that you've just got to be philosophical about it. I mean if we don't let them make their own mistakes how are they ever going to learn anything?"

Rex turned the car onto the main university boulevard. "It's not something that bothers me greatly. I'd never say that to your Uncle Ronald though," he added. "Live and let live and all that."

They drove up to the front door of the residence hall. The walls were yellow-white in the sunset, and shadowed with lush growths of jasmine and bougainvillea. Rex parked the car, and they walked inside, past a pair of palm trees which framed the entrance. Fans turned slowly on the high ceiling. Their shoes clicked on the polished parquet floor.

The room at the end of the hall was quiet, except for an irregular hum of stilted conversation. Rex headed straight for the bar, where a houseman stood in a smart white uniform with a red sash around his waist. Uncle Ronald appeared beside him a few seconds later. Grimmett walked over to a table set with soft drinks and hors d'oeuvres. He helped himself to some peanuts. He glanced around the room. His parents were talking now with Rex and the Registrar. About forty people were scattered across the room, standing in groups of four or five.

A man stood by himself, gazing through French windows into a stone-flagged courtyard. In the dying light of the sun his hair was like bleached straw, and a lens of his spectacles caught a trace of orange. One hand was grasping the wooden frame between the panes of window glass, as if to steady itself; his other hand held a glass of orange juice.

The man turned and looked straight at Grimmett, his eyes large through the lenses of his spectacles. Grimmett walked slowly round the table, and made his way towards him.

"It's rather beautiful don't you think?" said the man, indicating the jasmine growing up against the wall outside. "You can even smell it through the glass." He looked at Grimmett. "I'm sorry. I didn't introduce myself." He held out his hand. "My name is Alan Nunn May."

Grimmett stared at the hand for a second, then shook it.

"Oh, this cocktail party is for you then," he said.

The scientist turned and stared out of the window. "You could say that I suppose. So I can meet my new colleagues." He looked around, as if he'd forgotten something. The guests were congregated at the far side of the room, next to the bar and the food tables. There was a wide space between the new department head and his new colleagues.

Out of the corner of his eye Grimmett saw his mother beckoning him. He avoided her eye. He said, "I've just come here too. I don't know many people either."

Nunn May nodded. "These days you have to take work where you can get it; wherever it is." Without turning away from the window he continued, "I suppose it's the same for all of them too. None of them can get work in

84

Europe. All of us are exiles here whether we know it or not. Flotsam."

He went on. "We mustn't be too hard on them for supporting a system which has rejected them. They don't know any better."

The bitterness in Nunn May's voice made Grimmett feel awkward.

"But that's often the way it is," the scientist said. "The greater the rejection, the stronger the support which remains." He sighed. "But you'd think they would at least be curious about the new man wouldn't you? After all, we're in the same boat really."

In the reflection of the window Grimmett could see his mother and stepfather standing together, staring at his back. Uncle Ronald was glaring over the top of the glass that was raised to his mouth.

"What's it like?" said Grimmett. It was an impulse; as if he was seeking insight into his own situation.

"What's what like?" The physicist turned from the window.

Grimmett coughed, embarrassed at his question. But he carried on. "Being . . . free after all that time. What does it feel like?"

Nunn May nodded. "You know, you're the first person to ask me that. Everyone else avoids the question." He turned again to the window. "It's a nice thing to ask."

Grimmett waited. In the reflection he saw Rex Mayhew order another drink from the bar, and noticed Uncle Ronald lay his hand on his mother's arm. She had started to walk across the room.

"It's much as you might expect," said Nunn May. "For many years I was kept in a cell. I was only allowed outside once a day. It was the only time I got to see the sky. I was kept apart from the other prisoners. There was no one to talk with. And there still isn't now—at least not yet. It might change, I suppose. We'll see." He looked down at his empty glass. The dying light flashed again on his spectacles.

"The real answer to your question is that all the important conflicts are within you, and until you come to terms with that . . . well, nothing changes, wherever you are. That's really the only answer to your question." He passed his hand over his forehead. "The only important thing . . ."

Grimmett's mother was coming towards them. "My mother wants me now," said Grimmett. "I'd better go."

"Yes . . . yes, of course," said the physicist. He straightened his shoulders. "It was nice to meet you." He turned back again to gaze out of the French windows, at the geometric stones in the courtyard.

"Goodbye," said Grimmett, but the scientist only inclined his head a little.

Grimmett's mother glared past him in the direction of the French window. "I thought I told you not to speak to him," she said. Her lips were line-straight and firm.

"I didn't know it was him at first."

"You mustn't speak to him," she repeated, glancing over at her husband. "He's been sent to Coventry."

"He was a nice man," said Grimmett. "I liked him." He was aware of a hush in the conversation around him.

"He's a traitor," said Uncle Ronald, too loudly. "He's worked against everything our country stands for."

They left soon afterwards. Grimmett looked back as he walked out of the room. The old scientist was still standing by himself, looking silently out of the window. Then he turned, and gave Grimmett a small smile. Grimmett half raised his hand, and Nunn May nodded in farewell.

Chapter 12 – A Day at the Beach

"How was the flight?" Grimmett reached for Dunphy's overnight bag.

"All right I guess. Had a good sleep for a change. Can't usually get to sleep on aeroplanes." Dunphy yawned.

The airport terminal was crowded with disembarking passengers. A fan turned slowly overhead. A voice intoned indistinct messages over the tannoy system. Grimmett dropped the overnight bag at his feet. He'd looked earlier for his father without success. He saw him now, pushing through the passengers towards them.

"It's hot," said Dunphy. He pulled out a handkerchief and wiped his forehead. "Like stepping into an oven."

"You'll get used to it in a day or two," said Grimmett. "My father's coming."

"Your father? You mean your stepfather."

"No. My father. He's here too."

Dunphy followed Grimmett's gaze. He saw a tall man in a white, short-sleeved shirt with tabs in the shoulder epaulettes, and a flat, military-style cap on his head. He was easing his way through the crowded passenger hall.

"You must be George," said Grimmett's father, shaking his hand. Grimmett had not had any contact with his father since the day he'd arrived in West Africa. He wondered at the unknown communications system that seemed to transmit detailed messages between the two branches of his family that did not seem to recognise each other's existence.

"We've been so busy the last few days Arthur that I haven't had time to call," said Grimmett's father. "But on Sunday we're going up the coast to the saltwater pool at Winneba. Perhaps you and George would like to come with us? We can make a day of it."

There was an awkwardness in his father's voice, and Grimmett hesitated before replying. But Dunphy nodded.

"Great," he said. "If it's any cooler there than it is here I'll need it by then." And it was arranged.

"Right," said Grimmett's father. "Where's your suitcase?"

"I left it at Customs. They checked it. It's got a chalk mark on it."

"We should collect it then," said Grimmett. "My mother's waiting in the car." He realised why she hadn't wanted to come inside.

"I must go and get the aeroplane organised. See you on Sunday. We'll pick you up about nine." Grimmett's father dived back into the crowd.

Dunphy took off his jacket. "Phew! It's hot," he said. There were damp patches under his armpits.

"You can have a cold shower when we get home, and change into something cooler."

They collected Dunphy's suitcase and walked outside. Dunphy wiped the palm of his hand on the leg of his flannel trousers. He screwed up his eyes against the glare. "God. It's bright here," he said.

"We can get you some sunglasses," said Grimmett. His mother opened the door of the car. She stepped out as Grimmett put the suitcase in the boot. She gave Dunphy a kiss on the cheek.

"Welcome to West Africa dear," she said. "We're glad you could come. It'll be nice for Arthur to have a friend to play with. I'm sure he gets fed up with us grownups all the time."

Not for the first time, Grimmett wondered about the way her mind worked.

Dunphy smiled. He thanked her and slid into the back seat of the car. Grimmett started the engine, and drove slowly out of the airport car park.

"How was London?" said Grimmett's mother. "Did you have a nice time with your aunt and uncle?"

"It was totally boring," said Dunphy. "They go to church all the time and play a lot of Bridge. A week was about as much as I could handle."

"Don't you like Bridge dear?" said Grimmett's mother.

"No." They turned onto the main road and began to drive north, towards the university. Dunphy leaned forward and tapped Grimmett on the shoulder. "You're driving."

"Yes. You don't really need a licence here."

They passed through the elegant portico at the university's main entrance. "Quite a place," said Dunphy. "Looks a bit Chinese. The architecture I mean. Sort of pagoda style."

"That's the library," said Grimmett's mother, pointing to a building with a stepped roof. "The pond in front of it is full of tame goldfish. They'll eat out of your hand if you feed them."

Grimmett changed gear. They went round a roundabout, onto the main boulevard. Dunphy pointed ahead. "What's that thing at the top of the hill?"

"That's the Independence Tower," said Grimmett's mother, "although I can't imagine why they'd want to build a monument to the mess they've got themselves into since they took over their own government."

"Must be a great view from up there," said Dunphy, staring at the tall white tower.

"I wouldn't trust it to hold your weight," said Grimmett's mother. She adjusted her sunglasses, unaware that her comment might be taken as a reflection of Dunphy's physique. "Ronald says their construction people aren't very reliable."

Dunphy lapsed back into his seat. Grimmett turned the car off the main boulevard. They swept up the driveway beneath the jacaranda trees. Grimmett guided the Volkswagen into the garage and switched off the engine.

"Where are the houseboys? Campbell!" shouted Grimmett's mother. "Campbell!" Campbell appeared in the doorway.

"Take the suitcase please and put it in Arthur's room." She hesitated, and looked at Dunphy. "I should introduce you I suppose. Campbell. This is George Dunphy."

Campbell stuck out his hand. "I'm pleased sah!" He was a small wiry man. His thick, curly hair showed touches of grey at the temples, like frost.

"Er . . . yes. Pleased to meet you Mr. Campbell."

"It's just Campbell," said Grimmett's mother. "And this is Thank God." A thin youth in a knee-length cotton shirt stepped through the door.

Thank God bent forward in a bow. He swept the floor with his hand. He straightened up with a grin on his face. "The Diplomat," he said.

Dunphy gave him a startled look. Some of his father's activities were a mystery to him. "You've met him?"

"Suh?" Thank God's face went blank.

"He doesn't speak much English," said Grimmett's mother. "We've only taken him on for the holidays to give Campbell a hand. I think he must have heard us say that your father was a diplomat." She pointed at the car. "Take Mr. Dunphy's bag into the house please Thank God, and put it in his room."

Thank God didn't move.

"The bag." She reached into the car and pulled out Dunphy's black overnight bag. "Go with Campbell." She pointed at Campbell.

"Sometimes I don't think he speaks any English," she said. Thank God bumped down the corridor in front of them with the heavy suitcase. "In fact I don't think he's got much of a clue at all."

Grimmett shivered, and hoped that Thank God's English was as bad as his mother seemed to think it was. "What time will Uncle Ronald be home?" he said.

"In about an hour; then we can go off to the beach." She opened a door onto the interior garden. There was a loud crack and Dunphy jumped. Tiny bean pellets spattered across the tiled roof.

"Beanpods," said Grimmett's mother. "They spray their seeds all over the place."

"God it's hot," said Dunphy. "I feel like a piece of blotting paper."

"You can have a shower dear," said Grimmett's mother. "After lunch we can go down to the beach. It's a lot cooler down there."

A warm rain had begun to fall. It glossed the road so that it looked like a ribbon of flat, black water. The tyres hummed, and the wiper spread a thin grease across the windscreen. The high humidity made the inside of the car hot and sticky.

Uncle Ronald was driving. "Well, I got out of that one all right," he said. "I was supposed to go and see some Chief about his cattle this afternoon. I spend a lot of time advising the local Chiefs you know." Dunphy was sitting beside him in the front passenger seat.

They passed a woman with a brown pottery urn balanced on her head, her arms swinging easily at her sides. The wiper started to screech rhythmically on the glass.

"Hope there aren't too many Russians down at the beach today," said Grimmett's mother from the back seat.

"Russians?" said Dunphy.

"Too many of them dear," she said. "They've taken over the whole beach. Russian advisors to the government. All they seem to do is sell them aeroplanes and tractors." She gazed out of the window. "I do think it's too wet to be going to the beach dear," she said to her husband.

"Nonsense. It's just a spot of drizzle. It never rains properly before March. This will be over in five minutes."

A Mammy Wagon lurched along the tarmac towards them. Passengers hung from its sides, faces glistening in the wet. Dunphy stared at the truck's canopy, the words 'Stone The Crows' painted above the driver's cab in vivid yellow paint.

"What does that mean? Stone the Crows?"

"It's its name. It's a kind of bus. They've all got names," said Uncle Ronald, still pleased with himself for having avoided a steaming hot afternoon out on the plains.

The wagon's horn tootled as it swayed past. Dunphy turned and watched it receding behind them. The back of his seat suddenly gave way, pitching him backwards into Grimmett's lap.

"This car's a wreck dear," said Grimmett's mother as she helped Dunphy upright. "It's falling apart. You should get a decent one."

"Cars don't last long out here," said Uncle Ronald. "But I like this one. It doesn't need any maintenance at all."

They turned onto the coast road, and passed through a succession of small villages. The heavy fustiness of damp vegetation came through the window, punctuated with some musty sewage smells. Most of the huts were of the same construction: dilapidated mud walls and corrugated metal roofs. The old Volkswagen skidded lethargically as Uncle Ronald misjudged a corner.

"Steady," said Dunphy, unnerved by the collapsing seat. He gripped the handle on the dashboard. "It doesn't seem very reliable. I wouldn't be surprised if a wheel fell off." He coughed.

A small flock of chickens dashed out of some bushes at the side of the road. Uncle Ronald braked sharply and spun the wheel. The Volkswagen slithered on the wet surface. Dunphy's seat collapsed again as he pushed hard against the dashboard.

There was a succession of light thuds as the Volkswagen ploughed into the chickens and slewed sideways onto the dirt shoulder. Uncle Ronald stopped the car and pulled on the handbrake. One of the chickens was tottering about in front of them, screeching and trailing a wing. The survivors ran squawking into the trees.

"Now you've done it," said Dunphy. He levered himself out of Grimmett's lap.

Uncle Ronald opened the door and climbed out of the car. His foot slid out on a pile of feathers, and he nearly fell down. The injured chicken's cries pierced the quiet air. A trail of dead chickens littered the roadway behind them.

Uncle Ronald scratched his head. "Well, it wasn't my fault," he said. "I couldn't possibly have stopped. They ought to keep them under proper control."

"There doesn't seem to be anyone about," said Dunphy. He looked up and down the road.

"Come on dear," said Grimmett's mother from the back seat. "Let's get on to the beach. There's nothing you can do about it now. Besides, someone might come."

"Better beat it," agreed Dunphy. "No point in getting in trouble over some chickens." He looked nervously into the trees.

"Good morning." A cheerful face grinned at Dunphy from the edge of the woods.

"Er . . . morning . . . ah . . . afternoon. Are these your chickens?"

"I'll handle this George," said Uncle Ronald, stepping round the front of the car. He addressed the man at the side of the road. "You should keep these chickens under proper control you know. You've only got yourself to blame, letting them run wild like that." You had to be firm with these people. He hesitated. "They are your chickens?"

The man stepped out from the trees, onto the road. He was small and bent. His eyes darted quickly up and down the narrow highway. His smile widened to show grey teeth.

"Yessa."

Grimmett's mother leaned out of the window. "Ask him how much he wants for them dear and let's be off."

"Fi' pound," said the little man, holding up a hand with the fingers outstretched. He turned and looked behind him into the woods.

Uncle Ronald stared at him. These people could cause trouble. "That's a bit much," he said. "Look at them. They're just skin and bone."

The old man nodded. "They are now." His expression hardened. "Fi' pound." He pointed at the chicken with the broken wing. It subsided into the dirt at the side of the road. "My brudder's chicken." He wagged a finger at Uncle Ronald. "My brudder be very cross. He come soon. Big-big man."

Uncle Ronald reached for his hip pocket and pulled out his wallet. He quickly counted out five, one pound notes. The old man shot out a hand and snatched the money.

"I think we should get going," said Dunphy. He climbed into the car and wound up the window. "Not a good idea to hang about. His brother might turn up."

93

Grimmett watched the old man dart off through the trees, bent over, moving with surprising speed. Uncle Ronald started to move round to the driver's door. A shout came from the other side of the road. Dunphy groaned. A large man in a bright orange shirt ran across the road and skidded to a stop in front of the car.

Uncle Ronald's voice jumped an octave. "I gave the money to your brother," he said.

The big man looked at him. "That's not my brother," he said in a voice that rattled the car windows. "I ain't got no brother, and these are my chickens. You've got to pay me!" He looked at the mess on the road. "Seven chickens, seven pounds!" He held out his hand. "Damages!" Uncle Ronald reached for his wallet again. Behind the window, Dunphy's breath misted the glass.

"Come along dear," said Grimmett's mother again from the back seat, oblivious to the tension outside.

The big man snatched the money from Uncle Ronald's hand, and then tore off into the woods in pursuit of the old man. Uncle Ronald jumped in the car and started the engine.

"I think you gave the money to the wrong man dear," said Grimmett's mother needlessly. "I don't think he was his brother at all." Uncle Ronald gritted his teeth and gripped the steering wheel, and stared straight ahead.

"He might come back," said Dunphy. "He sure was big." The rain had stopped. Blue sky was pushing the clouds eastwards.

"Bandits," said Uncle Ronald. "We should never have handed the country over to them. Now they think they can do what they want."

They continued down the road in silence. Two miles further on they turned off the coast road onto a sandy track which wound through a grove of palm trees. They parked the Volkswagen beside a small salt- water lagoon and climbed out.

"This is it," said Grimmett's mother.

Dunphy gazed at the shallow inlet. "It's stagnant," he said.

"The beach is on the other side of it," said Uncle Ronald. "This is just a slough." He pointed at some low sand dunes on the far side of a rickety wooden bridge. "Over there. You can see the tops of the huts."

They changed by the beach in a hut made from palm fronds. The walls rattled softly in the sea breeze, and the surf grumbled powerfully against rocks. Uncle Ronald retired to a corner of the hut. Dunphy struggled into his bathing trunks.

"Haven't worn these for years," he said. "Must've shrunk. Don't seem to fit properly."

"They probably just need to get wet," said Grimmett. He looked out the door. "There's some of the Russians down there."

Dunphy went over to look. Three women were sitting under a bright red and yellow umbrella, beside a small salt-water swimming pool which had been built onto the rocks. The sea funnelled into it through a narrow cleft.

Grimmett looked at Dunphy's white skin. "I wouldn't spend too much time in the sun if I were you," he said. "It's best to work up to it slowly, a bit at a time. You can get an awful sunburn here without noticing it."

"Oh, I'll be all right," said Dunphy. "Our family never burns."

They walked across the warm sand towards Grimmett's mother, who was setting up a beach umbrella. The three Russian women looked over at them from where they were sitting beside the pool.

"I don't understand it," said Grimmett's mother. "They don't normally come down to this end of the beach."

Dunphy smiled as one of the Russians walked past. "Do svidaniya," he said. The Russian gave him a puzzled look, and walked on.

Grimmett spread his towel on the sand.

"Where are all the men?" Dunphy asked. "Don't they come down here too?"

"Only on weekends usually," said Grimmett's mother.

Uncle Ronald sank down beside them, pale and skinny down to his stomach, which folded over the top of his swimming trunks. "They're taking the place over. They're not supposed to mix with Europeans. That's what I've been told. Look at them. They look like something out of the nineteen-thirties in these swimsuits."

"You shouldn't stare at them dear," said Grimmett's mother.

"Why not? They're staring at us."

"What are these flags for?" asked Dunphy. "Something to do with the Russians?" He pointed up the beach at two red flags stuck deep in the sand. They were about fifty yards apart.

"Those are the lifeguard flags dear," said Grimmett's mother. She lay back in the sand and pulled a straw hat over her eyes. "You've got to stay in between them if you swim in the sea, or else the undertow will carry you off."

"Huh?" Dunphy stood up. "I think I'll go for a dip in the pool in that case. It's getting a bit hot." He walked off across the sand.

Grimmett propped himself up on one elbow and watched. Dunphy nodded to the Russian women, and clambered up on the side of the pool. He stood there for a moment, and launched himself at the water. There was a big splash and Dunphy's bottom bobbed out of the water, looking like the back of a seal in its shiny black trunks. Uncle Ronald lay back and closed his eyes.

A gust of wind blew sand particles in Grimmett's face. He realised he'd drifted off to sleep. He sat up. Dunphy was standing in the pool waving to him. Grimmett waved back, and turned to gaze out to sea.

A small open fishing boat was rising and falling on the swell, just beyond the surf line. The fishermen were hauling in a net. Sunlight flashed on silvery fish as they were emptied into the boat. The fishermen cast the net again as they paddled parallel to the shore. Dunphy waved again from the pool, more vigorously than before. One of the Russian women stood up and walked across the sand towards him. Grimmett picked up the short surfing board he'd brought from the changing hut, and walked down the beach towards the flags.

He ran through the shallow surf until the sea reached his thighs, and dived onto the board and paddled out towards the breakers. A tiny aeroplane sputtered overhead, following the line of the beach. Grimmett slid off the board and dived deep as the first big wave broke over him. He felt the strength of the undertow turning him around, and then he came back to the surface.

He paddled out further. It was easier out among the big swells. He lay just outside the surf line, rocking gently, waiting for a good wave to ride in to the shore.

The fishing boat turned in towards the beach. One of the fishermen was standing up in the stern, guiding the boat with a long steering oar. The boat bucked as it picked up a wave and slid, bow down, at the front of the crest. A white curl of foam flicked up behind the steersman's head, and blew back in a fine spray. The man on the port side of the boat dug in his paddle as the boat began to slew sideways. The helmsman leaned on the long rudder oar, and heaved the boat round. They rushed in towards the shore, trailing drops of sparkling spray in the sunshine behind them like a comet's tail.

Grimmett looked over at the pool. Dunphy was talking with the black-haired Russian woman. He turned and shouted something, but Grimmett couldn't hear him above the noise of the surf. Then he saw the wave he wanted and paddled hard to catch it. He met it just as it broke out white surf. He lay flat on his board and slid down the front of the wave, gathering speed, shooting in towards the shore.

Grimmett stood up in the shallows. He carried his surfboard over to the pool, the sand hot on the soles of his feet. One of the Russian women was standing near Dunphy, splashing water onto her face and shoulders to cool down.

"You're getting sunburned," said Grimmett. "You shouldn't stay out in the sun so long."

There was a pained expression on Dunphy's face. The Russian woman laughed. "He only stands there," she said in a thick accent. "He does not swim."

Dunphy was standing in the deep end of the pool, water up to his chest. His face and shoulders were bright red.

"She's a translator," said Dunphy. "Speaks English."

"You should get in the shade," said Grimmett, "or else you'll burn."

Dunphy gave Grimmett a pained look. "I . . . ah . . . my towel. I need my towel."

"I think you should come out," said Grimmett. "You won't be able to move tomorrow. Your towel's over where we're sitting."

"Can't," said Dunphy. "Can . . . you . . . bring . . . my . . . towel . . . here. Please." His teeth were clenched tightly together.

"What do you mean you can't?"

Dunphy winced. The Russian woman swam slowly to the other end of the pool. "I'm trapped," he said. "Swimsuit's disintegrated."

"Disintegrated!" Grimmett stared at him.

"Ssshh." Dunphy whipped a glance at the other end of the pool. "Completely vanished. Disappeared right after I dived in. Must've had salt in it from the last time I wore it."

Grimmett walked past one of the Russian woman on his way to get Dunphy's towel. "Your friend," she said. "No clothes. Niente. Nekked." She touched a finger to her eye.

"Sandwiches!" said Grimmett's mother from the umbrella. "Come and get them quickly, before the sand-flies eat them."

Chapter 13 – Accidents

"God, I can't stand it," said Dunphy. "My whole back's on fire. Isn't there anything else you can put on it?"

"You've got most of a tube of sunburn cream on it already. Any more's not going to make any difference." Grimmett levered himself onto an elbow and stared across at the other bed. Dunphy was lying on his stomach.

"It's only from your chest up," Grimmett said. "I told you to take it easy on your first day in the sun."

"There's got to be something I can do. I feel like I've been flayed alive."

"I suppose you could soak your bed sheet under the cold tap, and then wring it out and wrap it round you. That might help." Grimmett lay back. "It'll dry out again in this heat, but it'll probably stay cool long enough for you to get to sleep."

"I'll try it," said Dunphy. He went through to the bathroom, holding his body stiff to protect it from any errant breezes that might brush against his skin.

"It feels a bit better," said Dunphy the next morning. "At least I can get a shirt on today." It was two days since their visit to the beach at Labadi. Dunphy had spent most of the day before lying on his stomach in their room. "I think I'll be able to go to that place. . . Winnie something."

Grimmett had almost forgotten that his father was going to pick them up that morning. Now he brought it to the front of his mind. "Winneba," he said. It was about sixty miles up the coast; an interesting little seaside resort he'd only heard about. But a day with his father and his new wife was an uncertain prospect.

Grimmett's mother came into the dining room.

"How's breakfast?" Then, without waiting for a reply she said, "George, I've managed to dig you up a pair of swimming trunks. Rex dropped them off last night. He says he's never used them, so they're as good as new." She put a paper bag down on the table.

"I . . . er, don't know if I'll go in today," said Dunphy. Might be pushing it a bit with this sunburn." He sliced into an avocado with a spoon, and popped a piece of it into his mouth.

"Nonsense," she said. "You can put on another dollop of sun cream and you'll be as right as rain. They tell me the water's lovely at Winneba. Much cleaner than it is down here. Besides, the best thing for sunburn is to get into the salt water. It helps the healing process. Then when you're out of the water, you should keep a shirt on, and wear that big straw hat I got you."

With Dunphy organised, she turned and went out of the room, calling for Campbell.

The car came for them at half past nine. Grimmett's father didn't come into the house. He sat in the car in the driveway and honked the horn. Grimmett's mother called goodbye to them from the bathroom.

It was a big American Rambler station wagon with long bench seats. Grimmett's father made the introductions as they got in.

"Arthur," he said. "I think you met Hillevi at Famagusta . . . or was it Kyrenia."

"It was Larnaca," said his wife. She half-turned in her seat and offered a hand over her shoulder to Grimmett. She was larger than he remembered, and younger too. She showed her teeth when she smiled, as if she was trying to please him.

"And this is George." Dunphy stuck out a hand, and she took it, and turned round again to face the front. They drove off, passing under the jacaranda trees.

"It must be nice up here on the hill," said Hillevi. "You will get the cool breezes. Not like where we live. Down there it stinks."

"Hillevi! It's not as bad as all that."

There was a note of apology in his father's voice that Grimmett had never heard before.

"It's all to do with the airline," said Grimmett's father. He waved a hand over the steering wheel. "This is the official airline car. We live in the official airline house . . . and there's an official airline guest house next door for any VIP's who happen to come through here."

"With the Embassy we always get good accommodations," said Hillevi. "They make sure it's in a good district of the city. They give us air conditioning and a driver, and enough servants to run a house properly."

"Your English is very good," said Dunphy. Grimmett sat back in his seat. Not for the first time he wondered how Dunphy could be so oblivious to tension.

"Of course."

Dunphy couldn't tell whether she'd accepted the compliment or been offended by it. He tried again.

"Where did you learn it?"

"In Denmark all the children learn English from when they are young. And Swedish and German, and some of them learn French too. I have all of these and a little Hindi, some Spanish, and some Arabic. If we are to stay here for long, I will learn some Hausa. Enough to get by."

"Pretty good," said Dunphy. "Of course my father always reckoned that there should be one universal language." He paused. "English." He was the only one in the car who laughed.

They talked sparingly as they motored up the coast road. Grimmett stared out at the bush on the side of the highway. From time to time his father and his new stepmother spoke, but the talk was awkward. She was dissatisfied, Grimmett's father defensive. Nothing seemed to meet her expectations. Near the fishing hamlet of Winneba they found themselves

101

speeding along a new, metalled road. Then they rounded a corner, and came upon a scene of carnage.

A big, bright-coloured Mammy Wagon lay on its side in the ditch. A small, yellow car was squashed beneath it. A large grey cement truck was stopped, slewed sideways a few yards down the road. The accident had only just happened. Something that looked like red paint was running down the side of the cement truck.

Three bodies lay on the road. People were trying to climb out of the shattered windows of the bus, their eyes wide in shock. The name on the front of the bus stared out at them. 'High Times'. The Rambler slowed to a crawl. Grimmett's father detoured into the oncoming lane to avoid one of the bodies. Grimmett stared through the window. A sharp edge on the side of the cement truck had slit open a man's stomach; his entrails lay in coils on the hot pavement beside him. He was quite dead. Flies were already gathering. They passed the body of a young woman with her eyes open wide. There wasn't a mark on her. Grimmett could hear wailing from the bus.

"We should stop and help," he said. He couldn't take his eyes from it. He had never seen death so close.

"No! No, Jack. Keep going. There is nothing we can do. The ambulance will be here in a minute." It was his stepmother.

Grimmett's father drove past the cement truck. Above the red splashes, skin hung from the metal fairing like cloth.

They drove on in silence.

"They put too many people in these buses, like cattle," said Hillevi after a long time. "They are always having accidents. They are very unsafe to travel in. Of course you never see a European in one. No, there was nothing we could have done."

Grimmett stared out of the window. He was waiting for an ambulance to come past, but then he realised that he hadn't seen an ambulance in the two weeks he'd been in the country. His father was driving more slowly now. Grimmett found himself wondering about the passengers in the Mammy Wagon; about the people who had died. He hummed a small hymn from school quietly to himself, unaware of it.

"Stop that! Stop it now!" She was shouting. Grimmett's stepmother turned to her husband. "Tell him to stop! He is doing that to upset me. I will not allow it!"

"What's the matter Hillevi?" said Grimmett's father. "What's wrong?" He slowed the car and stared at her.

"He is doing it to annoy me. Make him stop!" She turned to Grimmett. "You are a spoiled, conceited young man. You know exactly what you are doing and I command you to stop!"

Grimmett had no idea what she was talking about.

"Hillevi," said his father. "What is it?"

"He is singing Deutschland Uber Alles. He knows it will upset me." She turned again to Grimmett. "That anthem is banned in my country. I heard it all through the war. I will not have it. You are doing it on purpose."

Grimmett swallowed. "It's a hymn," he said. "It's from school."

"It is the German anthem," she said. "You know what it is."

Grimmett didn't know what to say. After a minute, "It's a piece of music. I didn't mean to upset you."

She pulled a handkerchief from her handbag and blew her nose. "I was in Denmark all through the war. The Germans invaded us and they stayed for five years." She dabbed her eyes, and put the handkerchief away. Her voice hardened. "You think you know it all, but you don't know what it was like. I was only a little girl. It was awful. You could never understand." She was speaking to them all.

Some minutes later she reached out and put her hand on Grimmett's father's arm. She began talking to him about embassy matters, as if nothing had happened. She paid no more attention to Grimmett or Dunphy in the back seat.

They didn't stay at Winneba for long. It was too windy, said Hillevi. The sand was blowing in her face. Then she was hungry, but there were too many flies in the little safari café at the beach. By the time they got back to Accra, she had a headache. The houseboy at the airline house had prepared dinner for them, but it was his day off and his relief hadn't turned up. Hillevi brought cold plates out from the kitchen.

After dinner, when the others went to sit in the living room, Grimmett slipped into the kitchen. He began to wash the dishes. He had finished the big plates and had started on the cutlery when Hillevi came through the swing doors.

"What are you doing?" she said.

"I'm washing the dishes. I thought I would help. You said you had a headache."

"I don't want you to wash dishes. That is a job for servants. It's not something for the master's son to do." Her voice was controlled and low. It wouldn't carry to the next room. Her face was red.

"I'm sorry," said Grimmett. "I'll stop if you want me to."

"Yes, immediately. It is demeaning for you to do this. It is a job for the servants." She gave him a strange look. "Why do you do these things? To spite me? To show me up in front of your father?"

Again Grimmett didn't know what to say. He shook his head, and wiped his hands on a towel. She moved from the doorway, and he walked past her into the other room.

Later, Grimmett's father stopped the car at the University's main gate.

"I'll let you off here," he said. "I should get home to Hillevi. She's not herself today."

"I think I'll give the next excursion a miss," said Dunphy, as they watched the Rambler drive back towards Accra. "That one was something else." It was hot and sultry and not yet dark and there were no cars around; no people. The heat haze bounced off the ground. It gave the illusion that the buildings had been lifted onto stilts.

Dunphy glanced at Grimmett as they began to trudge up the long sloping boulevard. "You sure picked the right family," he said. "I've never seen anything like it." It was difficult to breathe in the heat after the air-conditioning in the car. The crickets were screeching.

Grimmett bent his head and said nothing.

"Don't go worrying about any of that," said Dunphy. "None of it's got anything to do with you. People like that are impossible to figure out. She's probably just jealous or something."

"I don't know . . ."

104

"We should stop in at the residence hall," said Dunphy. The heat was like a wall of hot mud; like an assault. You had to fight through it. "For a cold drink of something."

Grimmett shook his head. "You need to have an account there. It's only for members."

"We can put it on your Uncle Ronald's tab. He won't mind. We'll never make it all the way back to your house without something to cool us down. Besides, there might be someone in there who'll give us a ride."

There were always drums at Christmastime. The beat floated up the valley, drifting on the edge of consciousness like a faint, pleasant scent. It carried for miles; steady, rhythmic, haunting; mingled with the haze of laterite dust, a gentle bass to the buzz of the crickets, or the calls of cockatiels.

It was said that the people of the Accra plains could track a stranger anywhere with the drums, that they could send a message all the way to the north country in less than an hour.

Chapter 14 – Guests of Honour

Grimmett put his head round the door and looked into the darkened bedroom. Thin lines of light speared through the slats of the shutters.

"Come on," he said. "You'd better get up. It's eleven o'clock."

Dunphy stirred, and groaned. "Can't. Head's like a football." He pulled the sheet over his face and turned away.

Grimmett closed the door behind him and sat on the edge of Dunphy's bed. "Here, I've got some orange juice for you and some water with Alka-Seltzer in it. It'll make you feel better."

Dunphy rolled over and forced his eyes open. He sat up slowly and grimaced. "Eleven o'clock? It's not that late surely." He took the glass and gulped down the fizzing Alka-Seltzer.

"We've got to be at Montgomery's village at half past twelve," said Grimmett. "We can't keep them waiting."

"What? Who's Montgomery?"

"You remember. He's the local chief who works in Uncle Ronald's department. You told him last night you wanted to see his village."

"I did?" said Dunphy. "Don't remember that." He put the water glass down with a shaky hand and picked up the orange juice. He rolled the damp, cold glass across his forehead. "Head hurts."

"I warned you not to touch the palm wine. It's real firewater."

"Only had a little bit." Dunphy sagged back against the pillow.

"That's all it takes. One glass is enough if you're not used to it." Grimmett stood up and moved around the bed. "You had five." He pulled at the mosquito screen and threw the shutters open. Sunlight poured into the room, bringing with it the smell of dry earth. Dunphy moaned and passed a hand over his eyes.

"Don't you remember doing a cartwheel over the pole in the limbo contest?"

"Last night?" Dunphy had a dark twinge of memory. A frown crossed his face.

Grimmett sat down on the bed again. "You told Montgomery you wanted to visit an African village on behalf of your father because the Canadian government would be interested in their way of life."

Dunphy gave Grimmett an uncomfortable glance. "I said that?" He sat up and moved his legs carefully over the side of the bed.

"That's what you said. So now we're Montgomery's guests for lunch."

Dunphy stood up, and then sat down again. "Don't believe this," he said. "Must have a hangover."

"You'll feel better after you've had a shower. But you'd better get a move on. Montgomery will be upset if we don't show up."

Dunphy stood up again. "I can remember going into the residence hall," he said. "It was hot . . . and then we had a cold beer on Uncle Ronald's account."

"Yes, and then that faculty group came in and there was a party. That's when you started talking to Montgomery. I had to carry you most of the way home after you fell in the flood ditch."

Dunphy entered the living room, his hair plastered flat after his shower.

"Ah, good evening George!" said Uncle Ronald. "Come and sit down." He folded a tissue-paper airmail copy of the Daily Telegraph and put it down on the table beside him.

Dunphy lowered himself carefully into a wicker chair by the French doors.

"Had breakfast yet George?" said Uncle Ronald.

"Not hungry." Dunphy leaned his head back and folded his arms across his stomach. A grey-green gecko ran upside down across the ceiling and stopped in the corner. It flicked its tongue at a fly.

"So. I hear you're going down to Montgomery's village. You'll be batting for the visiting side there George," said Uncle Ronald. "Proper etiquette and all that. Eat and drink all they offer you and don't complain about anything. We're all on parade when you pay a formal visit like that." He turned as Grimmett came into the room. "Old George isn't very talkative today. Not at all like the man we saw in action last night."

"We'd better get going," said Grimmett. "We'll be late."

"Bush telegraph," said Uncle Ronald. "I shall hear about it soon enough if you put up a black." He reached for his newspaper. "What are you taking him?"

"Taking?" said Dunphy.

"You've got to take something; a gift. You must observe the proper protocol in these things."

"I never thought of that," said Grimmett. "We haven't got him anything."

"That awful cream soda that Mrs. Eldridge gave us," said Dunphy. "We can take him that. Even the thought of it makes me feel sick."

Uncle Ronald's old Volkswagen bounced down the pot-holed track, winding among scattered scrub bushes, and spired, laterite anthills.

"They have to dynamite these anthills when they clear the land," said Grimmett, wrestling with the steering wheel as they bumped around a washout. "Some of them they can't even knock down with a bulldozer. You wouldn't think ants could build anything that strong. They cement them with their saliva."

Dunphy grunted, his elbow propped against the windowsill, his head balanced on his hand. The cream soda bottles clinked in a crate on the back seat as the car lurched into a hole.

"They're just like concrete," said Grimmett.

"These bumps," said Dunphy. "Can't you drive round them?"

"Sorry. They're all over the place. It's hard to avoid them. Anyway we've not got far to go now." He peered through the dusty windscreen. "That's the village there."

The village danced in the noontime heat, as if a breath of wind could take it away. They drove into a dusty enclosure surrounded by mud-walled huts. Dunphy lifted his head and looked around as the car came to a stop. The mud had fallen away from some of the huts to expose crude, latticed frames. Corrugated metal roofs in stages of rusty deterioration deflected the rays of the sun.

Grimmett switched off the engine. They could hear the steady beat of drums. A bevy of small children dashed from the huts and surrounded the car.

"Drums," said Dunphy, passing his hand over his forehead.

The door of the closest hut fell open on a single hinge, and Montgomery stepped out. A small retinue of villagers took their places behind him. Montgomery's face broadened into a smile. He had abandoned his faculty suit for colourful robes which he gathered about him. He held out his hand and walked round to the passenger side of the car.

"Mister Dunphy," he said, and pulled the door open. "This is a great pleasure. You are most welcome to my village." He turned to his followers, and indicated the Volkswagen with a sweep of his arm. "My friends," he said. "Mister Dunphy and Mister Grimmett."

Dunphy stepped unsteadily from the car. Two small children immediately grabbed his hands. "Yes. Ah . . . Mister Montgomery. I'm pleased to be here," he said. He raised his voice over the thump of the drums. "Very pleased." He looked over at Grimmett.

Grimmett walked round the front of the car and shook Montgomery's hand. He ruffled the head of a little boy who was clutching Montgomery's robe. "He's a fine boy," he said.

Montgomery pulled his robes onto his shoulders. "All mine," he said. "All my boys."

Dunphy tried unsuccessfully to free his hands. Two more small boys attached themselves to his legs.

"They can see that you are an important man Mister Dunphy," said Montgomery. "Awuni, Kojo, leave Mister Dunphy alone." He swatted at them with a fly whisk. Dunphy straightened up gratefully as the children retreated.

"Oh, I nearly forgot," said Grimmett. He reached into the back of the Volkswagen and pulled out the case of cream soda. "This is for you." He presented it to Montgomery. "It's a present from us."

Montgomery smiled and waved his hand over his shoulder. One of the men behind him stepped forward and took the case from Grimmett.

"Come!" said Montgomery. "Let us go and sit in my grove." He led the way to a dusty corner of the compound where three bush trees offered a little shade. Two orange boxes and an armchair sat around an upturned wooden crate. There was hardly any upholstery left on the armchair. Metal springs stuck up dangerously from the seat.

"Mister Dunphy." Montgomery stretched out his arm. "Please take the Chief's chair."

Dunphy eased himself onto the springs. They twanged as they took his weight. Montgomery indicated one of the orange boxes for Grimmett. Then he arranged the folds of his robes around him and sat down between them.

They sat in silence for a few moments, a circle of children facing them. Dunphy was beginning to feel ill. He smiled at the children. The children grinned back at him. Montgomery observed this.

"You like children Mister Dunphy?"

"Yes . . . ah . . . oh, yes." After Uncle Ronald's warning Dunphy was anxious to please his host.

Montgomery clapped his hands. "Kojo, Awuni." The boys ran up and leaped onto Dunphy's knees. The springs clanged.

"Unngh!" Dunphy gritted his teeth. He reached up and patted one of the children on the head.

Montgomery clapped his hands twice more above his head. To Dunphy it sounded like rifle shots.

111

"Would you like a drink?" said Montgomery. "Some palm wine perhaps? I have very good palm wine."

"No, no thanks," said Dunphy. "Bit thirsty though. Wouldn't mind something else. Non-alcoholic though."

A man in a ragged pair of trousers ran up and stopped in front of them. Montgomery turned to Grimmett.

"The same for you?"

"Yes, that would be fine."

"And something to eat perhaps?"

"Er, yes. Thank you."

Montgomery rapped out an order in Hausa, and the man ran to one of the huts. Dunphy sat expressionlessly in the armchair; the two boys perched on his knees. One of them began to bounce gently up and down. The springs protested. A spasm of pain crossed Dunphy's face.

The background thud of drums stopped. The chief leaned forward and touched Dunphy on the arm. "Are you well?" he said. "You don't look well."

Dunphy's smile was weak. "Oh, I'm fine. A bit hot that's all. Be fine when I've had something cold to drink."

Montgomery nodded. "No refrigeration here in the village though, I regret." He pulled a packet of Tusk cigarettes from the folds of his robe, and offered it to Dunphy.

Dunphy turned his head away. "No. No thanks. Not just now."

The chief tapped a cigarette from the packet and placed it between his lips. He lit up, and the smoke drifted past Dunphy's nose.

"Ah. The drums," he said.

Some men were making their way among the huts. They were rolling black metal oil drums. They manoeuvred the big canisters towards the chief and his guests with much shouting, generating clouds of dust.

"A special demonstration for Mister Dunphy," said Montgomery. He flung his arms open to greet the musicians.

Dunphy watched. There were five of them. They jumped about in front of Dunphy, arranging the oil drums, tapping them exploratively with heavy sticks. Dunphy nudged the two boys off his knees while the chief's attention was distracted.

112

Grimmett stood up to take a closer look at the drums. Montgomery consulted with the leader of the band.

"They look a bit crazy to me," said Dunphy as Grimmett walked past. "Look at them." The group was acting up in front of the oil drums, waving their arms about, rolling their eyeballs.

"They're all right," said Grimmett. "They're just getting in the mood for it."

"Looks to me like they've been getting into the palm wine," said Dunphy. "Don't like the look of it."

The band leader danced away from Montgomery. He launched himself at the nearest drum and started beating it. Dunphy recoiled as a cacophony of noise erupted around him. In seconds all five men were thrashing at the drums. The sound came at Dunphy in waves. He slumped into the armchair.

"Here come the drinks," said Montgomery, raising his voice. The man in the tattered trousers ran up with three glasses and a plate of biscuits balanced on a board. He handed one of the glasses to Dunphy, and then offered the tray to the chief. Montgomery shook his head, and waved him towards Grimmett.

Dunphy took a deep draught to slake his parched throat. His tongue seemed to explode as the sweet liquid dissolved into a mouthful of warm gas. His stomach churned, and he fought back a huge belch as Mrs. Eldridge's cream soda worked its way through his delicate system. Montgomery smiled at him. Dunphy tried to smile back, and forced himself to drink some more. The noise of the drums pounded through his skull. Montgomery was stamping his feet and clapping his hands.

"Biscuit?" shouted Montgomery. He steered the man with the tray back to Dunphy. Dunphy reached out and took a small round cookie from the plate. He bit into it to remove the sickly taste of the cream soda. The biscuit was bone-dry. It removed every vestige of saliva from Dunphy's already dry mouth. Too late he realised that it was a dog biscuit. He bent round the side of the chair to spit it out and saw Montgomery watching him.

"Good oh, Mister Dunphy," said Montgomery. "Special treat for you. Special biscuits from Accra!"

113

Dunphy chewed at the indigestible biscuit and tried to swallow it. The drummers quickened the beat and raised the level of sound. Montgomery jumped to his feet and began a quick shuffling dance. He turned to Dunphy, holding out his arms.

"Hi Life!" said Montgomery. He waved Dunphy out of his seat. "Come Mister Dunphy. You do the Hi Life last night!" Mistaking Dunphy's reluctance for shyness he grabbed him by the wrists and hauled him out of his chair.

"No, no," said Dunphy. A shout went up from the bandsmen when they saw the guest of honour on his feet. They attacked the drums with redoubled energy. Dunphy stood irresolutely beside the chief for a moment, and then began to hop from one foot to the other. Montgomery took a couple of steps backwards and began to clap his hands to the rhythm of the drums.

"Go man go! Mister Dunphy you go one time now!" he shouted. Dunphy lumbered round the circle with his eyes closed; a look of anguish on his face. The drummers leaned into their instruments and battered their way to a crescendo as the guest of honour jumped about in front of them.

The drums stopped. Montgomery rushed forward and pumped Dunphy's hand. "Good stuff Mister Dunphy!" he said.

Dunphy staggered back to the armchair and collapsed.

"You tell your government that we are happy people," said the chief, overcome with the moment. He clapped Dunphy on the shoulder, re-arranged his robes, and sat down on the orange box. He let out a deep sigh.

Grimmett got to his feet. "I think we'd better be on our way now Mr. Montgomery. We want to thank you for your invitation. We won't forget this fine demonstration for a long time."

The Volkswagen bumped back up the dusty road. The sun was a crimson ball above the trees, distorted by the fine dust of the Harmattan winds which blow down the upper atmosphere each year before the rainy season.

"That was quite an honour for us to be invited to that," said Grimmett.

Dunphy grunted.

"It was interesting. Those rhythms from the drums take you right over, don't they? It's hard to keep still."

Dunphy folded over in his seat and put his head in his hands. "I can still hear them," he groaned. "Think I might be sick."

Chapter 15 – The Wayward Parrot

Grimmett had one more encounter with his father before he returned to Scotland. It was an odd, undefined meeting, preceded by a telephone call.

"I'll pick you up at the foot of your driveway at 6 o'clock," said Grimmett's father on the telephone. "You can tell your mother. It's all right."

Grimmett was waiting under the last jacaranda tree when his father drove up. He was alone. Grimmett climbed into the car and they drove down the valley towards Achimota.

"We'll go to the old golf club. We can have a drink there, and a chat," said Jack Grimmett.

At the golf club they sat in leather armchairs, on either side of a glass-topped table by a window in the corner. It was nearly dark. There were no golfers outside; only a green keeper far up the last fairway, tending the watering hoses. The high-pitched sound of evening crickets pierced the mesh screen over the open window.

Grimmett's father ordered two bottles of Club beer and began to speak.

"It has all been a bit awkward," he began. "I know that you and Hillevi don't get on very well. I'm at a bit of a loss as to why. I wish it could be different." He glanced over

116

at the door. It was a furtive movement, as if he were half expecting her to come into the club. Laughter came from a small group of men at the bar, embarking on an evening's entertainment.

One of the men looked over at them. "Jack Grimmett!" he said. "Come on Jack. What are you sitting over there for? Come and join us for a pint."

Grimmett's father shook his head. "Not tonight Alec. Mustn't stay late." The man at the bar waved a hand and turned back to his friends.

"I wanted to have a chat with you. Just you and me. We haven't really had a chance to do that, have we?"

No, thought Grimmett. It was funny how it didn't seem to matter so much any more.

"How are you getting on at school? It's a bit better now isn't it?" said his father. He fumbled in his pocket and brought out a packet of cigarettes. He cut the cellophane wrapper with his thumbnail and tapped a cigarette out of the packet.

"It's not much different than it ever was." Grimmett looked up at the ceiling. "Except that there's only half a year to go and then it'll be finished."

"This will be a better year, you'll see. You'll be a lot more independent, living in a flat instead of at home. You'll like it better."

Grimmett stared at his father. His mother had only told him the day before that she was going to stay in West Africa for several more months; that she had made arrangements to rent him an apartment in Edinburgh.

"No dear, you can't stay in the house," she had said. "I'm renting it out until I come back in the summer. Besides, the flat will suit you better. It's close to school and it will do you good to be self-sufficient, to look after yourself."

He wondered again how his mother and father communicated with each other. They avoided each other's company and yet they seemed to speak, make arrangements and reach apparently joint decisions on his future.

He made an effort. "It's a bit of a coincidence, you being posted out here."

117

"Yes. I suppose it is. But it's only a temporary arrangement while Geoff Weedmark is on leave. I will only be here for another two months."

"Where will you go then?"

"I don't know. Head Office in London will decide in the next few weeks. But it will probably be a long-term posting; five years or so. Maybe the Middle East."

"What about Uncle Ronald? How long do you think he'll stay here?"

"Oh, gosh. I've got no idea. I mean, this is where he works now, so unless he finds a job somewhere else I suppose he'll stay out here."

Grimmett gazed out of the window. A car came down the road from Legon. Its headlights shone through the water that was spraying from the sprinklers on the fairway and made a wide halo of light.

The parrot was hunched on its perch, its feathers fluffed, and its head under its wing. It was early and the low sun threw long morning shadows across the living room floor. Grimmett sat in one of the wicker chairs, staring out across the valley, one leg dangling over the arm of the chair. There had been no decisions from the evening before with his father, no conclusions. Nothing. He picked up the morning newspaper and leafed through the pages without reading it. A hawk hovered over the storm ditch at the bottom of the garden, hunting for small creatures.

Uncle Ronald came quietly into the room in his dressing gown. His bare feet made soft sucking sounds on the parquet floor. Grimmett put the paper down. His stepfather shuffled over to the table beside the aviary, his hair dishevelled, his eyes puffy from sleep. The parrot shifted on its perch and watched him with a dispassionate black eye.

Uncle Ronald pulled a tissue from a pink box on the table. He folded it carefully and applied it to his nose. The parrot straightened up and made a loud rasping noise. Uncle Ronald blew his nose and dropped the used tissue into the wastebasket.

"It's today you go isn't it?" he said, scratching his stomach. "I mustn't forget to get the big car from the department."

"Yes, the flight leaves at two o'clock."

The parrot stretched out a wing. It began to dig around in its food dish with its beak. It came up with a sunflower seed, and cracked the shell and flipped the husk through the wire onto the living room floor.

"Messy beast," said Uncle Ronald. He bent down to pick up the shell and dropped it in an ashtray. "I hope you won't have any trouble with him on the trip home. It's a bit of a risk of course. These quarantine regulations are so bloody tiresome, but you should be able to get him through without any fuss—as long as you can keep him quiet."

"What's yer game sunny?" shrieked the bird. "What's the score?"

Grimmett stood up and walked over to the aviary. He pushed his finger through the wire screen. The parrot stopped chewing and stared at him, unblinking, its head tilted to one side.

"He's quite good isn't he? The way he picks up your voice." About to leave Africa and faced with an uncertain time in Scotland, Grimmett felt a twinge of unaccustomed warmth towards his stepfather.

"I yam a talking parrot! Talking! Talking, I yam."

"He gets a bit confused sometimes," said Uncle Ronald, "but he will be nice for your mother to have when she goes back to Edinburgh." He lifted the bell from the table and rang it.

Dunphy stepped into the living room. He was wearing a pale yellow shirt and baggy khaki shorts.

"You rang sir?" he said.

Uncle Ronald ignored him and glared at the kitchen door.

"Campbell! Where the devil is he?"

The door swung open and Campbell jogged into the living room.

"Yes, Campbell." Uncle Ronald frowned. "Did you manage to dig up a cardboard box?"

"Yes!" Campbell stood with his arms at his sides.

"And have you punched some holes in it and put in some toilet paper?"

"Yes!"

"Well, Campbell," said Uncle Ronald, "would you go and fetch it please."

119

Campbell turned and marched from the room.

"We will have to give it some knockout drops of course," said Uncle Ronald. "That should help it sleep all the way to London."

The parrot coughed. Dunphy stared at it. "Taking the bird back with us are we?"

"Yes. It'll be all right in the box. You'll have to be a bit careful going through Customs in London because it's not . . . ah, exactly legal. But it should be all right. They're not going to tighten up the regulations until next summer."

Grimmett turned at the top of the aeroplane steps and waved. Dunphy hoisted his overnight bag onto his shoulder and stopped beside him. Below them in the spectator's enclosure Grimmett's mother waved a white handkerchief over her head.

"Let's go." Grimmett ducked into the aeroplane. He made his way up the aisle, scanning the seat numbers.

"Your father?" said Dunphy.

"Hillevi's sick with something. He said he might not be able to make it. His deputy's running things today."

Dunphy sat down in the aisle seat and manoeuvred the overnight bag between his feet.

"Is he all right?" whispered Grimmett.

Dunphy pulled the zipper back a few inches and peered into the bag. "Seems to be fine."

"Make sure he's got lots of air." Grimmett reached for his seat belt. One of the propellers began to turn. The engine hacked and spat out blue smoke. The next engine started up. The aeroplane began to vibrate. A stewardess hurried past checking the seatbelts. A faint cough came from the bag at Dunphy's feet.

An elegantly dressed, middle-aged woman was sitting across the aisle from Dunphy. She wore a purple hat and a purple dress, a string of pearls around her neck.

Dunphy nudged Grimmett's arm. "I think it coughed."

"It can't have. Uncle Ronald gave it something to put it to sleep until we get to London."

"I'm sure it coughed."

The aeroplane sped down the runway and lifted off the ground. Grimmett gazed out of the window as they climbed over the Accra plains. The university passed below them, its white tower on the hilltop, red-roofed houses scattered down the slope like small biscuit tins. Cars moved along the roads, slowly, like beetles. The landscape was like a child's plaything, neat and vulnerable.

Dunphy leaned over to look out of the window. The university rotated gently underneath them as the aeroplane banked onto a northerly course.

"Looks like Toytown from up here," said Dunphy. A belch came from the overnight bag. Dunphy quickly put a hand to his mouth and forced a cough. The lady in purple put down her magazine and stared at him.

"Pardon." said Dunphy. He fixed a smile on his face and waited for the lady to start reading again. As soon as she picked up her magazine, he turned to Grimmett.

"Look. We can't just sit here for the next eight hours or whatever it is if that bird's going to carry on like this. We've got to do something about it."

"What can we do? He's not supposed to be here. There'll be a lot of trouble if anyone finds out."

"That lady thought it was me." Dunphy glanced across the aisle. The woman was flicking through the pages of her magazine.

"It's just as well she did." The seat in front reclined back towards them. Dunphy caught a glimpse of a ruddy face with a moustache on its upper lip.

"Maybe it'll go to sleep in a minute," said Grimmett.

The aircraft levelled out at its cruising altitude and the engines settled into an immutable drone. Two of the cabin crew wheeled a trolley down the aisle, dispensing drinks.

"Would you like anything to drink?" The stewardess leaned over Dunphy, as she spoke to Grimmett. Inside the bag, the parrot let out a rasping hawk, followed by a spitting sound. The stewardess jerked upright and stared at Dunphy.

"I beg your pardon!"

"Sorry," said Dunphy. His face turned red. He covered his mouth with his hand.

"Er, no thank you," said Grimmett.

The stewardess frowned. "And you?" she said to Dunphy.

Dunphy had an idea. He patted his stomach and nodded. "A small glass of red wine please."

She lifted a bottle from the rack and poured some wine into a glass. She put it down on the tray in front of him. "Two shillings please." She held out her hand.

Dunphy reached into his pocket and handed over the money. The trolley moved on. The man in the seat in front of them opened his eyes for a second and grunted.

"It's too much," said Dunphy. He cast a glance at the woman across the aisle. She was staring at him.

"It's always expensive on airline flights," said Grimmett.

"Not the wine. The parrot." He felt a tap on his arm.

"I've got some indigestion pills," said the woman in purple. "Would you like one?"

"Talk-king! I yam talk-king!" called the parrot from the bag.

The woman snapped backwards. "I beg your pardon!" she said.

Dunphy rolled his eyes. "I . . . ah . . . sorry. It's the aeroplane. Flying. It does strange things to me."

A look somewhere between suspicion and understanding crossed the woman's face. She leaned over and patted Dunphy on the arm.

"I see," she said. "Well, there's no need to be afraid, young man. I'm sure the pilot knows what he's doing."

The parrot belched from the depths of the overnight bag. The woman snatched her hand away.

The parrot sniffed.

"I say old chap," said the man in the seat in front, without moving his head. He fixed Dunphy with one eye. The moustache twitched as he spoke. "Lay off the plonk for a bit will you. I'm trying to get some sleep." The eye closed.

"That's it," said Dunphy. "I'm going to wring its neck." He reached for the zipper.

"You can't do that," said Grimmett. "That bird's worth a lot of money. Besides, it's got a vicious beak. It could take your finger off."

"In that case I'm going to let it out when we stop in Rome. It can find its own way home from there."

"You can't do that either," said Grimmett. "It'll die. It's much too far for it to fly. I don't think it can fly anyway. I think it's had its wings clipped."

"I can't just sit here with it snorting and belching every few minutes. They'll put me off the plane if it goes on much longer."

"We'll have to think of something."

"Zip it right up," suggested Dunphy. "Tape its beak shut."

The parrot let out a whistle. The man in front jerked around to face them. He glared at Dunphy.

"Look here old man," he said. "If you must be a bloody pest why don't you move somewhere else. Outside for example, and take your wine with you."

Grimmett tapped the man on the shoulder.

The man twisted in his seat again. "What?"

Grimmett twitched his head in Dunphy's direction. He placed a finger on his temple and made a screwing motion.

"Nerves," he said. "It happens when he flies. He's got no control over it."

"Mwah. I see." The moustache flickered. "Well, try and keep him quiet will you. I've got an important meeting when I get to London. I want to catch some sleep before we get there." He punched his pillow and lay back in his seat.

Dunphy sipped the wine and scratched his chin.

"Brandy!"

"Brandy?"

"We'll give it some brandy. That's what your mother said she gave it when it had a cold. She said it liked it—and it put it to sleep. Remember?"

"How are you going to get it to drink it?"

"Eye dropper," said Dunphy.

"Where are we going to get an eye dropper?"

"First Aid Kit. They must have a First Aid Kit on board. I'll ask the stewardess." He heaved himself out of his seat and went up to the front of the cabin to speak to the stewardess.

"Got one," he said when he came back. He showed it to Grimmett: a small glass tube with a rubber bulb on the top. "This will do. Got a miniature of brandy too." He unscrewed the top of the bottle and dipped the eyedropper

123

in the brandy. He pulled the eyedropper out and studied it for a moment. He took a drop on his finger and touched it to his tongue. He made a face.

"Awful stuff. Don't know how it can stand it."

A faint sound like the ring of a distant telephone came from the black bag. Dunphy froze with his hand on the zipper and looked up at the seat in front. The telephone bell stopped and Dunphy quickly unzipped the bag. The Greenwich Time Signal pierced the cabin.

"For Pete's sake! What the hell are you playing at?" Dunphy whipped the zipper shut and stared up at the moustache shaking over the back of the seat in front. He shrugged his shoulders.

"Sorry," he said.

"Sorry!" The man's mouth opened and closed. "You need to show some bloody consideration for the other passengers young man!" He punched his pillow again and pulled the blanket over his head.

Dunphy unzipped the bag and lifted a corner of the parrot's cardboard box.

"You hold him," he said to Grimmett. "Get him round the neck and I'll shove this down his throat."

The man in the seat in front jerked upright, flinging his blanket away from him.

"I heard that," he said, swivelling round in his seat. He narrowed his eyes. "Lay a hand on me and you'll regret it I warn you. I'll have you put off this flight at the next stop." He pulled his seat upright, and pushed the button to summon the steward.

"Quick," whispered Dunphy. "Let's get this stuff into it before the steward comes."

Grimmett bent down and slipped his hand inside the bag. He took the parrot round the neck and tilted its head upwards. Dunphy pushed the eyedropper in its mouth and squirted the brandy down its throat.

"Here's the stewardess." Grimmett withdrew his hand.

Dunphy closed the lid of the box and fastened the tape. He drew the zipper shut as the stewardess came to the seat in front.

The man turned and pointed at Dunphy. "This . . . this lout is threatening me. He's been making strange noises and shouting, and keeping me awake."

The stewardess looked at Dunphy.

"He's just threatened to get me round the neck and punch me in the throat," the man went on. The stewardess's eyes widened.

"I'm not going to put up with this sort of hooliganism. It's disgraceful." He drew himself up in his seat. "I think you should put him off the plane. In the meantime I insist on sitting somewhere else. He's a menace; he's probably dangerous."

The stewardess stared at Dunphy for a moment. She turned her attention back to the passenger. "If you'd like to come with me sir, I'll take you to another seat further forward," she said.

Dunphy's face was crimson.

"I . . . ah . . . didn't mean it like that. Bit of a misunderstanding." His voice tailed away.

"It's all right," said the stewardess. "The chief steward will attend to you in a moment. You can explain it to him." She escorted the passenger up the aisle.

Hours later, Dunphy and Grimmett sat in an icy compartment on the Flying Scotsman as it raced across a Northumberland moor. Snow was falling past the windows, sifting the countryside into austere shades of grey and white. They gazed out at the pallid scenery.

"When you think of it," said Grimmett, "it's probably a good thing that you had all that trouble on the plane. There would have been an awful fuss if they'd discovered the parrot."

Dunphy grunted at the memory of it; of being escorted by the chief steward down the steps of the aeroplane when they reached London. He swayed against the window as the train rattled round a bend.

"With the steward seeing you off like that it probably helped when you went through Customs," continued Grimmett. "They probably thought you were a celebrity or something, getting the first class treatment. Did you see that sign which said there was a two hundred pound fine for bringing in livestock or vegetables without the proper permits?"

Dunphy pulled his coat over his chest. He'd said little since they left London.

"Wasn't necessary to treat me like an idiot," he said. He looked at the black bag. "Anyway, why didn't you carry the bird in the first place?"

Grimmett looked at him in surprise. "Because you said you wanted to. I thought you liked it."

The lights of a station flashed past the window, flickering into the compartment.

"It's your parrot. Your mother's anyway."

"You said it would look silly to carry a pink hatbox onto the aeroplane, and you offered to put it in your overnight bag."

Dunphy digested this. His face brightened. "It worked didn't it? The brandy. Would've been a lot worse without that."

"Do you think it's all right?"

"Yes. I looked at it when you were out getting coffee. It's still sleeping." A smile spread across his round face. "Actually, I've grown quite attached to it. I hope it won't be too cold for it in Scotland. I wouldn't like anything to happen to it after all we've been through."

Chapter 16 – Stark

George Dunphy, Canada's Vice-consul to Scotland, had a worried frown on his face as he scanned the carriages of the London train. The wind whistled down the platform, blasting under the open-ended Victorian canopy of Edinburgh's Waverley Station. Many of the roof's glass panels were cracked, and rainwater dripped from the high steel girders. He pulled up the collar of his raincoat, his mind occupied with the changes that were about to happen in his life. Political upheaval was a factor in his job, and once again it was about to disrupt his comfortable existence.

"I've got to fly out to Canada in the morning," he said to his son when they were in the car. "The government has changed, and the new people have recalled me. They're sending me on some kind of course. I wanted your mother to come with me because she hasn't been home for a couple of years—and anyway, with Arthur going into his flat it seemed like a good way to do things. You fellows can just buckle down and look after yourselves for a while."

He braked as a traffic light changed to red. He reached out to wipe condensation from the windscreen. "Back in the 'thirties, when I was your age George, I had to fend for myself. It was a lot rougher then than it is now.

127

There wasn't someone waiting at home to cook my meals and make my bed and iron my shirts and sew on buttons and things. It'll do you good."

"Why can't I come with you?" said Dunphy.

"Because you have to finish up at school. You've had enough changes in your schooling already. The way I see it you'll be hard pushed to pass your final exams in the summer as it is. Anyway, your mother and I will be back long before that."

The flat was in the city's New Town, among streets of looming tenements interspersed with green parks, and criss-crossed by uneven, cobble-stoned streets.

"Looks pretty ancient to me," said Dunphy, as he put the last of his boxes down in the hallway. "Can't see why they call it the New Town. And those stairs just about kill me, why didn't they put in elevators?"

"It's because it's only two hundred and fifty years old," said Grimmett.

"What?"

"It's why they call it the New Town—because it's only two hundred and fifty years old. They didn't have elevators then."

Grimmett pushed the bedcovers away from his face and forced his eyes open. His breath misted in the gloom. He groped on the table by his bed for a coin. He rolled over and dropped the coin in the slot of the electric meter, and lay back and stared at the ceiling. They had been in the flat for a week. His nose twitched at the sharp smell of sour milk.

Dunphy stirred as the red glow of the electric fire diffused into the winter morning dark. "What time is it?" His voice was husky with sleep.

"Eight o'clock."

"Too early." Dunphy pulled the covers over his head. "It's Saturday."

Grimmett slid out of bed. The clink of bottles came from a milk cart in the street. A vacuum cleaner started up on the floor above. The lady with the vacuum began to sing, secure in the knowledge that the noise of the cleaner was drowning out her voice.

Dunphy was easing himself out of his bed when Grimmett came back from the bathroom. He stepped across the wooden floor, shivering with cold. He opened the door of a cupboard in the corner. A powerful stench of sour milk wafted into the room.

"You've got to get rid of those bottles," said Grimmett. "Why don't you put them outside the front door so the milkman can take them away?"

"No way. Got to save them up. They're worth two-pence each these bottles." He took a shirt out of the cupboard and inspected the collar for dirt. Satisfied, he pulled the shirt over his head. Shivering still, he reached under a chair for his socks. He sniffed at them, and sat down and pulled them on.

Grimmett went to the window and looked down into the street. Three storeys down the cobblestones glistened with a whitening of frost. Black stone tenements lined the street. Some of the chimneys were already pushing grey smoke into the cold morning air above the frosted, slate roofs. He turned and looked round the room he shared with Dunphy.

It was a big rectangular room with a high ceiling. A marble fireplace took up part of one wall, but the chimney had been blocked up by a previous owner. Two tall windows overlooked the street. There were two beds in the room, and a pair of armchairs beside the fireplace. A thin red carpet covered part of a wood floor which hadn't been varnished for decades. A dresser stood against the wall at the foot of Grimmett's bed; a chest of drawers beside Dunphy's. As well as the bed-sitting room, they had a small kitchen and a bathroom.

Dunphy jumped to his feet at a loud crash from the apartment above. They heard the sound of heavy booted feet, and then another crash, followed by the sound of breaking glass.

"God," said Dunphy, staring up at the ceiling. "It's started already."

"What's started? What's all the noise about?"

"Stark. You know he lives up there?"

"I think so. But what's he doing?"

"He gets all wound up about his art. Mrs. Stark was telling me the other day that she's fed up with his temper tantrums. She says he gets them from trying to teach us."

Another crash reverberated across the ceiling. "She won't like that," said Grimmett.

"It's his Angry Room," said Dunphy. They listened to Stark's uneven tread on the floor above them. "He's got to go in there when he's cross. She's set it up for him so he won't frighten the children."

"You mean he just goes in there and breaks things?"

"Yes. You should see it. She showed it to me. I've never seen anything like it. Looks like a bomb's gone off in a paint factory." Dunphy sat down in the overstuffed armchair.

A door slammed upstairs. The ceiling light swung gently on its cord. Dunphy pointed upwards.

"You hear the boots? That's what he wears when he goes in there. Old army boots with steel toecaps. She showed them to me as well." He paused. "He's got to wear them in there because the floor's about six inches deep in broken glass." Dunphy motioned over his shoulder with his thumb. "It's why I keep the milk bottles. She gives me two-pence a bottle, to stock up his angry room."

"I've always rather liked him," said Grimmett. "He seemed like a decent sort to me. I didn't know he smashed his house up." They heard a shout from upstairs.

"He doesn't exactly smash it up," said Dunphy. "He just goes off the deep end once in a while when he gets upset with the school, or when one of his paintings doesn't go right. I'm sure he'll be all right now that she's got him his Angry Room."

There was a muted crash from the back of the flat above.

"Sounds like he's run out of bottles," said Dunphy. "Maybe I should take up some supplies. She said the war had something to do with it. She told me that's what he got his limp from." He went over to the cupboard. "Come on. Give me a hand."

Dunphy led the way up the stone stairs to the flat above. In his arms he was carrying a brown bag of pungent milk bottles. Grimmett knocked on the door. A moment later it was opened by the art master's wife. She was wearing an island-knit sweater and corduroy trousers. Her feet were bare. Long black hair fell straight to her waist.

She stuck two fingers in her mouth, turned, and whistled into the house.

"Jonathan," she called. "Two of your chaps here to see you." Grimmett hadn't met her before. Her accent was south of England.

Stark looked round the corner of the hallway. "Come in lads," he said. "You're just in time for coffee. We can give them coffee can't we Rosanna?"

"She irons her hair," whispered Dunphy as they followed her down the hall. "I saw her doing it."

Stark broke into song as they came into the kitchen. "Rrrooozanna . . . in the high-est . . ." He was standing at the sink with his back to them. His sleeves were rolled up to his elbows. He was washing a pile of dishes.

"I'll be with you in a minute." He waved his arm and scattered soapsuds across the floor. "Take a seat."

Stark's flat was close up under the eaves of the tenement, its ceiling slanted at angles to windows that were set in caverned alcoves. It was fuggy and warm from a heavy cast-iron cooking range. Sunshine fell from the window onto the kitchen floor.

They sat on stools round the kitchen table. The table's wooden surface was scratched and gouged with what looked like knife scars. Through the open door Grimmett could see into another room off the hallway, a room with a mattress on the floor and rumpled sheets and blankets. Rosanna followed his gaze. She closed the door with a push with her foot.

"I haven't made the beds yet," she said.

Stark lifted a steaming kettle from the stove. He poured hot water into four cups. He was a tall, raw-boned man with curly dark hair and a full beard. He brought the cups to the table two at a time. He limped badly when he walked.

"Make yourselves at home." Stark indicated a jug of milk and a sugar bowl. "I never did apologise to you did I?" he said, looking at Grimmett.

"What for sir?"

"You mustn't call me sir up here. Call me Jonathan."

"All right."

"I shouldn't have thrown that knife at you."

Rosanna turned from the cabinet, where she was stacking plates. "You threw a knife at him?" She stifled a laugh. "Jonathan, you mustn't do that. You're supposed to teach them, not kill them."

Grimmett laughed. "It wasn't as bad as it sounds." He looked at Stark. "You needn't apologise for that sir. I'd have been angry if I'd been you."

"What did you do?" Rosanna tossed the dishtowel on the draining board and sat down at the table.

"It was in the art class at the end of last term," said Grimmett. He spooned sugar from the bowl into his cup. "We were looking at slides. You know, projecting pictures of paintings onto the wall. Nudes and things. Some of the class started to laugh, and Mr. Stark got annoyed."

"Big buxom Ruebens' with overblown thighs and gigantic breasts," said Stark, making shapes with his hands in the air. "Some of these immature little philistines were laughing."

"The thing is sir," said Grimmett. "I didn't laugh at them. I wasn't laughing."

"No, I know you weren't. I was aiming at Rowland, but he ducked under the table just as I threw it, so it hit you instead."

Grimmett remembered it. The knife had hit him on the shoulder and clattered to the floor. The blade had been open, but the knife had hit him handle-first. He had seen, in that quick flash of temper, and the fast, reflexive way that Stark had flicked the knife off his table, that he had thrown it with a haunting expertise. Grimmett knew it was no accident that the handle had hit him, and not the blade.

"Sometimes I get a bit carried away with some of these hysterically prim attitudes," said Stark. "Sex-starved little heathens. But I'm sorry it hit you. I was too annoyed to apologise at the time."

He stood up and went to the window. Grimmett felt a twinge of sympathy for him. The stepped roofs outside were beginning to show slate-grey as the sun warmed off the frost. Beyond the chimney pots the river estuary sparkled blue in the sunshine. On the far shore invisible windows reflected the sunlight and shot it back at the city.

"'. . . the Forth wheels ample waters set with sacred isles, and populous Fife smokes with a score of towns.'" Stark turned back to the kitchen. "Robert Louis Stevenson. Now there was a fellow who thought for himself. They like to trot him out as one of the old boys, one of the star 'former pupils'. 'Look at what we can do for you if you just do what we tell you to do.'" He picked up his coffee cup. "Stevenson hated it so much that his family had to take him away from the school after a couple of years."

Rosanna patted him gently on the arm. "Settle down. Don't get worked up about it."

"Why not? It hasn't changed at all, even after a hundred years. This is the twentieth century, and they still stifle creative thought. They'll make you fit their mould—or else they'll ruin you for anything else." He glared round the table at them. "They do it all the time. Look at what they did to McCue—stamping all over that beautiful, sensitive mind and his brave explorations with their hobnailed boots."

He looked at Grimmett, and then at Dunphy. "They do it to you too. They do it to everyone, as if you're all made of stone, to be chipped and hammered into a bunch of statues. Young minds are delicate things. They should be encouraged and nurtured, and handled with care." He ran his hand through his hair.

"I . . . ah . . . brought up some bottles," said Dunphy.

Stark slapped his knee. "Ah-ha!" he roared, his mood changed in an instant. "Bottles for my Room. And they're just in time." He winked at his wife, and moved towards her with a lecherous look on his face. "You drive me so wild with passion that I can hardly control myself." He made a grab at her as she jumped up and skipped out the door. Stark wandered slowly back to his seat.

"I know what we'll do," he said. "We'll break some rules. I'll take you fellows out for a drink tonight. Eight o'clock at the Vaults."

Rosanna came back into the kitchen and dumped some coins on the table in front of Dunphy. He gathered them up and put them in his pocket.

"How much did you make?" Stark leaned over the table.

133

"I . . . ah . . . don't know," said Dunphy. "I didn't count it."

"Ah . . . you should always count any money you get from a beautiful woman," said Stark. "Beauty and virtue are quite different things. You must never confuse them." He stood up. "First round's on you then. I'll see you at eight. I've got to get back to work. I've just had a vision."

"I wonder what he meant about McCue," said Grimmett. They were walking down a narrow lane. The old Victorian stables on either side of them had been converted into garages. The street lamps threw pools of yellow light on the frosty cobblestones. It made Grimmett feel as if he was walking back through time.

"I don't know," said Dunphy. The air was sharp. He drew his coat tightly about him and sank his hands into the pockets. He clenched his teeth against the cold, and his breath punctuated the air like small smoke signals. "Keeps himself apart a lot, McCue. Spends most of his time in the art room by himself. Slow down a bit, can't you?"

Grimmett shortened his stride and hunched his shoulders against the wind. He was thinking.

"This is it isn't it? The pub he was talking about?" Dunphy stopped outside a dimly lit basement bar. He glanced up and down the street before darting down a short flight of steps.

They could see into the bar through a dusty window. The tiny, dank courtyard smelled faintly of urine.

"Prints!" They heard Stark's voice over the chatter as they pushed through the door. "Ersatz, plastic, fakery." Stark's bearded head loomed through the cigarette smoke at the far end of the bar. He waved his arm at a group of pictures on the wall behind the barman's head. They showed barefoot children, and fishwives in shawls; crowded 18th century alleyways full of people in plaid, with onlookers leaning from the windows of rickety buildings.

"The fellow who did these probably made a shilling or two for his talents," said Stark, squinting at the pictures. "He was quite a good draftsman. But they're not real you see."

"So why doesn't the artist get any money?" said the barman. He was wiping a glass with a dish towel.

Dunphy and Grimmett pushed their way to the bar.

Stark scooped up his mug and drank from it. "Because he's dead," he said. He wiped his mouth with the back of his hand. "Pint?" he said, turning to Grimmett.

He reached in his pocket and dumped a pile of loose change on the counter. "Two pints of your best heavy for my friends," he said to the barman. He had been in the pub for some time.

The bar's vaulted ceiling curved up through the smoke. What had once been whitewashed walls were tinged with brown and grey, and assorted stains. Small rooms and alcoves rambled into the gloom from either side of the main bar, furnished with battered armchairs, and barrels for tables. The air was thick with smoke and conversation. A scattering of sawdust covered the floor. Stark was wearing a black fisherman's sweater and big, scarred boots. His overcoat was crumpled on the floor, and his cane walking stick leaned against the side of the bar. A trick of the light threw half his face into shadow. To Grimmett he looked like an ancient pirate.

Stark raised his glass. "Prosit!" he said.

"Cheers."

"Slainthe!" said Stark, drinking deeply again. "A Scottish toast to you all." He studied his glass for a moment, and leaned towards Dunphy. "They don't give you froth up here. Down south you get froth. Up here you get beer."

Grimmett was staring at a small silver medal that was lying among Stark's change on the bar. It was elegant and fine-lined, and it was in the shape of a small, slightly flared, cross. Stark saw him looking at it. He picked it up and put it in his pocket, and muttered something Grimmett didn't catch.

"What was it?" asked Grimmett.

"Talisman," said Stark. "Small token of service." He pulled a packet of cigarettes from his pocket, and took one and lit it with a square, metal lighter. He held the cigarette upright between his fingers.

Dunphy had seen the medal too. "Did it come from the war?"

The buzz of conversation flowed over them and lapped at the chalky grey arches that led off to the adjacent rooms. Stark didn't answer. He took a swallow from a glass of whisky the barman had put down in front of him and leaned back against the bar and looked at them with dark eyes.

"Today," he said, "is Rommel's birthday." He took up his mug and washed the whisky down with a long draught of beer. "A great man. An artist at his trade."

Grimmett was intrigued. "How did you win the medal?" he said. Two men were playing darts in an alcove behind them. The projectiles thudded into the cork dartboard, one after the other.

"Oh, we're not interested in that sort of thing nowadays," said Stark. "It's not relevant to anything anymore, is it?" He gazed past them. Behind him a man spat on the floor.

"I'm interested," said Grimmett. "I'd like to hear about it." It occurred to him that Stark might be pretending to be more intoxicated than he was.

"Another pint Patrick!" Stark called to the barman, who was at the far end of the bar. "Drink up," he said. "Three, Patrick!" He held up three fingers. "It really is a dreadful, ratty place, isn't it?" he said, gazing round the room.

Grimmett wondered again at Stark's mood swings, whether they were cultivated to allow him a certain space and freedom. Or whether his irreverence and eccentricities came out of the things he had seen. Perhaps he didn't care about any of it.

"I could show you one of the tricks I picked up in the army," said Stark. "It would go down well in here, and it's much more useful than a bunch of silly war stories." He bent down and picked up his cane.

"With the assistance of this I can relieve myself without relinquishing my hard won place at the bar, and without shocking the 'sembled clientele—male or female."

Dunphy laughed. He was enjoying the beer. "How can you do that?"

"Simple." Stark took a sip from his mug, spilling some beer down the front of his sweater. His voice was thick, his words starting to run together. "A liquid will cling to a vertical surface: s'one of these laws of physics. They must've taught you it."

He drew the walking stick up in front of his chest and pushed it down inside the waistband of his trousers, down his leg. "I can pee down this stick and it'll run all the way down to the floor 'thout wetting my trousers." He looked at them. "Fi' do it properly that is."

He pulled the stick out again. "Not drunk enough yet. If you do it prop'ly it works. Learned it from a chap in the regiment."

The barman put down three fresh pint mugs. Grimmett watched Stark count out the money from a pile of change.

"How did you win the medal?" said Grimmett again. "I'd like to hear the story."

"S'a story all right," Stark said. He pushed a handful of coins at the barman and took a deep breath. "Not much to it. I was in the desert with an Intelligence lot called the Long Range Desert Group." He nodded as the barman slid another shot glass of whisky to him.

"We used to wander 'round in jeeps behind the lines. Pick up information on what the other side was doing. I was norm'ly in charge of our section, but a Colonel'd come up from Cairo to see what we were up to, and he wanted to join us on this p'ticular trip." He tapped a cigarette on top of the bar.

"The colonel was a bit of a nuisance. Wanted to do everything by the book. Made us shave every morning, even though we had more important things to do with our water, and we were never sure when we could re-supply."

He took another deep breath and went on. "After we'd been out for a few days—poking about really, hiding up in wadis in the daytime; pushing on at night—we ran into some Italians.

"Wasn't our job to get involved with the enemy 'less we couldn't help it, but this colonel ordered us up too close to them and they saw us. We got away all right, but we woke them up and that was stupid." He lit the cigarette with his metal lighter, and let the smoke drift out of his nostrils.

It seemed to Grimmett as if Stark was talking to someone else now; someone in another place, another time.

"They knew we were out there then. Nex' day at sunup the colonel hiked up the wadi to take a crap. We heard some shooting so we scrambled up to the top to take a look. Over the other side there were two German half-tracks and the Colonel running around with s' trousers round his ankles. Too prim and proper. Should've taken his morning dump right where we'd parked, 'stead of wandering off over the hill and getting in trouble. Anyway we fired back at them, 'though we should have left him to it."

Stark's eyes came back in focus as he looked at Grimmett. "The Germans pushed off when we popped up over the rim of the wadi and started shooting. Didn't know how many of us there were I s'pose." He took a drag of the cigarette. "Colonel was actually all right 'cept for a scratch on his arse."

Stark chuckled. "Trousers shot to rags though. Just tatters, flapping round his ankles." He was relaxed now. "Well I di'n't see that as a problem—C.O. with no trousers. I thought we should get out of there b'fore the Germans realised there weren't very many of us, and came back. But the colonel di'n't want to go anywhere without his trousers. 'Ventually we convinced him that he wasn't going to find new ones where we were, and that we could look'n some of the wrecks we came across from time to time to see if we could find him another pair.

"Nex' day we came across a burnt out jeep and an abandoned half-track, but there weren't any trousers in them. Colonel was a real nuisance by then. Seemed to think he was losing his authority 'cos he was trouserless. But the truth was he didn't have any 'thority anyway 'cos he hadn't got the faintest idea what he was doing out in the desert.

"Made us stop at every wreck we saw; made our lads poke about in them for stray trousers. That was dangerous 'cos the Germans sometimes booby-trapped them. Stupid, and it was all getting in the way of what we were s'posed to be doing out there."

Stark stared at the beer mug in his hand. He turned to face the bar and pushed the shot glass away. After a moment he pointed at it.

"Italians were over there," he set down a coin, "an' we were here an'. . . ", he placed the cigarette lighter between them, "an' the trousers were there." He looked up and smiled.

"We could see the trousers and the Italians, but they hadn't seen us. The colonel'd hardly noticed the Italians, he was so desp'rate for a pair of pants. They were on a dead body," added Stark. "It'd been partly uncovered by the wind; blown the sand off it."

He dropped his cigarette end on the floor and stabbed at it with the end of his walking stick. "I think he was a bit round the bend. Anyway he ordered my driver to go and get the trousers for him, but I told him we had to wait an hour or so 'til it was dark. Then I went and got them myself." He fingered the medal and put it back in his pocket.

"That's it. End of the story, 'cept that they fitted him quite well."

Dunphy thought about this for a moment and said, "They gave you a medal for that?"

"Yes. Cooked, of course. Cooked up. Citation said something about going to the aid of an officer . . . reckless disregard . . . That sort of thing. Weren't many real medals giv'n out for fighting the Italians." Stark hiccupped and said, "Maybe the Colonel thought the medal'd keep me quiet."

Stark picked up his lighter, swallowed the rest of the whisky and shovelled his change into his pocket. He straightened up, with his shoulders held back in an exaggerated military pose, and picked up his walking stick.

"Phoney's hell," he said, and turned and limped to the door.

Chapter 17 – The Shooting Gallery

"That was the most amazing story," said Dunphy, squinting against the glare of the sun. They were walking in front of the school's elaborate Grecian portico. It was a bright day, with a sharp wind. The two of them had just finished a class with Stark. He hadn't mentioned anything about the excursion to the bar on the Saturday night.

Sometimes, thought Dunphy, it was the contrasts in people that provided more mystery than the events they related.

"What a ridiculous way to win a medal," he said.

"You didn't believe it did you?" said Grimmett.

"What? Why? Didn't you?"

"Of course not. He made it up. Most of it anyway. He was pulling our legs."

Dunphy thought about this for a moment. "He can't have," he said. "He was too . . . sad."

"Tragic," said Grimmett.

"Well, yes," said Dunphy. "He was."

"Yes. Well, I think he's tragic about other things too. Life, for example."

Dunphy thought about this. Sometimes he thought it was all becoming clearer to him. Other times he wasn't so sure. He kicked at a pebble on the ground.

"I think it's more complicated than that," he said. "It's . . ." he searched for the right phrase. "It's more how he looks at himself. Maybe what he was really saying was that you shouldn't take things too seriously. That what other people think isn't as important as what you think about yourself and the things you do, and the way you do them." He looked up at the ranks of tenements that climbed the hillside; up and up, towards the castle.

"The system gets you in the end," said Grimmett. "It'll give you medals and prizes if it likes you, or it'll throw you out if it doesn't. That's what he was saying. Just look at him. He's an artist and he's got to teach us instead of doing his art. The system doesn't approve of artists, and artists don't often approve of the system."

Dunphy's face was a study in concentration. "Yes, but he was telling us more than that. He was telling us how to get past that point." He opened his mouth to continue but they were interrupted.

"Aha, Grimmett!" It was Mr. Forbes, the mathematics master. "You haven't forgotten the shooting have you? It starts in ten minutes."

Grimmett had forgotten all about it. "Uh, no sir," he said.

Forbes nodded. "Better get down to the range then," he said, and strode off.

Grimmett made his way down the steps to the shooting range at the back of the school. He pushed the door open and entered a long room hung with fading, brown photographs of the school's Shooting Eights, stretching back a hundred years. Black and white faces stared rigidly down at him from the walls, with the names noted neatly below. The poses were the same over the years. The back rows stood with their arms folded across their chests, eyes focused on a point above the photographer's head. The front rows sat behind rifles stacked like wheat sheaves, resting their hands on knees bared in Highland battledress.

The muffled crack of rifle shots filtered through the wall as a group of cadets shot at targets in the subterranean range. Grimmett sat down at a desk in the empty classroom, and waited for them to finish. The Combined Cadet Force was compulsory for all of them, and every year they had to shoot for their badges. The best of them were picked to represent the school at the national shooting championships at Bisley, in England.

"God, I don't have to shoot with you do I?" Grimmett hadn't heard the door open. Macgregor stepped smartly into the room. He had just been promoted to Sergeant. Grimmett ignored him.

"Trying to make the team are you?"

Grimmett shook his head. Macgregor had been on the school shooting team for two years. He wore crossed silver rifles on the sleeve of his battledress blouse. He was also a school Prefect, and he had never forgiven Dunphy for accidentally making a fool of him in the boxing ring.

Macgregor rarely missed an opportunity to make life difficult for either Dunphy or Grimmett. The week before he had made them both stay late at the school, cleaning rifles in the armoury.

The door to the shooting gallery opened, and the boys who had been shooting filed out. Macgregor pushed in front of Grimmett.

"Just you two?" said Forbes. He looked at his watch. "There should be a couple more of you shouldn't there?"

Forbes looked at Grimmett. Grimmett was a puzzle to him. Twice he had asked him to join the school's shooting team, and each time Grimmett had refused. He thought Grimmett was the best shot in the school, but he just didn't seem to have any drive or ambition.

"Aha, Phillips and Rowland." Forbes looked at them over the top of his spectacles. "You're late. You'd better take numbers three and four."

They climbed the steps to the shooting mats. Macgregor was already in the first bay, clipping his targets onto a wire frame. He always liked to shoot from number one.

Forbes sat at a counter behind the shooting bays. Grimmett collected three targets from him. He clipped them onto a metal frame, and spun a wheel to propel them down the dark gallery to its brightly-lit far wall, thirty yards away. When the targets reached the end, Grimmett turned and picked up a block of wood containing fifteen bullets, each one placed in a neat round hole. Behind him Forbes adjusted his telescope as he sighted it on the targets.

Grimmett lay down on the mat in bay number two, next to Macgregor. He rested on his elbows and lifted his rifle from the mat. It was a Lee Enfield .22, with a bolt action and a ring sight. He wound the leather strap round his arm until the butt rested firmly against his shoulder. His cheek brushed the stock as he sighted down the barrel at the targets.

"Right!" said Forbes. "Is everyone ready?" None of them answered. The four shooters lay prone with their rifles cradled, their legs splayed wide for stability.

"As usual, each of you has three targets," said Forbes. "The first target is for practice and sighting. The second is for grouping, and the third is straight scoring. Bull Eye's!" He waited for a response. Again, there was none.

"I shall watch your practice and sighting shots on the first target, then I'll give you instructions for adjusting your sights. The next two targets count, and you're on your own. Any questions?"

There were no questions. Forbes's speech never varied. All of them had shot before.

"Begin when you're ready." Forbes bent his eye to the telescope, and waited for them to start shooting.

"Shift your feet," said Macgregor. He kicked at Grimmett's ankle.

"Hey, take it easy," said Grimmett.

"Just keep out of my bloody way." Macgregor glared at him over his shoulder. Macgregor shot left-handed; his legs encroached well onto Grimmett's side of the mat.

Grimmett moved away so that he was brushing up against the pulley wire. He placed a bullet in the breech of his rifle. Rowland and Phillips began firing. The reports reverberated down the confined gallery. Grimmett could hear the telescope squeak on its tripod as Forbes moved it from one target to another.

Grimmett fired his first shots carefully, and felt the sharp sting of cordite in his nostrils.

Forbes spoke in tight, measured phrases. "Not bad Grimmett. They're close in, nicely grouped. Perhaps a little low at seven o'clock. Try one click clockwise on the top screw. One anti-clockwise on the side."

Grimmett adjusted his sights. The telescope squeaked as Forbes moved it over to study Macgregor's targets.

Grimmett put another bullet in the breech. He pushed the rifle bolt forward and down. The black circle on the bull centred in the rear sight. He held the pin on the fore-sight just below its middle. He squeezed the trigger slowly until he met the second pressure, and eased gently into it. The rifle jumped at his shoulder. He heard the rumble of Forbes' voice giving instructions to Macgregor. He fired again. When he had finished his sighting shots he lay still and waited for Forbes' clearance.

"That's fine Grimmett. We'll try one more click anti-clockwise on the side screw for elevation on the rear sight. But just keep on like that," murmured Forbes.

The telescope squeaked over to the targets at three and four. Grimmett felt another sharp pain in his ankle.

"I told you to keep your bloody feet out of my way," said Macgregor. "I won't bloody tell you again. Keep away from me!"

Grimmett massaged his ankle. He could hear Forbes directing Rowland at number four. Forbes acted as their eyes; the distance to the target was too great for the shooters to see bullet holes. Grimmett's ankle throbbed. He rolled on his side and waited for Rowland to finish.

"Right then," said Forbes, as the report from Rowland's last sighting shot died away. "You're on your own now. Fire whenever you're ready." He bent forward and placed his eye to the rubber eyepiece of the telescope.

Grimmett pushed his sixth bullet into the chamber with his thumb and moved the bolt home. His hand dropped to the trigger guard, as he felt for the curve of the trigger. Out beyond the fore-sight the bull wavered and then stilled as he pulled the stock of the rifle tight to his shoulder. He held his breath and squeezed. The muzzle jerked as he fired. A trace of smoke curled out of the end of the barrel. He selected another bullet and fired again. This target was for grouping. He shot the next three bullets quickly and moved on to the last target.

"Good shooting Grimmett," said Forbes behind him. "Good grouping."

144

Grimmett had fired four bullets at his last target when he heard Forbes.

"Well done Grimmett. They're all touching. You've got one big hole there. All in the bull." The telescope squeaked as Forbes traversed over to Phillips' targets.

Then Grimmett had an idea. He picked his last bullet out of the wood block with his thumb and forefinger. He pressed his thumbnail hard into the soft lead tip, and sawed it back and forth. He turned the bullet and scored his thumbnail across it again to make a deep cross in its nose.

Grimmett pushed the bullet into the breech. He glanced over at Macgregor's block of bullets. There were two left. Macgregor reached out and took one. He had his back to Grimmett, lying almost at right angles to the targets, taking up half of Grimmett's side of the mat.

Grimmett moved the barrel of his rifle over until the black bull of Macgregor's third target filled his sights. He lowered the muzzle and then squeezed the trigger for the last time. He pulled back the bolt and ejected the spent cartridge and set the rifle down, and turned on his side to wait for the others to finish.

The wires and pulleys shrieked as the shooters rolled the target frames back up the dark gallery towards them. Forbes leaned back in his chair and switched on the lights.

"Bring them up here and I'll mark them," he said.

Grimmett unclipped his two scoring targets and handed them to Forbes. Forbes looked them over, checking off the bullet holes with his pen. Then he frowned, and bent forward, and reached inside his drawer and pulled out a black-rimmed magnifying glass.

"Hmmm, I can see four of them clearly, but the fifth must have gone right through the middle. And your grouping is excellent." He looked up at Grimmett. "That's very good indeed." He handed the targets back to Grimmett, and wrote a figure in a blue exercise book.

Macgregor's face was white. Grimmett looked over his shoulder as he handed his targets to Forbes. There were four neat holes in the bull of Macgregor's second target, their white-ringed edges contrasting with the surrounding black background. But a huge, jagged tear split the target from just above the centre of the bull out to the bottom corner, shredding the thick-spun paper into strips. At the bottom right hand corner, just piercing the thin line of the outer circle, sat the perfect round hole of Grimmett's last bullet.

Grimmett picked up his empty cartridge cases. Macgregor's last shot must have gone right through the big ricochet tear in the lower half of the bull.

Forbes looked over the top of his spectacles at Macgregor, and pushed the magnifying glass to one side. "What on earth is this?"

Macgregor shook his head. "Something must have happened to the sights," he said. "Must have." He stared at the target on Forbes' counter-top.

"I can't give you a badge," said Forbes. He shook his head. "Not for that. And you won't make the team this year I'm afraid." He pushed his spectacles up onto his forehead. "We can't take a chance on that at Bisley. It's most extraordinary. You can do much better than that Macgregor."

Grimmett placed his spent cartridges on the counter and made to leave. Forbes took a small bundle from a drawer and extracted a badge of crossed red rifles from it. "Give me your old badge," he said to Grimmett.

Grimmett brought his old silver badge from his pocket and took the new one from Forbes.

"You'd better give me yours," Forbes turned to Macgregor. "I'll have to collect it."

A flush crept up Macgregor's pale face. "I . . . I didn't bring it with me sir."

"You're supposed to bring it when you do the annual test," said Forbes. "You'll have to find me tomorrow and give it to me."

Grimmett opened the door and stepped into the room of old photographs. The expressions on the faces in the pictures seemed more cheerful to him than when he had come in.

146

Chapter 18 – Dunphy's Field Day

"You put a dum-dum into his target!" said Dunphy. "What did that do to it?"

They were sitting in the armchairs in the flat, huddled over the electric fire. Flurries of snow blew against the window as the east wind rose and fell, making a moaning, whistling noise under the front door.

"Blew it to bits," said Grimmett. "The bullet explodes when it hits the back of the frame."

"That's why he was such a jerk this afternoon. You're sure he doesn't know? About the target I mean."

"He's got no idea. I was careful about it." He looked at Dunphy. Dunphy's face had lost its normal ruddy complexion; it was pale.

"You don't look very well. How did your Field Day go?" Dunphy was in the school's Air Force section. He had been out to Turnhouse airfield for an afternoon of flying.

Dunphy explained the terrible events of the day.

"He flew back upside down!" said Grimmett.

Dunphy looked at the floor.

"Yes." He shuffled his feet. "It's what they do, I suppose. Didn't make me feel any better."

Grimmett whistled through his teeth. "Why on earth did you join the Air Force section anyway?"

Dunphy hesitated. "It was the Diplomat. He was in the Air Force in the war."

Grimmett shook his head. "Well, it doesn't sound as if you're cut out for it; maybe you ought to stay on the ground." The meter on the wall clicked, and the glow of the electric fire began to fade. "Got any money?"

The only time Dunphy had ever seen his father inebriated was one night after a diplomatic reception. It was then that Vice-consul Dunphy had told him about his days in the Royal Canadian Air Force, when he had flown train-busting Typhoons across the breadth of France after D-Day.

The Typhoon, he'd said, swirling a nightcap whisky in his glass, his bow tie askew, made you feel like a God. It lifted you above the mud and grime of the common infantryman who lived in the cold and the rain. Vice-consul Dunphy made his son recite the Typhoon's cockpit drill with him—Brakes, Trim, Flaps, Contacts, Petrol, Undercarriage, Radiator.

Dunphy had never heard his father speak about any of this before. Slowly he allowed himself to be transported into the exclusive fraternity of the aviator.

Nothing, Vice-consul Dunphy had continued, overcome with nostalgia, could compare with the feeling that came from diving down canyons of cumulus, or banking hard around a church steeple, or dropping like a stone onto a column of tanks and scattering it with rocket and cannon fire. Nothing, not the fine cold air of the mountains, or the sensation of a fast hull angled beneath your feet and a mainsail stretched tight against the wind above your head. Not even a woman, he had added, confident that his wife was upstairs in bed.

Dunphy had joined the Air Force section of the school's Combined Cadet Force the next day.

Dunphy sat in a corner of the draughty hut and turned the pages of an aeronautical magazine. His eyes slid over the photographs and passed uncomprehendingly over the text. The clatter of aeroplane engines rose to a roar outside. A loose pane of glass rattled in the window. Two Chipmunks

148

from the training flight bumped across the grass field. Dunphy watched them as they climbed over the skyline. The noise faded, until he could hear the cheeping of sparrows.

"What's the matter?" asked Macgregor. "You're not scared are you?"

Dunphy looked down at the magazine and pretended not to hear. Macgregor started to say something else, when the door of the hut burst open and the two cadets who had just landed came in.

"Here," said Phillips, struggling with the release catch of his parachute harness. "Give me a hand with this."

Macgregor twisted the metal disc that locked the four parachute straps over Phillips' stomach, stepped back half a pace, and punched it hard with the heel of his hand. Phillips doubled over as the straps parted and dumped his parachute on the floor.

"I say," he said. "You didn't have to do it like that."

"It's the only way to get out of it quickly," said Macgregor.

Phillips rubbed his stomach.

Macgregor looked at Rowland, who had walked in with Phillips. "How was the flight?"

"It was good." Rowland turned to Dunphy. "You're next aren't you Dunphy? You should get him to do some aerobatics. They like to do that. They get bored when they just fly around showing off the view." He twisted his hands in front of his face, imitating the manoeuvres he'd been through. "Loops and rolls. It was marvellous."

Macgregor picked the tangled parachute off the floor. He held it out to Dunphy. "You'd better put this on. Mustn't keep them waiting."

Phillips took the parachute from him and draped it over a chair, arranging the straps. "I'll give you a hand," he said. "Sit down on that."

Dunphy sat on the bulky parachute pack. Phillips pulled the lower straps up between his legs, and reached behind him to pull the upper ones over his shoulders. He clipped all four straps into the lock on the disc at Dunphy's stomach.

"Stand up," said Macgregor. "Let's take a look."

Dunphy rose to his feet, bent slightly by the pressure of the straps.

"Much too loose," said Macgregor. He pulled hard on the webbing adjustments at Dunphy's shoulders and Dunphy bent more, almost double.

"Sit down." Macgregor pushed him back into the chair. He reached in and pulled the straps up tightly between Dunphy's legs. He gave another tug on the straps at Dunphy's shoulders.

"That's better." He stepped back. "You don't want to fall out of your parachute if you have to bale out do you?"

Dunphy heard the sound of an aeroplane flying towards the hut. The Chipmunk passed over the roof, rattling the window pane. Its shadow flitted across the glass and the aeroplane touched down on the grass in front of the hut. It slowed, and turned to taxi back.

"It's you now . . . Dunphy," said Macgregor. "You'd better get out there and . . ." The rest of his words were drowned out as the second Chipmunk roared over the hut and landed on the field.

Dunphy levered himself out of his chair and lurched towards the door. The Chipmunk was a small aeroplane with only room enough for two. The student sat behind the pilot, tandem style. The little aeroplane was standing thirty yards away, its propeller arcing in the watery sunlight. Dunphy waddled towards it, jack-knifed over by the straps of his parachute.

The cockpit canopy slid back and a student-cadet climbed out, onto the wing. He jumped down to the ground, and Dunphy clambered up.

"On the black bit!" The pilot leaned out of the cockpit and shouted over the noise of the engine. "For Christ's sake stand on the painted part!" He pointed, shaking his arm at a wide strip of black paint at the wing root.

Dunphy moved his foot off the silver wing surface and heaved himself into the cockpit. An aircraftsman jumped up beside him and began to fasten Dunphy's seat harness.

The aircraftsman shouted at him over the engine noise. "If you have to get out in a hurry, just twist this thing and the straps will fall away." He pointed at an arrow-shaped buckle and grinned. He had a gap in his teeth and a bent, boxer's nose. "Whatever you do don't touch it while you're flying about though. And don't get the bloody buckles mixed up. If you undo the wrong one you'll leave your parachute behind in the cockpit."

He jammed a leather helmet onto Dunphy's head, and reached across him to plug the microphone cord into its socket. The perspex hood slid over Dunphy's head and banged shut like a coffin lid, muffling the noise of the engine.

Dunphy heard a metallic voice in his earphones. "All set?" Without waiting for an answer the voice said, "I'm Flight Lieutenant Belcher. As soon as your pal's on board the other aircraft we'll take off." Dunphy looked over and watched Macgregor climb into the other Chipmunk, an expectant smile on his face.

A moment later they were bouncing across the grass. The seat straps bit into Dunphy's shoulders as they lifted over the airfield fence. Dunphy took a deep breath. The aeroplane smelled of metal and rubber and high-octane gasoline, and a sweet smell he couldn't place. His stomach sank as the Chipmunk soared upwards on an air current.

A burst of static came through his headphones. "If you want to speak," the voice crackled, "just flick the switch on the front of your face mask. If you're not talking, keep the bloody thing turned off. I don't like the sound of heavy breathing." Belcher chuckled tinnily in the earphones.

The ground tilted over the tip of the left wing as the Chipmunk banked. "So what do you want to do today? We can just stooge about for a bit and look at the sights, or we can go and have a bit of fun." Belcher chuckled down the intercom. "What's it to be then?"

Dunphy fumbled for the intercom switch as Belcher threw the Chipmunk over onto its other wing. "I'd like to go . . ." Dunphy had a sudden urge to clear his throat and did, ". . . flying about a bit." He was beginning to feel unwell.

"Fling her about a bit? Jolly good!" exclaimed Belcher. "That's the stuff. Just the ticket." The little aeroplane dropped sickeningly as it hit an air pocket. What sounded like a peal of insane laughter crackled through Dunphy's headphones.

"Ha, ha, ha," shouted Belcher. "That's the stuff all right."

151

The Chipmunk keeled hard onto its starboard wing and headed for the coast. "We can't do anything below three thousand feet. It's against the rules." Belcher laughed again. "I'll take you over the bridge first, and then we'll see what this little toy can do."

The thin line of the railway snaked through the fields below on its way towards the great jigsaw girders of the Forth Bridge. Dunphy could see the derricks at the naval base at Rosyth, standing black and gaunt like primordial beasts on the far side of the estuary. They crossed the shoreline, climbing steadily as the Chipmunk's Gipsy engine pulled them higher. A navy troop-carrier eased its cigar-shape under the bridge, scoring a chalky wake across the grey-green water. Smoke streamed from its funnel.

Dunphy was trying without success to communicate with his pilot. He flicked the switch on his facemask back and forth. Slowly he realised that Belcher must have forgotten to switch his microphone off; that his own microphone would not work when Belcher's was on.

"Right! Keep your hands off the stick and your knees apart so they don't get in the way. And keep your dirty big boots off the rudder." Belcher chortled erratically. "We can't have you pushing against me. It might get us into trouble."

The Chipmunk weaved smartly from side to side as Belcher checked the sky around him for other aircraft. Far off to the right, where the estuary fell into the open sea, Dunphy saw another Chipmunk flying along beneath a bank of cotton-white cloud. He watched it, fascinated. It was flying along in a perfectly straight line, rolling over and over as it passed under the cloud, its wings flashing in the sunlight.

"Hah! There's Rolly Stallworthy." Belcher lifted a gloved hand. "He'll do that for hours. He's got your pal in there with him. He tries to make them sick." He roared with laughter.

Dunphy fiddled furiously with his microphone switch. "I don't think I want to do that sir," he shouted. "I'd rather we just looked around the other shore down there."

The Flight Lieutenant was humming to himself. The Chipmunk dropped suddenly into a steep dive. Dunphy felt his stomach lift up under his ribs.

"Right! Let's get serious." Belcher's voice was clipped and businesslike. "We'll start with a loop and see where we go from there."

Dunphy gripped the sides of the cockpit. The engine roared and the pitch rose as they plummeted down towards the sea. The grey sea rose up until it seemed to fill the whole windscreen, then Dunphy's stomach was thrust violently down into his groin as he was rammed into his seat. The sea disappeared. The Chipmunk shuddered as it hung on its propeller, and then it soared over the top of the loop. Dunphy felt his face pulling and his eyeballs bulging as he dangled weightlessly in his seat straps. Red dots drifted from left to right in front of his eyes, and the sea slid over the top of the cockpit canopy.

Belcher was singing. Dunphy could see his head thrown back, his lips moving soundlessly in the noise of the engine, his facemask hanging below his ear. Dunphy swallowed and reached for his microphone switch. He tried to speak but his mouth was dry. The Chipmunk flicked over on one wing and the sun vanished below them, and then re-appeared from beneath the other wing. Dunphy's throat tightened. A bitter taste came into his mouth, and then he was crushed into a ball in his seat. The sea whipped over the top of the canopy again, and he was hanging on his straps with the webbing digging once more into his shoulders. The red cantilevered bridge spiralled dizzily through the windscreen, and vanished.

As they came out of a barrel roll Dunphy felt his stomach muscles weaken. He fumbled for the microphone switch but it was too late. Half way through the next loop he barked, and vomited all over the canopy.

Belcher reacted immediately. He pushed the control column forward with one hand so the Chipmunk remained flying upside down. His other hand reached for the microphone switch.

"Hey! What's this? What's going on old chap?" His voice was aggrieved. "You should have said something. Makes a hell of a mess you know."

Dunphy couldn't speak. He was hanging in his seat straps, holding his facemask away from him.

Belcher turned his head to look. "Looks bad," he said. "At least you took your oxygen mask off first."

They flew back to the airfield in silence, Dunphy staring morosely at the ground as it rushed past above his head, blurred by the contents of his stomach floating inside the canopy.

"I'm afraid you're going to get a bit messy when we land," said Belcher a few minutes later. "But I can't get any of it on me. I've got to keep on flying this afternoon." He twisted round again. "And we can't land upside down."

Chapter 19 – The Brothel

"The funny thing is, I sort of enjoyed it. Apart from being sick," said Dunphy. "My head kind of liked it, even if my stomach didn't." He stared at the fire. "It's almost as if I was supposed to like it, and so a part of me didn't want to."

"We've got our Field Day tomorrow," said Grimmett. "I know I won't like it. It's bound to rain."

Dunphy cocked his head to one side. "There's another one," he said. He was standing by the window. He pulled the curtain back. Grimmett joined him, and they stared down into the street.

Two sailors were climbing out of a taxi. The driver pushed down the arm of the meter. The sailors held a brief consultation beside the taxi, and then the taller one lurched forward, dipping his hand in his pocket. The taxi driver took the fare and drove off up the street. The two sailors walked unsteadily towards the door of a downstairs flat. The taller of the two cursed as he tripped on the front step.

"That's four taxis," said Dunphy, "all with sailors in them." He leaned forward to get a better view as the sailors disappeared inside the flat.

"There's an aircraft carrier in at the navy base at Rosyth," said Grimmett.

Dunphy looked at him. "What's that mean?"

"What do you think's in there?"

"I dunno. A club or something? For sailors?"

Grimmett laughed. "It's a brothel."

"Lower!" shouted the Sergeant Major. "Get yer arses doon. 'An you! Cradle that rifle properly. Yer fillin' the barrel wi' mud!"

Grimmett crawled through the wet grass, and tried to skirt a large cowpat.

"Yew! Ye dinnae wurry aboot shit when they're shootin' at ye!" roared the Sergeant Major. "This is supposed tae be the Leopard Crawl, no' the Guppy Shuftie." He banged his thigh with his swagger stick. "Ma goad! Yew young . . . gentlemen widnae last five minutes."

The staccato crackle of machine gun fire came from the other side of the ridge in front of them, drifting in and out of a wind that howled in bursts, snatched at their clothes and tossed sheets of rain in their faces. The Sergeant Major bobbed about among them, running up and down the wavering line.

"H'all right!" he screamed into the gale. "When ye get tae the top o' the slope ye'll see the targets and ye'll fire five rounds rapid. Right? You! Whit's your name?" He pointed his stick at McCue.

"McCue sir."

"Ah'm no a surr! Ah'm a Sergeant Major. An' yer no' tae stop and look at me when ah'm talkin'. Ye're tae keep movin'. Goat that? They'll shoot ye' if ye' dae things like that. Jeesus Christ!"

Grimmett crawled on, wet grass brushing his face. He stopped to wipe rainwater from his eyes.

"When ye've done that," said the Sergeant Major, "ye'll reload and ye'll wait fer ma order tae resume firing. When ye' resume ye'll fire snap shots. Five rounds each. Right? Clear? Goat that?"

It had been sunny when they'd started and they hadn't been issued with waterproof capes. It was raw now, and the rain was turning to sleet. Grimmett pushed himself doggedly forward on his elbows and knees. His saturated battledress clung to his skin, cold at his thighs and chafing at his neck. A ragged sheep dashed across the hillside in front of him, spraying water from its woolly back.

Grimmett dropped flat at the top of the slope and brought his rifle to his shoulder. He flicked off the safety catch, and sighted down through the rain onto the targets two hundred yards away. The valley chattered with automatic fire as the Bren light machine guns shot at a different set of targets off to their left.

Grimmett adjusted his aim to allow for the wind and distance. He squeezed the trigger, and worked the bolt back quickly, ignoring the sharp punch of the recoil. This was a .303 rifle, much more powerful than the weapons they used at the school's shooting range. He fired again.

The Sergeant Major strode up and down behind them. He swatted at Grimmett's legs with his stick. "Spread 'em!" he shouted. "Make yersel' intae a platform."

Grimmett pulled a fresh magazine from his pouch and jammed it into the slot on the rifle's stock. He squinted through the rain and waited for his target to pop up. When it appeared he'd have five seconds before it disappeared again. The target appeared suddenly above the bank, a few feet to the right of where it had been before. Grimmett held his breath and counted, adjusting his aim. At four, he squeezed the trigger. The target went down and then almost immediately popped back up. He sighted and fired again.

It was dark when Grimmett met Dunphy in the school yard. Water was still dripping from him as he climbed down from the bus that had brought them back from the army barracks at Dreghorn.

"How was it?" said Dunphy, as they trudged down the rain-slicked street to the flat.

Grimmett shook his head and shivered. They had made a four mile route march over mud and heather after shooting at the targets. His heavy military serge uniform had sponged up the rain, and the army kilt had chafed the back of his legs.

They walked on in silence. Grimmett looked over at the front of the ground floor flat as they turned into their stair. A curl of smoke was drifting from one of the windows.

"Smoke!" As they looked, a black cloud belched from the top of the open window. "The brothel's on fire. We should tell them." Grimmett ran up the steps and rang the bell. Dunphy stood uncertainly by the railings.

157

A big woman in a yellow dressing gown opened the door, bright red lipstick on her mouth, her hair piled in layers. "We're no' open yet dearie," she said.

A voice inside called, "Who is it Evie?"

The woman looked Grimmett up and down. "It's Andy Stewart," she said, without taking her eyes off him.

"No, no," said Grimmett. "Your flat's on fire." He pointed at the window. The woman took a step out of the doorway and stared upwards.

"Oh ma goad!" She ran back inside. Grimmett followed her into the flat, motioning Dunphy to come. He found himself in a dark hallway. The woman called Evie was running up a flight of stairs to his left. Grimmett followed her, taking two steps at a time.

Doors opened at the commotion. Before Grimmett realised what was happening, a hand reached out and pulled him into a dark room. Dunphy's heavy footsteps thumped past. Grimmett caught the scent of perfume.

"Hey, what's going on?" He couldn't see anything in the darkness.

"It's all right," said a soft voice. "It's company." A hand touched his knee and he jumped. "Besides, I need the money. Come to me."

Grimmett pulled away. Shouts came from the other side of the door. "I'm not a customer," he said. "There's a fire in one of the rooms."

He heard a gasp, and the light came on. Grimmett blinked. The room was almost filled by a big bed with brass rails. He looked at the girl beside him. She was wearing a light blue nurse's uniform. She didn't seem to be much older than he was.

"I've got to help them put it out," said Grimmett. He made a dash for the door.

He passed two women standing on the landing, and then he heard Dunphy calling. He ran into a room that overlooked the street. Dunphy was leaping up and down on top of a smouldering quilt. Evie rushed in and threw a bucket of water over the bed, drenching Dunphy's legs. She pushed him out of the way and hauled the quilt and mattress onto the floor. The room was thick with smoke. There was a big, smoking, black-ringed hole in the mattress.

Dunphy was coughing. His face was red. "Window," he said. "Open the window."

Grimmett threw the window open, and took several deep breaths of cold air. Evie tossed another bucket of water on the mattress.

"That Linda," she said. "Ah'll kill her when she gets back." She picked a sodden piece of cork-coloured cigarette filter out of the hole in the mattress. "She's only been gone ten minutes."

The doorway was crowded with women. The girl in the nurse's uniform pushed through them and smiled at Grimmett. "Is anyone hurt?" she said.

"No." Evie took charge. "All right, the fire's out. Everyone's had a good look at it. We're open in ten minutes. I want you all back in your rooms." She glared at them, and turned to Dunphy and Grimmett.

"Thank you," she said. "You've saved us a lot of trouble." She looked at Grimmett. "You live near here don't you?"

Grimmett nodded. "We live in one of the flats upstairs."

"I thought I'd seen you before." She ushered them out of the room, onto the landing. "Well, it's on the house. Next time you want it," she said. "You've got your pick, both of you." She smiled.

The girl in the nurse's uniform looked at Grimmett. She was almost as tall as he was, with a plain cheerful face and a kink in her nose that suggested it might have been broken once. She took his arm.

"You can come with me now if you want," she said.

Grimmett sneezed. "I'm sorry. I've been out in the rain all day." He cast about for an excuse. "I've got to go now. I've got an appointment." He edged towards the stairs. "Maybe later . . . another time. I can't stay now."

She looked at him, and let go his arm.

Grimmett followed Dunphy down the stairs. He stopped to look up at the girl from the front door. "Good bye," he said. She gave a small wave, and turned away.

As they climbed the dark stone stair to their own flat, Dunphy said, "Do you think she's a real nurse?"

"I don't know," said Grimmett. "How would I know?"

159

"Thought you knew her, that's all. She looked like an old friend."

"I've never seen her in my life before," said Grimmett. He put his key in the lock of the flat and opened the door.

"It's all right you know," said Dunphy. "It's all right to know girls."

Chapter 20 – McCue

A cold wind was blowing across the sports field. Grimmett stood at attention, and watched Dunphy's platoon as they marched towards an old brown hut at the far end of the field. It was the annual Army Cadet Force Day. A knot of parents and relatives stood and observed the proceedings from a roped off area beside the tennis courts.

"Oh God," said McCue. "There's my family."

Grimmett shifted his eyes to a heavyset man in a baggy suit who was walking past the cricket pavilion. A woman in a yellow coat and hat followed behind him. A young girl was with them, looking around the field.

"Damn! They said they wouldn't come."

Grimmett was looking at the girl. Her back was very straight, and there was something assertive about the way she held her head. Long dark hair danced around her neck. He noticed that she walked with a limp.

"Is that your sister?" he said.

"Uh-huh."

The family continued on to the enclosure. McCue's sister saw her brother, and waved.

"We've got a fifteen minute break while the Air Force gets itself organised to do its stuff," said the Corporal from the front. Grimmett focused his attention.

"Squad . . . Ordah . . . Arms!" shouted the Corporal. The rifles came down with a clatter.

"Squad . . . At . . . Ease! Wait for it! Fall out!"

McCue looked about as if he was trying to find a place to hide. He sighed. "Er, why don't you come over with me and meet them?"

Grimmett moved his rifle to his right hand. "All right," he said.

They walked across the grass.

"They're bringing out the glider," said Grimmett. He pointed towards the hut. The Air Force cadets were carrying pieces of the glider onto the field. Flight Lieutenant Ponsett was fussing about among them. In a few minutes they would start bolting the glider together.

McCue came up to his parents. "Hello," he said.

His mother reached out and gave him a kiss on the cheek. McCue took a step back. "Er, this is Grimmett," he said.

They shook hands. McCue's mother looked at Grimmett. "I've met you before haven't I?" she said. "Years ago. Weren't you with David at the Prep school?"

"Yes. But I don't think we've met," said Grimmett.

"Aren't you the one who had his tongue soaped for swearing?"

Grimmett's face reddened. "I . . . ah, that was a long time ago."

"Oh yes," she said. "I can remember it. It was the same teacher who tied David's left hand to his desk so he would learn to write with his right one." She smiled. "It didn't make any difference to him. I don't suppose it made any difference to you either, did it? How's your language now?"

"Janet!" said McCue's father. "You're embarrassing the fellow."

Grimmett wasn't sure if she was serious or if she was joking. "I don't think she liked either of us," he said.

"Did she really do that?" said McCue's sister. Grimmett looked at her. She was about the same age as he was. She had a high-boned face, and tiny laughter creases at the corners of her eyes.

"Sorry," said McCue. "This is my sister Fiona."

162

Fiona reached out and shook Grimmett's hand. "Did she?"

"Pardon?" said Grimmett. "Oh. Yes. She did. I'd forgotten about it."

A thunderflash exploded out on the field. A group of cadets ran through the smoke. Another explosion ripped across the sports ground, and then several more. Puffs of blue smoke spurted from the barrels of rifles, the air filling with the pop of blank ammunition. McCue's parents turned to speak to some people beside them.

"What are they doing?" McCue's sister touched Grimmett's arm.

"It's an attack on the platoon up there." He pointed up the field towards a small copse. "They're supposed to cross over all these obstacles too." He indicated rows of truck tires, brushwood fencing, and a heavy net strung between trees. "It's a kind of competition to see who can do it fastest."

The cadets wriggled through the tires and ran towards the fences.

"It seems a bit silly," she said.

"Yes." Grimmett gazed across the field. "I suppose it is. But they seem to think it's important. Your group loses points if anyone doesn't make it."

"They're not firing real bullets surely?"

"No, no. I didn't mean that." Grimmett turned. He saw that she was smiling. "Sometimes they get stuck, or their equipment catches in something."

"They're going to launch the glider," said McCue.

The Air Force platoon trundled the little glider over the grass. Flight Lieutenant Ponsett strode out in front, tapping his leg with his swagger stick. He ordered the platoon to halt, and saluted at the distant figure of the Colonel.

"Who on earth is that?" said Fiona.

"Flight Lieutenant Ponsett," said Grimmett. "He teaches Geography."

The glider sank onto one wing as the platoon sprang to attention. Dunphy was standing in the front row. He looked over at them and winked. The colonel hurried across the field towards the platoon.

163

"Are you going to launch her today Flight Lieutenant, or just show her off?" said the Colonel. He laughed. He knew the glider never actually flew.

Ponsett looked at the Colonel. "I shall be taking her up myself sir," he said. "We're ready when you give us the word."

"Yes, well, carry on then," said the Colonel. A group of cadets ran past. Another thunderflash exploded. The Colonel looked at them. "These chaps will be out of your way in a minute or two."

Ponsett swung round to face the Air Force platoon. He began shouting orders. "You and you. On the wingtips. And don't let them droop like that. You and you." He pointed at Dunphy and Phillips. "Stand by the ropes at the nose. You two there." The swagger stick swung round and pointed. "On the tail. And don't get your hands stuck in the elevators. The rest of you at one yard intervals on the ropes."

He stuck his forefinger in the air, holding it up to the breeze. He pointed up the field. "Line her up to the right of the cricket pitch." He spun on his heel and marched off in the opposite direction, towards the cricket pavilion.

"He's quite a performer," said Fiona. "Is he really going to fly in it?"

Dunphy was coming towards them.

"It only gets a couple of feet off the ground," said Grimmett. "They put spoilers on the wings to stop it taking off properly."

"Maybe he's nervous," she said. "I think he's gone to the bathroom."

Dunphy smiled at McCue's sister. "Hi. I'm George." He stuck out his hand. Fiona shook it.

Fiona's mother called and she turned and walked over to join her parents.

"Bye!" Dunphy stepped over the rope barrier, and made his way back to the glider.

Grimmett was watching Fiona, the way she carried herself. There was a dignity to it.

Fiona turned back after she had spoken to her mother. When she reached Grimmett, he said, "Did you hurt your leg playing hockey or something?"

164

She shook her head, and the fall and sway of her hair gave him a curious sensation. "No. I had polio when I was little. I can't play hockey."

He felt his face hot. "Oh . . . I'm sorry."

"It's all right," she said. "I don't think about it. It doesn't bother me. It just doesn't allow me to play sports, that's all."

Grimmett stared across the field.

Fiona touched his arm. "Why don't you join us for tea when you've finished these . . ." she waved her hand, ". . . these exercises. You can tell me what my brother's been up to." She reached out and took McCue's hand, so that she was holding onto them both.

Grimmett swallowed, and turned to face her. "All right," he said.

McCue brushed his hand through his hair. "I suppose we'd better get back to the platoon. We've got Bren gun drills now."

Grimmett sat on the damp grass and contemplated the scene in front of him. The attack exercise was nearly finished, except for one cadet who was dangling upside down between two trees. He was scrabbling at the netting which held him, his movements only entangling him more. His colleagues were already staging a mock attack on simulated dugouts beside the Garden Club's allotments. The Colonel strolled across the field towards the cadet who was stuck in the netting.

"Where's the bolt?" said McCue, feeling around on the grass with his hands. "Damn." He was sitting on the ground, blindfolded, trying to re-assemble a Bren light machine gun. "God! I hate this stuff."

Grimmett slid the bolt under McCue's hand. He let his eyes wander to the spectator enclosure. McCue's sister was watching the glider. It was standing in the centre of the field, resplendent in its blue-grey paint, bright red, white and blue roundels on its wings. McCue continued his struggle with the Bren gun.

Ponsett climbed into the glider's seat and fastened his safety harness. "Take the strain!" he called, waggling the control column. "Easy now! This is just a test." The glider moved forward a few feet and stopped.

Ponsett moved the rudder bar with his feet. He looked behind him to make sure that there was a corresponding movement at the glider's tail. He pushed the control column forward once more.

"Right. Cockpit check complete." He stuck his hand in the air with his thumb extended. The spectators waited. Two lines of cadets were strung out at an angle of forty-five degrees in front of the glider, holding elasticised ropes that were attached to the glider's nose. Ponsett sat at the head of the vee like an expectant charioteer.

"Are you ready?" The cadets at the end of the ropes waved back. "Right," shouted Ponsett. "Move out slowly." The cadets marched away from him. The ropes made musical twanging noises as they stretched.

"What's going on?" said McCue behind his blindfold.

Grimmett had forgotten about him. McCue had almost finished re-assembling the Bren gun.

"It's just the glider. They're going to launch it now."

McCue snapped the tripod support under the front of the gun barrel, and reached back to untie the blindfold. He blinked in the sunlight. "That won't beat any records," he said. "But that's fine." He stared at the glider.

"There's something funny about it," he said. "You know, I think they've forgotten to put the spoilers on."

The cadets strained on the ropes as they stretched to three times their original length.

"That will do," shouted Ponsett. "Take the strain and stand fast." He moved the joystick forward. They heard a click as he let off the brake.

The ropes contracted and the glider sped off like a toy aeroplane fired from an elastic band. The tail lifted and bounced once. Ponsett eased the control column back into his crotch, and then the glider was airborne. The spectators began to clap.

"He'll fly properly if he's not careful," said McCue. "It won't stay on the ground without the spoilers." The glider caught the wind at the end of a line of trees, and soared skywards.

"He's dropped the tow ropes," said McCue. "I hope he knows how to fly."

"I don't think he does," said Grimmett.

166

They heard a shout from the glider as its nose dipped, and it dived suddenly towards the ground. The crowd cheered as Ponsett tilted spectacularly onto one wing and shot back across the field towards them. They could see him sitting rigidly at the controls, with both hands on the joystick, and a sheet-white face as he passed overhead. He flashed over the spectators and headed for the centre of the games field.

"He's going to come down on the cricket pitch," said McCue. "There'll be trouble about that."

The glider lurched dangerously towards the ground, swooping over the ropes which quarantined the finely cut cricket square from the rest of the playing fields. It landed heavily, bounced, dug in a wing and with a gentle tearing sound, ripped across the manicured turf like a rogue plough, grinding slowly to a stop in a tangle of ropes and metal picquets. Ponsett climbed from the cockpit and stood unsteadily at the end of the jagged brown furrow he had made. The cadets ran up and helped him off towards the pavilion.

Grimmett pushed his way into the pavilion, and looked across the crowded tearoom for McCue's sister. The room was filled with a hum of conversation, and the sound of teacups rattling on saucers; the air with vague smell of dried sweat mingled with scents of perfume and mothballs. A white-aproned crew of ladies stood behind a row of trestle tables, distributing curled sandwiches, hard buns and tea.

Dunphy was standing beside Fiona, talking. He had a half-eaten bun in his hand. A line of cream ringed his mouth.

"Ah," said Dunphy, "you made it. Enjoy the air show?" He chuckled to himself, and began to cough. Tears came into his eyes, and particles of bun flew out of his mouth. Grimmett slapped him hard on the back.

"Thanks," said Dunphy. "Buns are a bit dry." He took another one from the table. "Starving though. Haven't eaten anything since lunchtime." McCue's sister wiped damp crumbs from her blouse.

McCue eased through the crowd towards them. "Well, what do you think of it all?" he said to his sister.

"Pretty barbaric isn't it; all this running around, playing at soldiers."

Fiona looked at him, and a small shadow crossed her eyes. Grimmett saw it; saw that it was concern, not disapproval. He picked up a plate of sandwiches and offered her one. She shook her head. "No thanks. I've had one already." She looked at her brother.

"I think it's kind of interesting," she said. "To watch, I mean. I don't think I'd like to get all dressed up in uniform and march about a parade ground, but all that other stuff looks as though it could be fun if you don't take it too seriously."

"Fun!" There was something like anger in McCue's voice. "You understand what we're doing here?" he said. "We're training for fighting; we're being taught how to kill people. You'd think we'd have found a better way of dealing with our problems by now than by fighting about them; a better way than training young people to do it."

Dunphy buried his teeth in another bun. Grimmett realised that he'd come upon something more than a filial disagreement. There was an instability to it, and Mc Cue's sister was trying to level it out; trying to calm her brother.

"It's fun for me at least," said Fiona. "I get to meet some of your friends." She smiled.

McCue shook his head. "What's the use," he said, his anger gone as suddenly as it had come. "You don't understand. All this stuff is designed to kick us into shape so we'll conform, and not make waves when we get out into the real world. But it's like everything else around here. It's fifty years behind the times."

Fiona took a step towards him. She tugged at the front of his battledress. "Come on," she said. "Don't take it so seriously. You don't need to pay that much attention to it." She dropped her voice, and Grimmett could hardly hear what she said. "Just carry on doing what you do, and thinking the way you think."

She put her head close to her brother's ear, and Grimmett wasn't sure what she said then, but he thought it was something like, ". . .and remember that we love you." Which seemed to Grimmett to be an enormous thing for someone to say.

168

She stepped back, and held out her hand to Dunphy. "I've got to go now," she said. Dunphy wiped his palm on his trousers, and shook her hand. She turned to Grimmett. "Please come and see us. We don't live far away from the city. The train goes there, and the bus." She smiled, but the laughter was gone from her eyes. Grimmett watched her make her way through the crowd until she passed out of the door.

Several days later, Grimmett walked into the art room during a break. McCue was smoking a cigarette. He quickly dropped his hand behind the work bench to hide it. But a thin trail of smoke lingered in the air.

"I thought you were someone else," he said.

"No. It's okay. I won't say anything."

"Do you want one? Stark doesn't mind if we smoke in here."

Grimmett shook his head. "Is he around? I was looking for him."

"He went out about five minutes ago." McCue blew a fleck of ash off the sketch paper in front of him.

Grimmett looked round the room. It was a simple room, with a wood floor and white walls, and paintings pinned haphazardly to the plaster. Brushes sat in jars of dirty water on trestle benches covered with multi-coloured splashes of paint.

His eyes were drawn to a big canvas standing by itself on an easel in a corner. It showed a violent landscape of torn earth and shattered, leafless trees. Pieces of people and animals hung from skeletal branches; an arm here, a leg, part of a torso. Some of the fragments were large, but most of them small and undersized. Grimmett couldn't take his eyes from the painting. It fascinated and horrified him at the same time. He realised that the anatomy came from lambs, colts, calves. Life which had not reached its maturity. Children. The picture was painted in jagged oils. Brown, slate-grey, black. Except for a dull red glow along a horizon behind some trees there were no other colours. The painting dominated the room, and haunted it.

"Is it one of yours?" he said.

McCue turned and looked at it. He held his head to one side as if he was trying to make up his mind. He took a pull of the cigarette and blew out the smoke.

"Yes. I've been working on it for a while."

"It's strong," said Grimmett. He wasn't sure what else to say. "Bleak."

"Stark doesn't like it," said McCue. His tone was detached, offhand. "He thinks I should be doing other things. Not stuff like that."

They heard the sound of footsteps outside the door. The footsteps faded as they passed by.

"It's risky to smoke in here isn't it?"

McCue shrugged. "Who cares? Anyway I only do it when Stark's around, or if he's just left. He smokes in here all the time."

They stared at the painting for a time, thinking separate thoughts.

McCue stood up. He walked to the back of the room. "Look. See what I found yesterday." He opened a small wooden cabinet on the wall. Inside was a black-painted electrical box, and a breaker switch. Cobwebs hung around them. A conduit line ran up to the ceiling. "It's the switch for the organ," he said.

"That was you then."

"I should've been in there to see it, but I can't stand their self-serving sermons, and those hypocritical services they go through every morning." McCue ran a hand through his hair. "I'm not sure what the bloody point of it was though."

"You'd have laughed if you'd been in the Hall," said Grimmett. "When we all stood up for the hymn, and Hubble banged down on the keys, and there was dead silence. He got into a panic and started pulling out all the organ stops and kicking at the pedals, and still nothing happened. You could have heard a pin drop." He paused. "They had to stop the service."

Grimmett thought of the great oval Hall with its walls adorned with ancient trophies, and forbidding paintings of old boys and past Headmasters. The magnificent rosewood organ and its huge brass and steel pipes filled one end of the Hall, and overshadowed the stage.

170

Despite the frantic coaxing of the music master it had remained majestically silent.

McCue turned on the tap in the sink, and the cigarette end hissed as he held it under a stream of water. He reached up and closed the cabinet door.

Grimmett searched for something to say. "That was risky. There will be a fuss if they find out."

He knew right away it was the wrong thing to have said.

McCue stared at him for a moment, and then the fight went from him, and his shoulders hunched and he turned away.

"It doesn't matter," he said.

A few days afterwards, McCue asked Grimmett to come with him to the farm for the weekend. But the way the invitation was put made it sound odd, so that Grimmett was puzzled by it.

McCue's father met the train at the country station. McCue's father settled into the driver's seat, his son beside him in the front. Fiona was sitting in the back of the Land Rover among dusty sacks and coils of rope. Grimmett climbed in beside her. They shook hands as formally as they had done at their first meeting.

Fiona said, "I'm glad you could come," but she said nothing more on the drive to the farm. They bounced on the hard metal seats and listened to desultory talk between McCue and his father as the Land Rover made its way along country roads. A mile or two from the station they turned onto a rutted track, and followed a line of poplar trees to a clutch of farm buildings.

Most of the domestic activity at the farm took place in the big stone-floored kitchen. A big, cream-coloured, coal burning stove stood against one wall. A kettle simmered constantly on its top. No one paid particular attention to Grimmett at the farmhouse, and yet no one ignored him. His presence was simply accepted, and an outsider might have taken him as one of the family.

Mrs. McCue handed Grimmett a pair of black gum boots, and a weathered duffle coat that smelled of earth. "You should wear these while you're here," she said. "You'll know by our road why David sometimes wears Wellingtons to school. He doesn't always get a lift to the station." She smiled. "Try them on. You'll need them as soon as you step out the door."

Fiona ate quietly at supper. She had hardly spoken since the drive from the station. When the plates were cleared from the table she said, "I should take you out and show you around, so you can get your bearings."

"That's a good idea," said her mother. "We'll get on with the dishes. Besides we've got some things to talk to David about."

McCue looked up, but he didn't say anything.

It was cold outside, and Grimmett fastened the horn toggles of the duffle coat. The sun had dropped from sight, but it was not yet dark, and the trees stood out like photographic negatives against an amber skyline.

"Let's go this way," said Fiona. She led him past a cattle byre to a barred gate. She fastened the gate behind them when they had passed through. In front of them lay the flat black water of the Forth-Clyde Canal.

"It was me who asked him to invite you here," she said as they walked along the bank. "I thought you might be someone I could talk to. I thought you might be able to help."

Unbalanced by her directness Grimmett wasn't sure how to respond. He waited for her to continue.

"It's my brother," she said. "I'm so terribly worried about him. He's been withdrawn for a long time now. He's not been himself. We used to have so much fun together, and now we don't laugh any more. I keep trying to talk to him, to find out what's troubling him, but to him . . . now," she hesitated, ". . . I'm just his sister. You know?" She looked at him. "Do you understand?"

"I think so," said Grimmett, although he knew that he didn't. "But I don't know him very well really. I don't know who does—at school I mean."

"He seems . . . well, so negative about things. He used to laugh and make jokes all the time. I thought he was the wittiest person I knew. But now he's so deadly serious about everything." She gave a small laugh, but there was no humour in it.

"Maybe it's my imagination; but we used to be very close. Good friends with each other, and now . . ." She

172

stopped. Somewhere far off, across the water, a curlew called in the stillness, ". . . now I just worry about him, all the time."

They walked on.

"Have you seen his paintings?" said Grimmett.

"Yes. They worry me. I don't like the things he sees. It's part of what I mean."

And Grimmett saw that there was an unfathomable difficulty, and he had no idea what to say to her.

"You must be cold," she said. "We should go back."

"No," he said. "I think I know what you're telling me, but I'm not sure what I can do." They walked on. "I can try and talk to him; see if I can get anywhere."

"He wants to be an artist," she said, "but my parents don't want that, and neither do the teachers at your school. Except for the Art Master. I don't know what David would have done without him; having someone like that believe in what he can do. Understand what he's thinking."

"What do they want him to do then? Your parents, I mean."

"Oh, they want him to do something much more conventional." There was an edge to her voice. "They want him to become a draughtsman or a designer of some sort."

"But your parents don't seem like the kind of people who would mind what he does."

"My mother perhaps. But don't let them fool you. My father is very traditional, strong-willed. He didn't have a particularly good schooling himself. He never went to university. Sometimes I think he wants us to be what he couldn't be."

She stopped, and looked out across the darkening fields. "That's what they're talking to him about now. A friend of my father's has offered to take David on with his architectural firm when he leaves school in the summer."

A small gaggle of ducks battled across the water in front of them, and disappeared into the reeds at the far bank. Dark, widening ripples glittered across the water. They watched the ripples flatten out and die away.

"We should be getting back," said Fiona. "They'll be wondering what's happened to us."

She bumped into Grimmett as she turned. "Sorry," she said, and Grimmett thought again of his gaffe at the

Army Cadet Force Day, and felt his face warm again despite the bite in the air. She took his hand and they walked back along the bank towards the farm, and he felt he could do anything then.

The next morning, Grimmett went for a walk with McCue along the old canal. McCue was preoccupied, his eyes on the ground in front of him. The air was sharp, the tufted grasses in the pastures white with frost.

Grimmett breathed in the clear air. "You must like it out here."

McCue lifted his head and gave him a puzzled look. He looked about him as if he hadn't seen any of it for a long time. "Yes. Yes, I like it. I love it in fact. I love the canal and the fields. Sometimes it moves me in ways I don't understand. It's a shame they don't use it any more."

"Don't use what?"

"The canal. Years ago it was busy with barges hauling coal and potatoes and all kinds of things between Edinburgh and Glasgow. Now they've filled most of it in and they don't use it any more. They should have thought about it before they did that. They could have used it for other things."

"I suppose they could," Grimmett said.

"It was a brilliant piece of engineering when they built it. You forget that, being full of water, it had to follow the same contour line between the two cities. It's funny. We never think that they had the brains to work out complicated things like that a hundred and fifty years ago."

He watched a sparrow splashing in the shallows among the reeds on the other side. "But I think our ancestors might have been a lot smarter than we are. The Romans built canals and aqueducts; the Egyptians too. And the Arabs put sophisticated gravity and vacuum irrigation systems in place in all the countries they lived in. They even devised water-based air-conditioning for the streets of their cities.

"I like it out here at night," McCue went on. "You can imagine the ghosts of old horses pulling barges along the towpath; a whole way of life with its own skills and customs and manners. All gone now."

174

They walked round a low hill and McCue pointed to a spot where the canal curved behind distant trees. "The farm stretches as far as these woods." He shook his head. "It's a pity they didn't leave the canal alone near the cities. That's where they need it most. It brought life, and a unique aesthetic. At least out here we've got other things of beauty to enjoy. In the cities they need to have more natural things around them. They need to take all the energy that comes with that."

He stopped and looked at Grimmett. "It's a different kind of thing," he said. "Different from the sort of man-made vitality you see. That always seems so . . . destructive." He fell silent.

They continued on for a while, and then McCue suggested that they go back to the farm. He'd said nothing about his conversation with his parents the night before, and Grimmett couldn't think of a way to bring it up.

As they came up to the farm buildings McCue's sister drove a tractor out of the yard. "She's putting out turnips for the sheep," said McCue. "We should help her.

"I think she rather likes you," he said after a minute. "She was keen for you to come out here." He was about to say something more, but he turned away.

The next evening, the three of them walked along the canal bank again: McCue and his sister, and Grimmett. The sun was slipping behind a bank of cloud, and the canal was blood red with its colour, and black with the shadows of trees. In an hour Grimmett would have to catch the train back to Edinburgh.

"Just look at that," said McCue. "It's magnificent. I could paint all my life and I'd never be able to duplicate that richness. It's so . . . unpredictable."

"Yes, you will," said Fiona. "You have the learning. It only takes work, and time . . . It can take a long time, but you can do that with the gifts you have."

"And patience," said Grimmett. He breathed in the clean smell of damp grass. The evening was warmer than the day had been, the air heavy and textured. A fish rose to the surface of the water and left a bubble.

"It seems to me," said Grimmett, "that most artists and writers have done other things first. They've had other

175

jobs, sometimes because they had to—to earn money to live on . . . and then they've found a way to work into their art."

The fish-bubble burst, sending tiny ripples out to the bank. Orange and crimson, shimmering in the last sunlight.

"Not true," said McCue. "It's only in recent generations that writers and artists haven't been in the forefront of society; the absolute forefront." He paused.

"It used to be that they were recognised and respected for their inventiveness, for their learning and progressiveness."

He turned towards them, and his face was flushed. "Look at Michelangelo. And da Vinci with all his ideas about flight, and his incredibly advanced anatomical drawings, and his inventions that were still hundreds of years in the future. The Popes used to go to him for advice. Look at the Greeks; all the thinkers they brought into government. The Greeks thought of philosophy as a science—not as an indulgence. Great people like Plato and Aristotle; they'd be swamped and buried and battered into line in a society like ours."

He turned away as his passion subsided. A small hawk hovered over the path in front of them and its wings caught the last of the sun. Grimmett fancied he could hear the hawk's wings beating against the air. It flew off across the wheat stubble and hovered again above a hedge at the far side of the field.

Grimmett caught a quick, anxious glance from Fiona. "Maybe we should just concentrate on what we have," she said. "We're young, and we need time to be young. Maybe that's the secret."

"The secret of life is the utter realisation of death," said McCue. His voice was flat and certain, without tone. "Parents keep it from their children."

"Oh David," said Fiona, and Grimmett could hear the anguish in her voice. "Look around you. It's so beautiful here. Look what you can see and hear, and smell and touch. It's here for you to do what you want with. A world with all this can't be bad."

"The world's all right," said McCue. "It's the people in it that are the trouble. Rushing about on their tiny treadmills, earning money and more money so they can buy even more useless things. There's no place for ideas any more, no room for the abstract. It's all rationalisation. No one has vision, and if they have it gets stifled anyway. No wonder they call it the age of anxiety." He walked on.

A train rumbled through the gathering dusk several fields away. They could hear it clatter over some points as it joined the line from Grangemouth.

"Listen . . . I'm sorry . . . going on like this." McCue's voice was sombre. "I suppose you should be getting back to the house. You've got to catch your train soon."

"It's all right," said Grimmett. "It doesn't go for a bit yet." He searched for something to say, something to make a connection. "I'm enjoying the walk. And you've got a . . . different way of looking at things."

"I don't see what's so different about it," said McCue, as if everything were a challenge. "I think it's quite realistic." He stared down the canal, and the lights of Edinburgh glowing faintly in the distance.

"My parents want me to be an architect or something like that. They don't see a future in Art, certainly not any kind of career. Of course they don't." He laughed. "It's beyond their comprehension. And it's the same at school, but that's only what you'd expect from a place that prides itself on the number of lawyers and army officers and Oxford scholarships it turns out. Stark's the only one with any idea at all. Only . . . only, he's given up too." He said it so quietly that they hardly heard him.

McCue turned to his sister. "Look, why don't you walk back with him. I think I'll go on for a bit yet; there are things I want to work out. I'll be back in a little while." He thrust his hands in his pockets, and without waiting for an answer, he walked down the towpath, towards the darkness.

Fiona stood watching him. Grimmett cast around for something to say; for words to fill the silence. "He'll be all right," he said. "He's bound to get depressed trying to work out what he's going to do and no one being any help. But it's the kind of thing you've got to sort out for yourself." Again, he knew it was the wrong thing to say.

A frog skittered across the pathway and splashed into the water. Fiona spoke and her voice was flat. "I'm not sure if he'll be all right. I'm not sure about anything any

177

more. I only know I'm frightened for him, and there doesn't seem to be anything I can do."

There was nothing more to say then, and they walked back to the farmhouse in their separate silences. Yellow light from the kitchen window fell onto the cobbles in the farmyard. Without looking at her Grimmett said, "I'd like to see you again." As soon as the words were out they sounded hollow and inappropriate, and he wanted to take them back.

She touched his arm and said, "I'd like that too." Then, "you will try won't you? To talk to him I mean. Try to be his friend?"

"Yes."

She pushed open the door and they went in.

A pot of tea and a plate of sandwiches were set out on the kitchen table. The kettle spouted steam on top of the coal range. After a few minutes Grimmett excused himself and climbed the narrow zigzag staircase to his bedroom. He packed his bag and stood in front of the window, and listened to the night sounds. The sun had gone, leaving only a faint red halo behind a leafless beech tree standing by itself across the canal. He picked up his bag and went downstairs.

Mrs. McCue was talking about sheep and the early lambs that were due. McCue came in as they were finishing their tea. He sat down and bit into a sandwich. Then it was time for Grimmett to leave, and they went outside and climbed into the Land Rover. This time Grimmett squashed into the middle seat in front, while Mrs. McCue and Fiona arranged themselves among the sacking and ropes in the back.

Under the bright lights of the station, Grimmett felt suddenly tired. He said goodbye to them and stepped onto the Edinburgh train. There was no one else in his compartment, and he fell asleep until he was woken up by a porter at Edinburgh's Waverley station.

Chapter 21 – The Dashing White Sergeant

"But I don't know how to do these kinds of dances," said Dunphy. They were taking a short cut to the flat, up a steep, cobbled lane behind the school. The granite setts were slippery with drizzle.

"You'll learn soon enough," said Grimmett. "Anyway, we haven't got a choice. We've got to go to it."

"It's that girl isn't it?" Said Dunphy. "You just want to see her again."

Grimmett's face flushed.

"What girl?" he said.

"McCue's sister. She goes to St. Joseph's."

"St. Joseph's is our sister school. They've got the same Board of Governors as we've got. We've got to go. They made it a rule."

"Huh!" Dunphy's voice showed his disbelief. "Since when did you start worrying about the rules? It's a convent school too. I didn't think nuns were allowed to go dancing."

"It used to be a convent school," said Grimmett. "This dance has been held for years, and because no one from our place ever went to it they've made it compulsory now. The upper two years in the school have got to go."

"Scottish country dancing! I don't know anything about it." Dunphy fumbled in his pocket. "What are the girls like?"

"Not great. But you've got to go anyway so it doesn't matter. It's not all country dancing; they throw in some modern stuff as well."

Dunphy looked furtively up and down the lane, and took a packet of cigarettes from his pocket. He pulled up the collar of his jacket against the wind, and hunched over and struck a match and held it to a cigarette in his mouth.

"What on earth are you doing?" Grimmett had never seen Dunphy smoke a cigarette before.

Dunphy began to cough. Smoke poured out of his mouth and nose. "McCue gave them to me . . . thought I'd give it a try."

"You're daft. You'd better put it out. They'll kick you out of the school if they catch you doing that around here." Dunphy was seized by a paroxysm of coughing. Tears ran from his eyes, spittle flew from his mouth.

"Diplomat smokes," he croaked, his voice in the back of his throat. "Wouldn't give me a bad time about it."

"He would if they threw you out. Besides it's not the Diplomat we're worried about." He looked down the lane. "I'm telling you, if they catch you there'll be a lot of trouble."

Dunphy gagged as he sucked at the cigarette a second time. He blew the smoke down inside his coat to hide it. Grimmett watched as the smoke billowed out around his waist and neck and swirled about him. Dunphy punched himself in the chest.

"Stupid," said Grimmett.

Dunphy dropped the cigarette in a puddle. It hissed and went out.

"Wanted to try it," he said, wiping his eyes. "You get fed up with their stupid rules all the time. Sometimes you've just got to do something about it. It's a matter of principle." He cleared his throat and patted his chest. "Don't think I'll take it up though."

They continued up the steep lane, placing their feet carefully on the glistening cobblestones. Grey stone tenements leaned over them, water dribbling down the walls in dark patches. The gutter was littered with soggy papers. A gust of wind pulled the acrid smell of coal fires down into the street from rooftop chimneys.

"What are we supposed to wear?" said Dunphy when they reached the top of the lane.

"Wear?" Grimmett was thinking of other things.

"Yes. To the dance."

"Oh, yes, the dance. Well, it's a bit formal. You're supposed to wear a suit or something. They made an announcement about it on Monday."

"Didn't hear it." Dunphy took a boiled sweet from his pocket. He unwrapped it and popped it in his mouth. "I don't remember them saying we had to go to it."

It was dusk. The days were beginning to lengthen. A last ray of sunlight reflected off a window high up in the castle, like an explosion. It flickered for a few moments and disappeared. Grimmett was sitting upstairs on the bus. He was on his way to the dance. The city's lights were coming on, and he looked down at the shop windows as the bus rattled down the bumpy streets.

The bus stopped by the railway station and he saw her. She was wearing a raincoat over a long dress. In the reflection of the lights from the bus he could see that she was wearing makeup. He turned round to watch her in the convex mirror as she climbed the stairs, and her face seemed to leap upwards at him, drawn out of proportion by the curvature of the glass. Then she was there, and she saw him and smiled.

"Hello, are you going to the dance?"

"Yes." And then, "how did you know that?" He moved along the seat to make room for her.

"David said something about it; that they'd told you that you had to go. They more or less said the same to us."

There was no make-up he decided. It must have been the effect of the lights at the stop. There were shadows under her eyes, and he thought back to the weekend he'd spent at the farm. He had tried to talk to McCue since then, but it had gone nowhere.

"Where's David?" he asked. They never called each other by their christian names at school, but with her it was different.

"He's not coming." She didn't add to it.

Grimmett nodded. McCue was going his own direction. No one seemed to be able to change it.

She changed the subject. "You look very smart."

Grimmett shrugged his shoulders. It was a borrowed suit. It felt tight and uncomfortable.

"Where's your friend? The one you share a flat with."

"He'll meet us there. He's picking up a suit at a rental place."

They sat in silence for a while. "We're nearly there," she said. "Do you mind if I walk in with you?"

"No. No, of course not."

They saw Dunphy as soon as they stepped into the gymnasium at St. Josephs. He was sitting at the end of a row of chairs with a fixed expression on his face. The gym had been decorated for the dance. Flags hung limply from the wallbars, and streamers dangled from trapezes. A composite band, made up of student musicians from the two schools, was sitting on a small stage at one end of the hall.

A line of teachers from both schools sat along one wall. Some of them had brought wives or husbands with them. None of them looked happy. Most of them sat with their hands folded in front of them. Most of the men wore suits; one or two wearing the kilt. Some of the women wore starched white dresses, with tartan sashes which fell diagonally from their shoulders to their waists.

Grimmett started to walk over to Dunphy, and sensed Fiona hanging back. He turned to her.

"I don't think I should," she said. "I should go and sit with the other girls." She smiled. "At first anyway."

"All right," said Grimmett. "Maybe we can have a dance in a little while?"

"Yes. I'd like that." She walked across the floor, and he watched her, and realised he had forgotten about her disability since that first day they had met.

"Why isn't anyone dancing?" said Dunphy when Grimmett sat down.

"The band's not playing." Grimmett looked over at the band; an accordionist, two fiddlers, a pianist and a drummer. They were talking among themselves. Opposite them the headmaster was deep in conversation with a woman in a nun's habit.

182

"Have they played anything yet?" said Grimmett.

"They played two pieces, but no one danced."

About forty boys were sitting and standing along one wall of the gymnasium. The girls from St. Josephs were arranged along the opposite side of the hall. The two groups watched each other carefully, like rugby teams waiting for the referee's whistle. The band played a chord, and launched into 'Heilan Laddie'. The notes echoed into the rafters. Dunphy scratched his nose.

"Can't sit here all night like this," he said. "Why doesn't anyone get up and dance?"

"It's always like this," said Grimmett. "Someone will dance in a minute."

The headmaster stood up and took a step towards the woman in the nun's habit. He bowed, and extended his arm. She shook her head, and the headmaster's face turned red. Mr. Forbes stood up, scraping his chair on the floor. He advanced towards a group of St. Joseph's teachers. One of them stood, and a moment later the two of them were moving around the floor, holding each other at arm's length. Encouraged, the band picked up the tempo.

Mr. Fisher stepped onto the floor with his wife. Dunphy had already seen her. He was careful to avoid her gaze. The death of the Fisher's cat had etched itself onto his mind. In moments of insecurity he found himself imagining what might happen if the corpse should ever come to light. The Fishers shuffled around the floor. After a few moments the French teacher loosened up, and began to pilot his wife past the other dancing couples, swooping and whirling from one end of the gym to the other.

"Didn't know Fisher could dance like that," said Dunphy.

"He makes it look quite easy," Grimmett agreed.

"It's probably not that difficult. Just takes a bit of practice, that's all." Dunphy looked across the hall for a likely partner. "We should give it a go." He stood up.

Grimmett saw Fiona, and walked over to her. "I'm not very good at this," he said, "but would you like to dance?"

"I'm not very good at it either," said Fiona. "We'll just have to go at our own pace." She brushed her hair from her face. He put his hand on her waist and took her onto the floor. She seemed to float in front of him. He concentrated on not stepping on her toes.

"Try and slow down a little bit," she said, resting her arm on his shoulder. "We can find our own rhythm if we listen to the music. It's the only way I can do it."

Grimmett was concentrating on the steps, his head down, his eyes on their feet. "I've not done it like this before," he said. It was difficult to dance and talk at the same time.

She pulled him round. "Follow my feet," she said, and stepped to the music.

"You see," she said. "It's not so hard." She spoke close to his ear, so that he could hear her over the noise of the band, and he found himself being folded into her presence in a way that had never happened to him before.

They stayed on the floor after the dance finished, waiting for the next piece. "Do you still want to get away?" she said.

"What do you mean?" He had never spoken to her about it.

She looked at him with the direct gaze he had seen before. "You don't have to leave here to get away from them. They can't touch you inside if you don't let them." He only just knew what she was saying to him.

The music started up and they began to dance. This one was slower. Dunphy danced past flush-faced, holding a red-haired girl at arm's length, as if he was steering a car. Out of the corner of his eye Grimmett saw him bump into Mr. Forbes. Forbes was doing the same step as he'd danced to the waltz. The headmaster spun past, locked in an automatic gait, his kilt swirling about his knees. Grimmett felt a thump in his back as Dunphy careered past, the red-haired girl trying to act as a brake.

Fiona sat down beside Grimmett when the dance ended. She waited until the band started another tune, and then she said, "David will try and leave home at the end of the term, and you'll go away too and neither of you have to."

He didn't know what to say at first. After a moment he said, "I don't know what I'm going to do when I've finished here."

"No. But you want to get away."

"Yes . . . I don't know," he said.

184

"Listen Arthur." She took his hand, and then put it down because she saw that he was embarrassed, and she knew too that her teachers were watching. "All this is just part of a straitjacket they try to put us in so we can't see properly, and can't feel things. You don't have to pay attention to it. Inside, you can just be what you want to be. They can't decide what you think."

The music ended, and Dunphy came over with the red-haired girl. "This is Judith," he said. He was breathing hard. Grimmett stood up and shook her hand. It was damp and soft.

The band leader moved to the front of the stage and waved his fiddle. "The next dance," he said, "is the Dashing White Sergeant. Everyone on their feet please for the next dance."

The red-haired girl pulled at Dunphy. "Come on," she said. "This one's fun."

The dancers formed themselves into two parallel lines, partners facing each other. The band waited while the lines jostled and sorted themselves out.

"I won't do this one," said Fiona. "You go ahead if you want to."

Grimmett shook his head. "That was enough for me. I don't really like to dance all that much. I'm not any good at it."

Out on the dance floor, Dunphy leaned across to Judith. "How do you do this?"

"It's easy. Just watch the others. You take it in turns with your partner, and you just sort of dash down the aisle between the lines. You'll get the hang of it in a minute."

The band began to play a lively tune and the first couple danced down between the rows. Mr. Fisher moved forward to meet his wife, and took her hand high over his shoulder. He stepped down the line with his feet darting left and right in time to the music.

"See? It's simple," said the red-haired girl. The tempo picked up and Dunphy turned to look at the band. When he looked back again his partner had gone, and he realised he was late for his turn. Judith was already travelling up behind her line.

Dunphy sprinted down behind the dancers to catch up with her. He turned the corner and tore into the centre of the floor and his feet slid out from under him. He skidded across the gym, pirouetting on one leg. But his momentum was too great, and he fell onto the floor and began to scythe down one of the lines, felling dancers liked dominoes. A plume of smoke came from his hip pocket, trailing out behind him. Mrs. Fisher jumped out of his way with a shout.

Dunphy came to a stop and leaped to his feet and began beating furiously at his bottom. Clouds of blue smoke rose up behind him. The music tailed off and stopped.

"What on earth happened to him?" Fiona was laughing. "I didn't think he was going fast enough to create that kind of friction."

A group of people were swatting at Dunphy's rear. A big hole had burned in the seat of his rented trousers. It was charred round its edges, showing the white of his underpants. The headmaster took off his jacket, and wrapped it round Dunphy's waist. He led Dunphy off the dance floor and out the door.

"Matches," said Grimmett. "There'll be a fuss about that."

"Matches?" Fiona held her hand up to her mouth. Tears were running down her face.

"Ssshh. Not so loud."

"Sorry," said Fiona. She wiped her eyes. "But it's kind of obvious."

"They were probably left in the suit at the renters." And then he regretted not sharing it with her.

Chapter 22 – Arthur's Seat

Grimmett folded the letter and put it back in the envelope. "They'll be back here in four weeks," he said.

"For how long?" Dunphy was reclining in an armchair, his feet propped against the side of the mantelpiece. A bag of potato chips sat on his lap, and a history book. He ate steadily, periodically turning the pages of the history book. They had scavenged some wood from the park at the top of the street, and a small fire sputtered in the grate. The previous week they had pried off the hardboard cover that was sealing off the chimney.

"They don't really say. But it sounds as if Uncle Ronald will just be back on leave for a while, and my mother will stay over here for the summer."

"Diplomat will be back in about a month too," said Dunphy. "Then we'll just about be finished." He crunched a potato chip. "Will you have to move in with them then?"

"I don't know," said Grimmett. He stared at the fire, his thoughts turning over.

"Two letters in one day. That's more'n I get in a month. Quite a thing with your Father." Dunphy shook the chip bag. He put another chip in his mouth.

Grimmett didn't say anything. "Breaking up with that other woman," Dunphy went on. "I'm not surprised though. I don't see how he could've lasted more than five minutes with her. What'll he do now?"

Grimmett shook his head. "Don't know," he said.

"Probably get another posting. Africa was just a temporary one wasn't it? Mebbe you can go and spend some time with him. Take a break from here while you figure out what you're going to do."

Grimmett stared into the fire. It was too late for that now. A year or two before he had wanted it more than anything else in the world. There had been a cheque from Barclay's Bank inside his father's letter. It was for two hundred pounds; a huge amount of money. It came to him like an apology, with a sense of discomfort and guilt.

"No," he said. "It's what I wanted once. I think I want to do something different now."

"She's a beauty." Dunphy brushed his hand across the saddle. "What kind is it?"

"Norton," said Grimmett. He pointed at the faded lettering on the scratched paintwork of the petrol tank. "Norton two-fifty. It doesn't go all that fast, but it'll get me about. It's better than waiting for buses all the time."

Dunphy gazed at the small beige motorcycle. The leather saddle was scratched and scarred, the glass on the speedometer was cracked, and the brake cable hung loose from the handlebars where the clip had broken.

"What's the 'L' for?" He pointed at a square white placard with a big red letter 'L' on it. It was tied onto the front forks of the motorbike with a piece of string.

"Learner. It means I haven't passed the test yet."

Dunphy walked round the machine, examining it. He patted the seat again. "Start it up. I want to hear what it sounds like."

Grimmett swung his leg over the saddle. He turned the key on the panel and waved Dunphy out of the way. He bent down to pull the pedal out on the kick starter. Grasping the handlebars, he leaped upwards, and came down hard on the starter pedal. The engine sputtered. Grimmett rubbed his hands together. He jumped up in the air and came down on the pedal again. The motorbike made a tired, wattling noise.

188

"It's a bit temperamental." He tried again. The engine gave a long drawn out sigh and a hacking cough.

"Doesn't seem to work," said Dunphy.

"You've got to give it a minute." Grimmett twisted the hand throttle. He jumped on the pedal for a fourth time. The engine caught for a second, and quickly choked into silence. "It'll start this time," he said.

Dunphy took a step backwards. The motorbike roared into life, spat black smoke from its exhaust, and fell off its stand. Grimmett just managed to stop it from falling onto the road.

"Sounds good doesn't it," he shouted. He twisted the handgrip and the engine crackled like tearing canvas, and the motorbike shook with a series of tremors.

Dunphy stepped forward and shouted in Grimmett's ear. "Take me for a ride on it."

Grimmett switched off the engine. "I can't. I'm not allowed to take passengers on it until I've passed the test."

"When's that?"

"This evening at five o'clock."

Grimmett met the Examiner in the forecourt at the Haymarket railway station. The Examiner was a thin man with a raincoat buttoned to his chin. He was carrying a clipboard in his hand, and wearing a white crash helmet with leather flaps over his ears. He noted the details of Grimmett's name and address carefully on his clipboard.

"Right," he said, when he had finished writing. "Let's get on with this shall we? I'll come along on the pillion for a while and watch how you go. I'll be checking you for your driving abilities, as well as your hand signals and your practical knowledge of the Highway Code."

He fastened the strap of his crash helmet. "When we've done that I'll get off and set you some simple manoeuvres, and test you on emergency procedures." He consulted the clipboard. "We'll finish with some questions on the Highway Code."

The Examiner climbed onto the pillion seat behind Grimmett, and arranged his raincoat about himself. He tucked the clipboard into his coat and pulled on a pair of goggles. "All right," he said. "Take me up here whenever you're ready." He pointed up the Glasgow Road.

189

Grimmett turned round to look at the traffic. He waited until a bus drove past, and then stuck out his hand and moved into the roadway. The Examiner gripped him round the waist. They drove up the hill at a steady thirty miles an hour.

In five minutes they came to the suburb of Corstorphine. The Examiner called out, "This will do. Pull in at the traffic lights and I'll get off."

When the motorbike came to a stop the Examiner dismounted.

"How have I done?" said Grimmett.

"All right so far," said the Examiner. "You should be a bit more definite about your hand signals. But we're only halfway through the test. Turn into this car park. I want to set you some manoeuvres." He walked over to a low wall at the edge of the car park.

The Examiner consulted his clipboard. "Right. Drive round in a big circle."

He made notes on his board while Grimmett slowly circled the car park. Then he asked Grimmett to do some stopping and starting drills, and to follow closely along the painted white lines. After a few minutes he waved Grimmett over. "Show me what you do if you get into a skid."

Grimmett started to drive off.

"No, no!" shouted the Examiner. "I don't want you to actually go into a skid. Just show me with the bike stationary."

Grimmett leaned the motorbike on its side and turned the front wheel in the direction of the slide. The Examiner made another note on his board.

"Right. Just the emergency braking and some questions on the Highway Code and we're finished." He looked at his watch. Three large black limousines drove into the car park. Dark curtains were drawn over the windows of the front car.

"Funeral," said the Examiner. He frowned. "We can't do it in here then." He looked around. "We'll go back onto the road, and you can drive round the block. Go round it a couple of times until you see me step out in front of you. Then I want you to stop immediately, as if it were an emergency. Right?"

Grimmett nodded. He followed the Examiner through the gate.

When they were out in the street the Examiner shouted over the noise of the motorcycle's engine. "Keep an eye out, because it won't necessarily be here. I might go round the corner and try to catch you napping, so be on your guard." He patted the seat behind Grimmett. "Off you go then."

Grimmett opened the throttle and moved out into the traffic. His coat filled with wind, and drops of rain spattered on his face. He pulled the visor down over his eyes and hunched over the handlebars.

The traffic light was red. Grimmett stopped, and waited for it to change. When it turned green, he accelerated out onto the main road. He looked for the thin figure of the Examiner. Several pedestrians were walking along the pavement in front of the shops, but the Examiner was nowhere in sight. Grimmett turned off the main road, and began another circuit of the block.

When he reached the main road again there was still no sign of the Examiner. He changed gears and pulled into the side street for the third time. He wiped his hand across the visor. The rain was coming down harder now.

In front of him a small crowd of people were bending over a prone figure in the road. A brown motorbike lay on its side in the gutter. Grimmett pulled up and dismounted. He went over to the group.

"Jumped right out in front of me!" The motorcyclist's voice was high-pitched and excited. He was wearing a blue raincoat. He pulled his white helmet off his head and cradled it under his arm. "I didn't have a chance. Honest. I couldn't possibly have stopped in time."

The Examiner moaned as someone placed a folded jacket under his head. "My leg," he groaned. "I think it's broken."

"I can't give you a lift home," said Grimmett. "I still haven't passed my test." He explained what had happened to the Examiner.

"You're kidding," said Dunphy. "The guy jumped out in front of the wrong bike! I don't believe it. So when do you take the test again?"

"Some time next week. They said they'd get in touch with me."

Dunphy took a chip from the newspaper wrapping in his hand, and popped it into his mouth. He offered one to Grimmett. Grimmett shook his head.

"Anyway, that's the story. I'm still a learner, so I can't take anyone on the back."

"Oh, come on! You can't just leave me here. You told me you'd give me a lift home. I can't walk all the way back to the flat. It's miles from here."

"It's not that far. We do it every day."

"It's pouring with rain."

"You can always take the bus."

Dunphy gazed at the fish supper in his hands. "Spent all my bus money getting that suit invisibly mended after the dance." He ate another chip. "Unless you can lend me some. Anyway, you promised to give me a lift."

Grimmett looked up and down the road. Reflections from the streetlights bounced off the wet cobblestones, and rainwater coursed down the gutter. There was hardly anyone about, almost no traffic.

"Take the 'L' plate off the back then. We'll chance it." He struggled to untie the plate on the front forks. He tried to break the string but it was too strong. "Have you got a penknife?"

'No."

"Go on then, jump on the back. I'll just have to leave the front one on." He let out the clutch. "Hold on tight," he said.

The headlight threw a wobbly beam into the darkness as they roared up the lane and turned onto the main road. The noise of the engine echoed back from the tenement walls on either side of them. A black car was coming slowly down the street towards them.

"Police," shouted Grimmett, and Dunphy crouched low on the pillion seat. He turned to look at the police car as it drove past.

"They saw us," said Dunphy, twisting in the seat. "They're turning round."

Grimmett opened up the throttle and sped up the hill. He turned left into a side street, and then left again into some back mews. The motorcycle bounced across the cobbles. Dunphy held on. Grimmett turned down a narrow alley, struggling to hold the motorbike on the slippery road.

"I think we lost them," shouted Dunphy.

They roared past derelict tenements, down a gloomy street with no lighting, and Dunphy caught glimpses of broken windows and walls shining with rainwater. The back wheel skidded as Grimmett stamped on the brake. The police car was parked in front of them, blocking the exit from the lane. Like a scene from an old film, the police driver flicked on the headlamps, lighting them up like criminals. Grimmett switched off the motorbike's engine.

The car doors opened and two policemen climbed out, putting their policeman's hats on their heads. Grimmett could hear the crackle of the police radio in the car. Dunphy fumbled in the newspaper on his lap and put a chip in his mouth.

One of the policemen flashed a light over the motorbike. Then he shone it in Dunphy's eyes. "Right. What are you boys up to then? Coming up here in the middle of the night eh?"

"Trying to get away Jack," said the other policeman. He reached down at the front forks and flicked the 'L' placard. "That's a learner plate there right enough." He walked round to the back of the bike. "Where's the other one?"

Dunphy dismounted. "It must've come off."

"Don't be cheeky sonny." He pointed at Grimmett's coat. "What's that sticking out of your pocket then?"

Grimmett reached for his pocket. "Oh yes. That's right. I put it in my pocket after it came off."

The second policeman reached out and took the remains of the fish supper from Dunphy's hand. He wrinkled his nose. "I shall require this as evidence," he said.

"It's my supper," said Dunphy.

"Evidence," said the policeman.

His colleague stared at Grimmett. "Licence?" He held out his hand.

Grimmett reached in his pocket and pulled out his licence. The policeman took it. Grimmett sat astride the bike and watched the rain fall through the light at the end of the street. It seemed as if the fates were working to ensure that he would never leave the city. A van came down the hill at the end of the lane, throwing spray from its wheels. The policeman wrote in his notebook.

"Right," said the policeman when he had finished writing. "You young lads are in a spot of bother." He held the notebook up to the light from the police car. "Charge number one. Carrying a passenger on the pillion when not licensed to do so. Charge number two. Insufficient insurance. Charge number three. Not displaying learner plates when required by law to do so. Charge number four. Rear light not working. Charge number five. Speeding. Charge number six." He looked up from his notebook at Grimmett. "Trying to evade arrest. Charge number seven. Passenger seated on the pillion in a manner unsafe and liable to be a danger to the public." He closed the book and stared at Dunphy. "Eating fish and chips."

That was it. Grimmett got off the motorbike and took off his helmet. He felt the cold rain on his face. Suddenly he felt very tired. None of it seemed to matter now.

The policeman was speaking again. "Any one of these charges will see that you don't ride this bike again for a long time," he said. "And I can make them all stick. What have you got to say about that?"

Grimmett shook his head and stared out at the end of the lane. His real thoughts were far away. "I don't have anything to say."

"No, I don't expect you have, so I'm going to tell you what will happen next." He closed his notebook. "There will be a letter to the headmaster of your school, and no doubt he will have something to say to you about this. Next, I'm going to put my book away and Constable Fairbrother and I will forget to file a report." He saw his partner's mouth fall open. "So get out of here before we change our minds. Separate like. You on your bike, and you," he turned to Dunphy, "on your feet."

The two policemen watched Grimmett push the bike off through the rain, Dunphy walking beside him.

"What the hell did you do that for Jack?" said the second policeman.

There was a bemused expression on the senior man's face. "Dunno really." He shook his head. "My boy's about that age. Some of these kids need a little break . . . Maybe that's it."

The headmaster leaned on the lectern and surveyed the morning Assembly. His eyes scanned the faces below, moving from one side of the great hall to the other.

"I have here," he said, in a grave voice, "a serious complaint from the Lothian and Borders Police." He rustled a piece of paper, lowered his head, and stared over the top of his spectacles. "It informs me about a breach of the law perpetrated by two of our pupils last Wednesday evening."

The cadence of his voice rose and his spectacles caught the overhead lights. "I shall take steps to ensure that incidents of this nature do not besmirch the name of this school again. Unfortunately," he continued, "the precise details of the offence have not been disclosed to me, nor do I have the names of the offenders. They alone know who they are, and I expect them as gentlemen to step forward privately before the end of the day and announce themselves to me in order to receive appropriate punishment."

His eyes roved the Assembly and he cleared his throat. There was complete silence in the hall.

"In the meantime I shall take this opportunity to announce a new school rule which will become effective immediately. As of today, no boy from this school will give a ride in a motor car, or on a motor cycle, or in any type of motor vehicle, to any other pupil." He paused. "There will be no exceptions."

The headmaster turned, and the school rose. With his gown billowing behind him, he strode out of the door.

"I guess we'd better go along to his study," said Dunphy as they waited for the row of seats to clear.

"What!" There was a feeling of elation with all this. Grimmett felt an overpowering need to laugh out loud. McCue looked at him, but said nothing.

"We ought to," said Dunphy. "It's the proper thing to do."

Grimmett laughed as they went out into the fresh air. It was a happy sound, carefree and wild. The sun was shining. "Are you mad? To hell with him. He just wants to beat the hell out of your backside. Don't you see? That policeman was a decent man. He's let us off, not because he wants someone else to punish us. God! He didn't even tell the Head our names!"

Dunphy's voice was doubtful. "I don't know."

"I do," said Grimmett.

Grimmett was waiting for her at the gates of her school. She didn't show any surprise.

"Where are we going?" she said, and they walked down the street together.

"Arthur's Seat. Is that all right?"

"Yes. I can manage it." And then, after a few seconds, "Has something good happened today?"

He took her bag, and she unbuttoned her coat and let the air surround her.

"I think so," he said. "I think so. Some things sort of fell into place." They came to a bus stop. "We can leave your bag in a locker at the station if you like." The sun had warmth in it for the first time. "It's all right isn't it? For you to come?"

"Yes. I can catch a later train."

She stopped in front of an outcrop of polished rock. "Help me up this bit Arthur."

Grimmett reached down and took her hand and helped her. She stopped halfway, holding onto his hand.

"I can't call you Arthur," she said.

"Why not?"

"It's too formal. Arthur's too proper a name." She let him pull her up the rest of the way. "Art's too American. Ari . . . Airy, like the wind. Maybe I'll call you that." She stopped and looked at him. "You don't mind do you?"

He held her eyes. Her cheeks were flushed. She looked happy and well. He liked her name for him, and he wanted to hold her. "No," he said, "I don't mind."

The moment passed and they climbed the last gentle incline to the summit.

Below them, a thin harr was creeping up the river estuary. Its advancing tendrils had enveloped the distant village of Aberlady, and they were pushing on towards Port Seton and the links at Musselburgh. Further down the coast, beyond that, only the top of North Berwick Law poked through the ground mist.

A benign southwest wind shuffled over the top of the hill, and the late afternoon sun was shining. They sat with their backs against the Ordnance Survey marker at the summit.

"Look at that," said Fiona. "What a view."

"It makes you think doesn't it," said Grimmett, gazing over the broad river to the fields of Fife. He had an urge to laugh out loud again. The sun caught a windowpane on the far shore and reflected back at them, over miles of water.

"The ships look like toys." He pointed at a tanker moving over the plate-glass sea, heading for the oil terminal at Grangemouth.

They sat and listened to the wind, and the city sounds floated up at them. Somewhere far below a door slammed, and a church clock chimed over the hum of traffic. The sounds seemed to be coming from a long way away.

"You know," she said, "when you look at all this it makes everything seem simple—for a little while at least. Whoever put it all together got the important things right."

Grimmett looked at her. Her hair was blowing in the wind, and the wind brought with it the smell of the hills. The things she said to him were different, and it was fine.

Fiona cast her arm at the broad river and the darkening northern hills. "I mean," she continued, searching for the words, "all the hustle; all the commerce. The people cutting each other's throats, climbing over each other like rats. That's how it seems sometimes. But on a day like this you can see that there's no point to that—no point to that sort of avarice and greed. All of it comes from the same thinking as the kinds of controls people try to put on you to shape your life to fit their own images.

"Whoever put all this together worked it out pretty well. We're all in the same boat, and in the end we'll all die. And when we all die, what do we take with us?" She didn't wait for him to answer. "We don't take anything. We leave it the same way we came. With nothing to show for a lifetime of work except the memory of what we've done for the people we leave behind us. Not much more than that, and even that's temporal; it doesn't last. The biggest monuments and

197

buildings all come down in the end to make way for new things."

She took his hand. It felt warm. "I'm sorry," she said. "I go on a bit sometimes."

"No. It's all right. I want you to go on. I haven't thought of it like that."

He was comfortable with her. Other people were climbing up towards the summit. He didn't want them to come near.

"There's lots more." She smiled.

"If it's as simple as that, why is there still murder and stealing and wars and things?"

"I suppose that's the flaw," she said. "Whoever or whatever it was that put all this together gave us brains, but not everyone was gifted with vision. Most people don't see that there's just no point in any other attitude than being decent and considerate. The bad things only cause misery, and they never benefit anyone for long." Her head went back and she closed her eyes. "Least of all the people who cause them."

The sounds of evening traffic were beginning to fade. Somewhere down among the tenements in Abbeyhill a dog barked. Some children were playing in Hunter's Bog at the bottom of the lion's head cliff, their shouts and laughter floating up the hill. The other climbers started down again.

"Are you talking about religion?" Grimmett felt as if he had woken from a sleep; he wanted to understand the things she was saying, wanted her to keep talking.

"I don't think so. Not in the conventional sense anyway. It seems clear to me, but I'm not very good at expressing it. The way I put it, it just sounds heavy. You know?"

She took her hand away, and he felt the leaving of it.

"All of it is so beautifully thought out; only most of us aren't smart enough to see the point of it." She leaned back against the concrete trig marker. "You see, if we all knew what was going to happen when we died . . . you have to think about that.

"What would happen for example if you knew that when you died, there was just nothing? A black hole; a sleep without dreams?" Again, she didn't wait for him to answer.

"If people knew that, they'd be frightened and depressed. There wouldn't be any motivation to do anything. The world would be in a worse mess than it is.

"On the other hand if you knew absolutely that when you died you didn't really die, but you went somewhere else—call it Heaven, or Paradise, if you want—then people would have no particular motivation to be thought well of after death . . . and because we think materially they'd just want to accumulate possessions . . . or power. Or perhaps do extreme and dangerous things. Then the world would be even more grasping, more dogmatic, than it already is."

She shook her head. "No, the genius in the thing is the uncertainty of it. That's what makes most people hedge their bets—the fact that no one knows what happens in the end. And there is an end to it. Everyone knows that. Most of us just don't think about it. Most people avoid it until they have to, which is right at the very end."

"'You can go through life fudging and evading, indulging and slacking, never really hungry nor frightened nor passionately stirred, your highest moment a mere sentimental orgasm, and your first real contact with primary and elemental necessities the sweat of your deathbed.' Is that what you mean?" Grimmett was surprised that he remembered it.

Fiona looked at him, but there was no surprise on her face. "Something like that. Where did it come from?"

"H.G. Wells wrote it; a long time ago."

She smiled, and her teeth were white and even and he wanted to kiss her, but he didn't know how to do it.

"You see," she said. "It's what you do inside that's important. No one can take that away from you."

She sat up. "I think I should go and get my train now. I'm glad you came to meet me this afternoon." She turned to face him. She held his eyes for a long moment. "Eyes of rain," she whispered. She got to her feet, then "I like you Airy Grimmett; I'd like to be your friend." She started to walk away, down the path.

Chapter 23 – A Fiery Parting

Grimmett carried Dunphy's suitcase down the stairs to the street. Dunphy's father was waiting in his car. He got out and opened the trunk.

"You're sure you'll be all right here by yourself," he said.

"Yes," said Grimmett. "I'll be leaving too, soon."

"It's just that we've got to get George sorted out before he flies back to Canada, and it's difficult to do that with all his things in different places." Vice-consul Dunphy sounded apologetic. "I must say you fellows seem to have done quite well looking after yourselves. I'm impressed."

Dunphy struggled through the front door, carrying a bag overflowing with clothes. "Couldn't get the zipper done up," he said. Socks and items of underwear fell onto the pavement. He thrust the bag at his father and turned to Grimmett.

"What'll you do? At the end of term I mean?" he said.

"I'm not sure yet. I'll let you know when I've worked it out."

They shook hands, and then Dunphy and his father drove off in the big consular car. Grimmett watched as it motored smoothly up the hill and disappeared round the corner.

"It's not the same. Living at home I mean. It's quite difficult in fact." Dunphy pushed his way through the swing doors into the dining hall. "They keep going on about manners and stuff." He raised his voice over the chatter in the hall. "I miss living in the flat. How're things there?"

"They're fine," said Grimmett. "It's a bit different since you left, but I'll be out of there by the end of the week anyway. Uncle Ronald and my mother will be back then."

"That reminds me. Diplomat's given me some money. Thought we might like to go out for dinner. Sort of a celebration, since we're about to be finished with this place."

"That was good of him." Grimmett elbowed his way through a group of students standing in the aisle between the long tables.

"He likes you," Dunphy said. "For some reason he thinks you're a good influence on me." He pulled out a wooden bench and stepped over it and sat down.

The tables were covered with clean white cloths, each place neatly set with cutlery and a napkin, a half-slice of bread at each setting. The benches quickly filled up.

"He didn't specifically say dinner," Dunphy went on, as Grimmett squeezed in next to him. "He said dinner, or the theatre." He broke off a piece of bread and put it in his mouth. "Or he said we could just go out and get bloody well drunk. That was how he put it when my mother was out of the room. I thought dinner would be better."

The headmaster swept through the door at the head of the hall, followed by an entourage of masters and senior boys. They climbed the steps onto the stage and stood around the top table like birds of prey in their black academic gowns. The headmaster stepped forward and the school rose with a scraping of benches. The boys lowered their heads.

"Benedicus, Benedicat."

"Deo gratias," came the response from the rest of the dining hall.

The headmaster sat down at the head of the head table, and everyone else sat down after him.

Grimmett passed a plate of soup up the table. "Have you got a place in mind?"

201

Dunphy chewed on a piece of bread. He picked up a spoon as Grimmett placed a bowl of soup in front of him. "Lentil. You'd think they'd give us something special on the last day." He made a face. "There's a new German place in the Old Town called the Gasthaus; in the Canongate. We could go there." He supped his soup.

"What about Scottish food?" said Grimmett. "Since you're leaving soon you should try some good Scottish food."

Dunphy turned and stared at him, his spoon part way to his mouth. "You've got to be kidding."

"No. Scottish food's fine when it's done properly. You should try it."

Dunphy pushed his plate away from him. "Scottish food's what I've been eating here for the last year. It's probably done me lasting damage."

The main course came up the table, passed from hand to hand. Dunphy surveyed his plate with a pained expression. The mince was a pale grey colour. A small pile of yellow-green beans sat to one side of it, and a heap of overcooked, brown potatoes to the other. The food was surrounded by a moat of watery gravy. Dunphy poked a potato with his fork.

Grimmett mashed the mixture together and began shovelling it in his mouth. "This isn't real Scottish food. When they do it properly it's more like French cuisine. Scotland and France have had cultural associations for centuries."

Dunphy stared at him.

"It's quite delicate really," Grimmett went on. "It's not all porridge and potatoes." He noticed Dunphy staring at him. "When it's done properly."

Dunphy moved some mince across his plate with his fork. "For twenty-five pounds we can have a decent dinner," he said. "We'll go to the Gasthaus."

At the end of the meal, the headmaster approached the front of the stage. He cleared his throat and his black gown hung unevenly from his shoulders and gave him a lopsided, hunch-backed appearance. He held a small piece of paper in his hand, and stood for a moment, gazing around the hall.

Then he spoke, and Grimmett had to strain to hear him. "This last day of school," he said, "I would like us to think of one of our colleagues who is not with us. It is with deep regret and sadness that I have to inform you of the untimely death of David McCue." He paused and his eyes travelled the hall.

"Many of you knew David—some of you were his friends. But all of us are diminished by his death. He was drowned yesterday evening in the canal near his home at Linlithgow. David was not a brilliant student, but he was a . . . ah . . . an imaginative one, and I am sure . . ."

But Grimmett didn't hear the rest of it as his mind drifted back to the banks of the canal on a spring evening with rising trout rippling the water, and the ghosts of old draw horses on the towpath.

"You were a good friend to him," said Dunphy. "I mean, he did keep himself pretty much apart." He sat down on the top of Grimmett's desk in a corner of the classroom.

Grimmett gazed out of the window. Outside the traffic rumbled past, setting up vibrations in the room. Tiny flecks of dust floated in a sunbeam filtering through the high window.

"His sister knew," said Grimmett. Someone shouted something in the corridor. Last day celebrations had begun. "It's funny how everything just goes on. I suppose they'll all forget about him in a few days."

"I don't know," said Dunphy. "It depends on how well you knew him I think. I mean, if you didn't know someone all that well . . ." He left the sentence unfinished.

"She wanted me to talk to him; to try and help make things right for him. And I wasn't able to do anything. Nothing at all."

Dunphy realised that Grimmett was talking to himself.

Grimmett knew that he had to see her. That was the most important thing. And then he understood that it probably wouldn't be possible for a while. The family would have its own grief to deal with first.

"I think I know what you mean," said Dunphy.

Grimmett was already walking out of the door to find a telephone.

He walked for a long time without paying attention to where he was going. He walked down narrow streets and along the path through the park by the Water of Leith, and he didn't see any of it. It was late when he climbed the stairs to the flat.

"What a mess this place is." She was standing in the hallway when he opened the door, a cigarette in her hand. She'd been pacing up and down.

Uncle Ronald came out of the kitchen. "This is a disgrace," he said. "I've never seen anything like it. Look at that." He motioned at the kitchen. "The place is full of bottles. Wine bottles, beer bottles. Milk bottles. It stinks." He glared at his stepson. "You need a firm hand my boy. It's a wonder to me that they haven't kicked you out of the school while we've been away."

"I'm very disappointed in you Arthur," said his mother. "Very disappointed. Living in squalor like this."

He stared at them. He hadn't expected them until the end of the week; and not here. "How did you get in?"

She stared back at him and her eyes widened. "With a key. We've got a key." She turned again, agitated, shaking her head. She looked as if she might cry. "How could you live like this?"

"You've let us down. You know that, don't you! Let us down." Uncle Ronald strode into the bathroom, continuing his explorations.

Grimmett hadn't moved from the front door. "I can't talk to you just now," he said. "You'll have to go."

"That's no way to speak to your mother after she's been away. We're not going anywhere until we've cleaned this place up," said Uncle Ronald. "It'll take us a couple of hours. At least." He looked at his wife. "We'll have to forego the dinner we were going to treat him to." He shook his head. "What a disgrace."

Grimmett looked at them as if they'd come from another world. Then he turned and went out the front door, shutting it behind him. He ran down the stairs and heard the door open behind him, and his mother calling, but he didn't stop, and then he was in the street, running.

Stark was very drunk when Grimmett found him in the Vaults. There were only a few customers in the bar.

"Best leave him be son," the barman said to Grimmett. "He's in a strange place tonight right enough. I've not seen him like this before."

Grimmett reached in his pocket and pulled out a five pound note. "I'll have a pint of beer and a whisky," he said. "And give him the same."

Stark's head was down and his forearms were resting on the bar. He looked asleep, but Grimmett could see his body was full of tension, like a spring. The barman brought the drinks.

Stark looked up. He reached for the whisky and poured it into the beer and drank deeply from it.

"The bastards got him in the end," he said, and Grimmett had to lean close to hear him. "The god-fearing, self-righteous bastards. Oh, what a waste . . . what a bloody waste."

There was nothing to say, and so Grimmett drank from his beer, and took a sip of the whisky and it burned his throat and made him shudder because he had never had whisky before.

Stark raised his head. Staring down at the counter top, he spoke in the same voice, and it sounded featureless like the desert he had spoken to them about in that place before. Again, Grimmett had to strain to hear him. "He was such a talent; such a beautiful talent. He could have been so good. So good. If only he'd been able to give it some time."

He turned his eyes on Grimmett. "I was all he had and I let him down." Stark drank, and the beer with the whisky in it vanished. "He'd have been fine if it had all been more obvious. Less subtle."

His words were running together, but Grimmett understood them. He caught the barman's eye and nodded. He touched Stark on the arm.

"You weren't all he had," he said. "He had a sister who loved him, and understood what was happening. And I was his friend too. I knew what was going on." He wanted to share in it.

Tears were running down Stark's face, sliding down his cheeks into his beard. He made no effort to wipe them away.

He nodded. "Yes," he said. And then, "He'd have been all right with me in the desert. You could see things clearly there and deal with them. Even though there wasn't anything out there, matters of importance were all about; gave you perspective. Elemental things. 'S different here. Takes a special deviance to understand them. A special deviance. . ."

Stark sat up. He lifted his fresh beer and poured the whisky into it. "We'll drink to him and we'll not forget him." He emptied his glass, and Grimmett finished his as well. "We mustn't forget him." And after that they had more drinks and they both got drunk, so that Grimmett didn't remember leaving the place, and woke up in Stark's flat in the spare room the next morning with a dry mouth and a sore head.

"What will you do now?" said Fiona. They were sitting on hard chairs in front of an empty grate in a coffee shop on Hanover Street.

"I don't know. Go away for a while. Maybe go to France and clear out my system." He was finding it difficult to look at her, but he'd seen the dark rings under her eyes, the redness round her eyelids, her pale face.

He realised all of a sudden that he was only thinking of himself. "It's me who should be asking you things like that," he said taking her hand.

"You know why I had to come to Edinburgh today?" Fiona said.

"No."

"To pick up his things from the school." She hesitated. "You wouldn't come with me would you? To help? It's difficult for me to go there by myself."

Now he looked at her, and her eyes held his, and he saw the effort she was making, and felt his way into her grief. "Of course I will. When do you have to go there?"

"Soon. In a few minutes." She looked up at the clock on the wall. It was ticking loudly through the seconds, filling the spaces in their conversation.

Grimmett stood up. He walked to the counter and paid for the coffee. She was ready when he came back, and they went out the door together. An east wind swirled up the street from the river. Grimmett held her hand without thinking of it, and they walked down the hill.

She held his hand and he could feel her body shaking. He stopped her under the trees at some gardens and put his arms round her and held her, and she cried for a long time. He brushed her hair with his hand and tried to think of a way to take away her sadness, but he knew that nothing would do that.

They started walking again, and she let the wind dry her tears.

"It was such a bloody selfish thing to do," she said at last. "He was so good about thinking of other people, most of the time." She sighed, a great shaking sigh. "I don't know what I'll do now, without him."

The Janitor was waiting at the school gate. Grimmett had never seen him without his top hat and tailcoat, a legacy from the pre-Victorian beginnings of the school. Today, with school finished for the year, he was wearing a brown lab coat. He escorted them to the Headmaster's office. He knocked on the door.

The meeting with the Headmaster was brief and awkward. He greeted Fiona with a handshake, and gave a nod of recognition to Grimmett. He told Fiona that he was sorry about her brother. It seemed to Grimmett as if he was substituting formality for sorrow.

Fiona thanked him, and the Headmaster picked up a brown parcel from his desk and handed it to her. They stood looking at each other, and then Fiona turned away and went to the door. The Headmaster jumped in front of her and opened the door, and then she and Grimmett were outside in the sunshine.

They walked together down the street. Grimmett wanted to say something to make her feel better, but he was lost.

"Do you know Stark?" said Grimmett. The question came out before he realised it.

She walked on beside him, and he thought she hadn't heard him.

He was about to say something else, when she said, "No. But I would like to meet him."

"We could go there. To his place. It's not far from here." It would be warm there, and Stark would be better today.

207

"Yes. I don't have to go home yet. It doesn't matter what train I get."

They climbed the stairs to Stark's flat, and Rosanna opened the door. She took them through to the kitchen. Stark was sitting at the table with an empty bowl in front of him, a mug of coffee in his hand.

"You're Fiona," he said. He stood up and went to her and wrapped his arms around her. He held her, and his eyes were closed. "I'm sorry. I'm so terribly sorry."

When they drew apart Stark poured out two mugs of coffee, and reached into a cupboard and pulled out a bottle of whisky. "This is what they do on the islands. It's more civilised than the way we deal with things in the city." He unscrewed the top of the bottle, and poured a tot into each mug.

It was mid-afternoon and they talked for a while about Fiona's brother. They didn't avoid the subject of death. Fiona sat close to Grimmett, and it wasn't the whisky but her closeness that made him feel light-headed. Later he was never sure how it had happened, but he and Fiona went to lie down together on the bed in Stark's spare room and it was what they wanted. It was tender and awkward and inconclusive because neither of them had done anything like it before. But both of them knew then that it was what they wanted, and that a time would come for it.

Grimmett went with Fiona on the bus to the station. Walking down the ramp from the Waverley Bridge his step was light. They didn't speak to each other for long minutes and it was all right. Fiona held his hand and there had been nothing wrong in any of it. When the train came he found himself climbing onto it to take the thirty-minute ride out to the farm with her, and she said nothing to stop him because she understood why he was there. At the country station they said goodbye, and he crossed the bridge to the other track to catch the next train back to Edinburgh and watched her as she left, and she looked back at him as she climbed into the green bus that was waiting to take her down the road to the farm.

Grimmett was late for the dinner with Dunphy. Dunphy was standing at the top of a close in the High Street, waiting, flapping his arms and stamping his feet against the east wind. It was swirling cold up and down alleyways, whisking litter and bits of paper from the street up towards the high garrets.

"Sorry I'm late."

"It's okay," said Dunphy. "At least it would be if it hadn't gone back to winter again." He pointed down the close. "It's down here. I don't think they're busy. I've been waiting here for twenty minutes and I haven't seen anyone go in yet."

"You should've gone ahead. I'd have found you."

They walked down the alley, and the walls converged on them, clammy and damp.

"It's a funny place to have a German restaurant," said Grimmett.

"Diplomat recommended it," said Dunphy. "He's been here a few times." He stopped in front of a black oak door and turned the handle. The door creaked open and they stepped into a shadowed vestibule. The door swung closed behind them.

"It's a bit dark." Grimmett looked around. A faded mask hung on the wall above his head, two pointed molars protruding from its mouth. A silver bolt dangled on a cord from a picture rail above it. "Strange."

"German," said Dunphy. He rubbed his hands together. "Old German." A hairy werewolf mask leered down at him from the plastered, yellow wall. He looked away. "Diplomat likes it."

"I thought he fought them in the war."

"Well he did, but that was a long time ago. He likes them now." He coughed. "Doesn't seem to be anyone about." Dunphy sat down on a carved wooden chair.

A velvet curtain swept to one side and a girl in a white blouse and a short black skirt came into the vestibule. Dunphy pulled himself out of the chair. The girl was taller than he was. She had a dark, gypsy face. She was taller than Grimmett.

"Good evening," she said. "Have you got a booking?" She had a deep voice.

"Dunphy's the name."

The girl smiled. "Of course. Mr. Dunphy and Guest." She nodded at Grimmett. "Come with me please." She held the curtain aside for them.

"Mind the step," she said, as Dunphy stumbled into a thick-carpeted, low-beamed room. Candles were burning in holders, on tables set in wood-panelled booths. There didn't seem to be any other lighting. The girl showed them to a corner of the room. She waited while they seated themselves on benches at their table.

"Would you like anything from the bar while you look at the menu?" she asked.

Dunphy extended his arm towards Grimmett and his sleeve caught the top of the salt cellar and knocked it over. He picked it up, and began to scoop the salt back inside.

"I would like a beer please," said Grimmett. "Beck's."

"And you Mr. Dunphy?"

Dunphy smiled. "I think I would like a glass of wine please. Perhaps a Schloss Laderhausen."

The girl frowned. "Oh no sir, we don't carry ordinary table wines in here. I'm afraid we don't have it."

Dunphy put the lid back on the salt cellar. He drummed his fingers on the table. "Course not. Silly of me. What would you recommend?"

"I'd recommend the Moselle—as long as you were buying it of course." She smiled.

"Oh yes, a Moselle. That will do fine."

The girl handed them menus in thick leather covers embossed with gothic script.

"How did you know about that? Beck's beer?" said Dunphy when the girl had gone. "I've never heard of it."

"I had it when I was with my father; a long time ago when I was staying with him in Cyprus. It's a German beer."

"I didn't know your father had been in Cyprus." Dunphy paused. "Where is he now?"

"I don't know. South America I think."

They watched as the girl navigated her way back to them in the semi-darkness. She was carrying a silver tray. "You need radar to see where you're going in here," said Dunphy.

The girl placed a porcelain stein with a pewter lid in front of Grimmett. Then she put the bottle of Moselle on the table in front of Dunphy. She took a small silver knife from a pocket in her skirt. Expertly, she sliced round the leaded paper at the top of the bottle and tore it off and tucked it in her skirt pocket. She unscrewed the cork, and it pulled out with a plop.

"Would you like to taste it first?"

"Yes, please," said Dunphy. He picked up his glass and took a sip, swirling the wine around the inside of his mouth. "Good. Excellent." She poured more wine into his glass.

"You're not going to drink the whole bottle," said Grimmett when the girl had gone.

Dunphy looked at him over the candle flame. "To tell you the truth I didn't expect a bottle of the stuff. I thought she'd just bring me a glass of it. You'll have to help me out. We can't waste it."

Grimmett looked round the room. The decor was growing more distinct as his eyes became accustomed to the dim light. He could pick out heavy weavings on the walls. Half a dozen tables were tucked away in alcoves, three or four more in the centre of the room. There were more diners than he had thought; the restaurant was half full.

"Have you been in here before?"

"No. The Diplomat has." Dunphy stared up at a print of a mist-wreathed castle set in a dark Teutonic landscape. He shifted in his seat. "Seems an unlikely place for him to come when you think about it."

The girl came back. She picked up the bottle and poured more wine into Dunphy's glass. "Are you ready to order yet?" she asked.

"The Black Forest pâté," said Grimmett.

Dunphy opened the menu again. "I'd like the snails please, to start with." He watched her walk away, and leaned forward and put his elbows down on the table. "What are you going to do now that school's all finished?"

Grimmett took a sip of his beer. "I'm not sure. I haven't really thought about it."

"You must have," said Dunphy. "You've got to move out of the flat in a day or two, and I can't see you wanting to go and live with your mother and Uncle Ronald." Grimmett had told him about the incident at the flat the day before.

"What about you?" said Grimmett. They had hardly spoken about life after school, but there might be some inspiration for him in Dunphy's plans.

"Well, I won't miss Edinburgh much I don't think. Ottawa's not a bad place, except for the winters. They're pretty cold, but then we go skating, and have parties out on the ice on the canal. You know, hockey games and bands and stuff." Dunphy grinned. "I like the girls better there than the ones here."

Grimmett smiled at a vision of Dunphy skating. "Maybe I'll come and visit you sometime."

"I'll be going to university in the fall. There's two of them in Ottawa, but I think I'll probably go to Carleton. It's more English."

"Yes." Grimmett was thoughtful. "The school didn't really fit us out for much else but university, did it? University and accounting, or stock-broking; things like that, and nothing that we'd actually want to do with our lives. Sometimes I feel as if I don't know anything useful at all."

"You should come out and visit me in Ottawa," said Dunphy. "We've got a big house there, just outside town. It's by the river. There's lots of room in it. You could stay as long as you wanted."

A small, muscular waiter came up to the table. He was carrying two plates. "My name is 'Elmoot," he said. He put the plates down in front of them. "I am your personal vaiter for ziss effenink. If you vant anyzink zen you must let me know." He bowed and left.

"I wonder what happened to the girl?" said Dunphy.

"She must be the hostess. Perhaps she just shows people to the tables and gets them drinks."

Helmut reappeared like a ghost. He rubbed his hands together. "'Ave you decided on ze entrée?"

Dunphy put down his fork. "Yes. I'll have the shish kebab flambé. I like the sound of that."

Helmut peered at Grimmett. "New York steak please, with chips."

Helmut disappeared into the gloom.

"Creepy sort of chap," said Dunphy. "See those scars on his cheeks? Old duelling scars I bet."

"When do you go back to Canada?" Grimmett said.

"Monday." Dunphy chewed on a snail. A dribble of garlic butter worked its way down his chin, reflecting the candlelight. "Thought you knew. Flight from here to London, and then off to Toronto and Ottawa." He reached for his wine glass. "What about the girl? McCue's sister."

Dunphy's question took Grimmett by surprise. It showed on his face. He was thoughtful for a moment, remembering the climb down the windswept track from the crags, with the city's twinkling lights spread out below them like a cake with candles. He thought of the afternoon at Stark's flat. It wasn't something he wanted to talk about with anyone else.

"I think she's going to go to university too," he said. "St. Andrews."

"That's not what I meant."

"No," said Grimmett. "It's all you'll get just now though." He took a drink from the stein.

Dunphy smiled. He wasn't offended by Grimmett's answer. He changed the subject. "Well, it's been interesting, being over here, going to school. Not what I expected when I came. More like going back in time. All the stone buildings, the damp; no central heating. Even the cars are old. And the people too; bent under the weight of history."

"Tradition," said Grimmett. "They're weighed down by tradition."

"It's much more regimented here," Dunphy went on. "Not at all like it is in Canada. Especially at the school. They were just waiting at that place for us to step out of line."

They heard a rattling noise as Helmut pushed a trolley across the dining room. The wheels squeaked as he coaxed the trolley between the tables.

"Now sirs," he said. "Ve haf ze main course. Ze shish kebab for you," he nodded to Dunphy, "and ze New York stek for you." He bowed slightly, and straightened up. He began to pull off his white gloves, tugging one finger at a time.

"Zis vill tek a minute so ve vill remain ze stek in ze varm offen." He bent down and lifted the lid from a warming cabinet on the lower shelf of the trolley to display Grimmett's steak. Then he picked up a long, gold-plated rapier from the trolley. He stepped back and swished it experimentally over his head.

"It iss a performance ziss," said Helmut smiling.

Dunphy leaned back in his seat.

"You vill not see its like in Schottland at any ozzer place." He flashed the blade over his head again, and glanced round to make sure the other diners were paying attention.

"Vatch!" he commanded. He set the rapier down beside a thick wood cutting board. Cubes of marinated meat lay in a dish at one end of the board, and sausages wrapped in bacon, onions, carrots, peppers and other assorted vegetables. Helmut whipped out a dangerous looking, short-bladed dirk. Expertly he began to slice the vegetables into chunks.

Dunphy watched the flashing knife.

Helmut put the knife back on the board. He picked up the rapier again, grunting with concentration as he skewered the meats and vegetables one by one, sliding them up the blade towards the hilt.

"You haf neffer seen zis, ja?"

"No. Can't say I have," said Dunphy, fascinated.

Helmut waved the sword, added a final piece of meat, and stepped back and bowed. Dunphy clapped.

Helmut reached under the trolley and extracted a heavy brass gravy boat. Wisps of steam curled from it.

"Ja! Now ve are ready." His eyes opened wide.

Grimmett thought it gave him a crazed look.

"Now ist der fieur!"

Helmut took a silver Zippo cigarette lighter from his pocket, and flicked it at the top of the gravy. There was a pop and a flash, and a blue flame danced across the dish, and caught and enveloped the surface of the gravy. Helmut picked up the rapier again, and held it in front of him and lifted the gravy boat with his left hand. The conversation in the room died as the other diners turned in their seats to watch.

Dunphy leaned forward in his chair, his face animated by the flames. Shadows leaped across the walls.

Helmut moved the rapier round in a wide arc, and brought the flaming gravy cruet up to it. He tilted the cruet over the top of the blade in order to pour the gravy over the meat and vegetables.

214

Nothing came out. Helmut tilted the gravy boat some more. Still nothing. Impatiently he jerked the gravy boat. A blob of fiery gravy leaped from the cruet and landed on Helmut's sleeve. Immediately the rest of the flaming gravy gushed un-dammed from the cruet and splashed down the front of his trousers. Helmut jumped as a pool of fire enveloped his feet. His crotch burst into flames. He jerked into a panicky dance and began stamping his feet frantically on the floor.

With great presence of mind Grimmett threw his beer at the front of Helmut's trousers, and Helmut pirouetted away and ran across the room in a cloud of smoke, and disappeared through the curtains. Grimmett was emptying the wine bottle over the fire on the carpet when a white-hatted chef ran up with a fire extinguisher.

A buzz of chatter filled the room.

"Did you see Helmut's jacket?" said Dunphy, when the chef had gone. "His sleeve was in tatters." He picked up the empty wine bottle and put it down again. "And his trousers too. That was a performance all right. He could have cooked us all."

"The chef's taken the food away," said Grimmett.

"And the wine's gone, and your beer," said Dunphy as he inspected the charred carpet.

"At least you won't have to pay for the wine," said Grimmett. "It would have broken your budget."

"What do you mean?"

"I looked it up a few minutes ago," said Grimmett. "It was seventeen pounds a bottle. We'd have had to wash dishes."

A waiter they hadn't seen before came towards them with a pair of plates. When he reached the table he said, "Shish kebab?"

"Yes, here please," said Dunphy.

"And yours must be the steak sir." He put the plate down in front of Grimmett and left.

"No flames."

"No flambé," agreed Dunphy. "Too risky."

"It was a good meal, in spite of the excitement," said Grimmett. They were walking slowly up the High Street.

Dunphy patted his stomach. "Very good. Just as well they didn't charge us for the drinks."

"Yes. Well, we saved the place from burning down." A car drove past, its tyres whining on the cobblestones. "It's a good job we weren't drinking whisky. Helmut would have gone up like a torch if we'd thrown that on him."

They walked on up the rain-slicked hill. The wind had picked up. A newspaper fluttered down the pavement towards them. Grimmett stuck out a foot to stop it. He picked it up and stuffed it into a litter bin. A door slammed up the street, and a drunken voice crooned softly from the darkness of an alleyway.

"It could be such a great place, this town," said Dunphy. "It's a shame they don't take care of it." He turned to Grimmett. "Maybe I will miss it after all."

Grimmett nodded. "You probably will."

They stopped by the Tron kirk. Dunphy looked up at the tall spire. "It's my bus stop here," he said. "Don't suppose I'll be seeing you for a while." He held out his hand. "We'll meet up?"

Grimmett took Dunphy's hand and shook it. "Yes. Yes, we will."

They looked at each other for a moment, and then Grimmett turned away and walked on, up the narrow street. Dunphy watched him fade in and out of the streetlights, shadowed and dwarfed by the high stone tenements. A gust of wind made him blink, and when he looked again Grimmett had gone.

"Good luck," he called. But there was no answer.

Acknowledgements

"Eyes of Rain and Ragged Dreams" is a work of fiction, but it would be wrong to claim that all the characters are fictitious. A couple of them are not, and some of the others are composites. Almost all the events in the book occurred more or less as they've been depicted—in the nineteen-sixties in Edinburgh, where I went to school; where I grew up.

There are several people to thank:
First of all, for help with the writing and editing of this book, my wife Marilyn Bowering—for taking the time to go over the chapters, and the whole, many times, and for her gentleness and tact. The book has been a long time in the coming, and I know it wasn't easy for her.

My late Mother, with apologies, because the character in the novel is decidedly not her, but another mother, who had best remain anonymous. My Mother showed me my native land when I was young, joined me to it in inexpressible ways of the spirit, and fought for me every day of her life.

My late Father, for sharing firesides and beer and wonderful stories with me, and for linking past things to the present. And who was nothing like any of the fathers depicted in the novel.

My much loved stepfather—Uncle Stew—who was nothing like Grimmett's stepfather in the novel, but who contributed enormously to the health and well-being of the people of Ghana through his work in animal husbandry, in irrigation and the growing of crops.

The book is also for the friends who survived the ordeals of coming-of-age in Edinburgh in the nineteen-sixties. Friends like Windy, who created great adventures, and became a master of his surgical trade. Friends like Johnnie, who was possessed of the most subtle humour and wit, who was irrepressibly opposed to cant and convention, and whose exploits live on in legend. For friends like Kenny, an artist who knows better than most the tribulations of those who wanted to take an alternate route to the one that was prescribed. For Max in Edinburgh, and Jerry in Pitlochry, for Willie the Pea, Olly and Peter, and for Nobby, who is no longer with us.

It is also for the late John Firth, a teacher who quietly gave his support to the unconventional. And for Doc Isaacs, who pretty well did the same in a more academic role. They're both gone now, but Harry—John Harrison—is still around I think, and if he encounters this he should know that we are forever grateful for the trust he placed in us. It has not been forgotten.

And the book is for those friends who are not here now. They shouldn't be forgotten—Alan, Bobby, Hugh, Rollie—and Charles, who I went to France with when I was sixteen, and who died later.

Michael Elcock was born in Forres, Scotland, and grew up in Edinburgh and West Africa. He emigrated to Canada when he was twenty-one and worked in pulp mills, as a tree faller, on west coast fishing boats, and as a ski instructor—earning along the way a B.A. and M. Ed degree at the University of Victoria. Since then he has travelled widely, and worked and lived in Canada, the US, Spain and Scotland. He has published many articles in periodicals, newspapers and magazines in Canada and the UK, two works of non-fiction—*A Perfectly Beautiful Place* and *Writing on Stone*—and a novel, *The Gate* (all with Oolichan Books).

Michael has served on several Boards of Directors, including the National Council of Canada's Writers Union, and the Board of Access Copyright, Canada's copyright licensing agency. He lives in Victoria, British Columbia.

Printed in Great Britain
by Amazon